HALLOW

Book Two of the "Celestial Creatures" series.

Olga Gibbs

RAGING BEAR
PUBLISHING

Hallow.

Published in 2019 by Raging Bear Publishing.

A CIP catalogue record for this title is available from the British Library.

Paperback ISBN 978-1-9164710-1-6

Cover design by Perie Wolford.

For upcoming publications visit www.OlgaGibbs.com

Under the sky
Here I lie,
Under the sky
My sister and I
Trees above us and the bottomless sky
Here we'll live – my sister and I.

(Adopted from traditional of an unknown author)

About the book.

"It's always the darkest before the dawn" – Thomas Fuller.

"It's going to get worse before it will get better. And today is no exception" – Ariel.

Curse like an angel.

Urbat Manzazu – Dwelling place of the dog of death.
Damu Azeru – Cursed child.
Irtu Etu Dalkhu – Demons' dark boobs.
Zu ku Izi – Flesh eating fire.
Pagru di mursu sadhu – Corpse of a diseased pig.

All the above were created using the known elements of Sumerian language and its loose English translations. All of these phrases are used by our fearless characters throughout this book.

Full glossary of terms, the celestial words and phrases introduced and used in "Heavenward" and "Hallow" and their translations, can be found at the end of this book.

Chapter 1

chre yellow empty polystyrene cartons from a local fish and chip shop litter the pavement, dimly glowing in the dark like little islands amongst a dark, night sea.

Small pieces of rubbish, sweet wrappers and old newspapers twirl and dance under our feet, but when picked up by a gust of wind, they would race past us, as if alive, hurrying like a morning herd of commuters flooding a platform at Victoria station on their way to work.

The streets are pitch-black as the street lamps are already turned off for the night. It must be well past midnight. But the steady, soft, pearly glow coming off Rafe's body, dimly illuminates the pavement and the surrounding air, as if we are followed along by a personal street lamp.

The streets of the town are filled with the salty smell of the sea and a faint stench of rotting rubbish from nearby takeaways and restaurants that are already closed for the night. Rats rustle and squeak in the bins, fighting for the juiciest scraps.

The air has the faint, crisp smell of the upcoming winter and it probably will be a week before rain puddles begin to freeze at night, giving young children the acute satisfaction of jumping onto the thin crust of bright ice in the mornings and hearing it crunch under their feet. And a week after that, the snow will come.

The day of the fire in the science class, the day when my life irreversibly changed and I learnt not only that angels exist, but I am one of them, was a breezy English summer day. Somehow it is late autumn now. Somehow, somewhere I've lost half a year.

A chilling easterly wind throws fine drizzle in my face, whipping my damp hair around, seeping its numbing cold fingers through my muddy jeans and the sweatshirt. I didn't have a chance to change earlier and now I'm paying for it with the smelly and crusted over attire, which stands rigid like stinky armour.

My wings are behind me.

It's weird to have them there.

Most of the time I don't even think about them, don't feel them. But now and again, they would flutter ever so slightly behind my back, move my hair or brush past my shoulders or arms, reminding me of their presence. They are there like long hair over the back of my neck, constant, familiar and inconspicuous. I only notice and think about them in the moments like now, when they gently rise and spread, covering me from the wind and rain.

But I'm still cold.

A few streets back my teeth began to chatter. At first it was short, sporadic clucks of a convulsing chicken, but now the chatter has upgraded to a steady rhythmic pulse. The shiver descends over my body, raking over me, twisting and shortening my muscles as if I'm touching exposed wires.

I need to get warm. I need to get to warmth, but I don't know what to do or where to go next.

I left Uras decisively.

I made the decision and now I need to follow through with it. The problem is that I knew I needed to leave, and I knew I needed to come here, to see my sister, to make sure that she is alright, safe, but that was as far as I went in my preparations or in my planning.

I have no idea what to do next or even where to begin.

Rafe's heavy footsteps echo behind my back and I can hear his laboured breathing.

I can feel his presence. I sense him with the hair at my nape, and I can smell the scent of ripe fruits and sun around me. I can feel his pulsating life energy with my wings.

My wings know without a shadow of a doubt that it is him behind me. My wings know that he is in pain and they know that the pain is bad.

But he doesn't share it with me. He doesn't say a word.

He just walks behind me, keeping up with my intentionally shortened steps. He didn't want to share his pain with me then, and he is not sharing it now. He is just here for me, insistent and constant, even after everything I put him through.

Without question, he followed me on the path that I chose for us, and the earlier guilt stirs up again.

The swords that Sam gave me are awkwardly stashed away, looped through the belt at the back of my jeans. I've never carried weapons before nor have I used them until today.

I sober in an instant thinking of Mia. I still can't believe that I've done it, done to another human, to another living being.

And as if answering my call, the memories of our fight rush back, spreading the dark chill from within, matching the chill of the autumnal wet wind. The memories bring the crisp stabbing details of her beautiful porcelain pixie face. Her face frozen in shock, with her eyes and red mouth wide open, her surprised gaze locked to mine.

I remember watching her body folded unnaturally on the floor, twisted at the weird angle. I remember that feeling, that knowledge: she is dead.

The heavy weight of guilt pushes in next. It expands, bulges inside like a poisonous cyst about to burst.

I have never killed anyone or anything in my life. Even annoying buzzing flies on windows were carefully caught under a cup and pushed out of an open window. Spiders were released into woods and the local foxes were regularly fed with old bread and leftover sandwiches in the home's back garden.

I cried for days when I found a dead hedgehog outside our house, hit by a car, his little unmoving body pressed against the curb.

This was my first experience of death.

I was very little then and remember touching the sharp little prickles on the hedgehog's body, calling for "Mr Hedgehog" to wake up, and my dad dragging me away, slamming the door shut behind us.

And that night he spoke about death. My dad, the man of a very few words and even fewer expressions, said that night with the stern face (my tears always bothered him): "That hedgehog was already dead. Nothing we could've done. Everything and everyone dies eventually, such is life."

Then he tucked me in, turned off the light and left the room. That was the only week in my life I didn't have my usual nightmares, because that was the week when I barely slept, scared and confused, staring into the dark emptiness of the night, wondering about mechanics of death, the finality of it all, falling into an exhausted oblivion only just before dawn.

Since then I was so careful not to harm, not to kill – anyone or anything. Ever.

But now I've crossed that line. I have killed. This thought churns my stomach and I think I might throw up.

What am I turning into? Who am I becoming?

Every step I take, every decision that I make changes me, taking me further away from myself, turning me into something completely different, new, alien. Nothing is "me" about me anymore: I wear a stranger's clothes with a stranger's *weapons* tucked in at the back of my jeans, fighting a stranger's battles. And oh, yeah, and I have two pairs of wings now as well.

Will there be any of "*me*" left? How far will this road lead me? How much more will I change? What more will I do? And ultimately, am I still a good person if I have done evil things?

And then the sobering thought like a slap rings in my head.

Maybe now and here I am my true self? The self I was always meant to be, just like Baza said? Maybe all that I was before was just an accident, a dream, a mistake, a pretence?

Maybe now I am me, and maybe, just maybe, I'm not a good person after all?

Maybe I was never good...

"*Bad things don't happen to good girls*", my mother's stern reciting voice echoes in my head and I can feel again, years later, a heavy pull of Bible in my hands and the stabbing of sharp shards of salt in the skin of my knees.

Rain water washes my face, running down my lips and my chin. I lick the rain off my lips, startled to taste the salt. Only now I realise that my eyes are sore and the crazy 'house of mirrors' film distorts my vision.

The influx of memories is so powerful, the stress of the last few hours is so draining and doubt is so crippling, that I want to drop to my knees right here, in the middle of the street, and wail head up to the sky like a wolf, to mourn myself, for everyone to hear my misery.

Again I feel like there is not enough air in the world to fill my lungs, like the darkness of the night around me is a tight metal box.

I force myself not to bolt. I force myself not to drop to my knees. I force my feet to keep the pace, my knees to bend in time as I count my steps, finding the rhythm in it and drowning my thoughts: one – two, one – two.

I rub at my eyes, wipe at my face, forcing my breathing.

"Do you know what date it is today?" I glance at Rafe over my shoulder once I manage to restore my breathing.

The beads of rain or maybe sweat dot his forehead, glistening in the light.

Only the one wing pokes above his shoulder, and that large purple wing, illuminated by Rafe's glow, looks so lonely and odd, that remorse washes over me again as I am confronted by the sight of his wing and the sight of his tightly set jaw and half-hooded eyes.

I quickly drop my gaze and turn around.

"It's the third of November", he answers.

The breath hitches in his throat between the words, just in time with his footsteps, as if each step stabs him. But he keeps his voice toneless and flat, like only a person in pain would.

But I'm suffering too and it's not only a physical pain. My arm still hurts where Mia had slashed at it with her sword. The wound had started to heal but I think it will be a good few hours before the pain will dissipate completely.

And on top of everything else, away from Sam and his magical, unexplainable hold on me, everything he did, everything he said comes to me with a ringing clarity, bringing self-loathing in its wake. I want to kick myself for wanting him, for needing him and for being so placid and melting in his arms.

Away from him I bitterly regret the *"I love you"* I uttered. The space apart, like a wise grandma helpfully reminds me of everything he had done. Now, with space apart, I don't know if I can trust him, or who can I trust at all.

With unexpected sadness I realise that I'm just like my mum, falling for a guy and his empty promises.

Bloody genetics, huh?! What a gullible fool!

Self-loathing is flogging me hard and I desperately want to purge that feeling. I want to open the gates and release it. I want to hit something, I want to scream but instead I just ball the fists by my sides and keep on marching down the familiar street, counting the steps, keeping my eyes on the cracked asphalt under my feet, lit up by Rafe's pearly glow.

I steal another glance at him over my shoulder.

At least he is not pretending to love me.

He was honest and upfront with me from the start. It's his soul mate's essence he is after, it's her he wants. Very simple, very straight forward, very clear cut.

In anger I kick a stone from under my foot. It bounces away into the darkness of the street with a melodious juicy beat.

I'm tired of it all. I am walking down an empty street but I don't know where I'm going or where I want to be. I think now is the time to admit to myself and to Rafe, that I don't know where I am leading him, I don't know where I am going.

I had to leave Uras. And although it was *my* decision to leave, it was a forced decision of a 'tactical withdrawal'. I didn't have a plan then and I don't have one now. I was so busy leaving, so busy to be the leader they all prophesise me to be, that I didn't think past the open door.

In my mind, I haven't envisioned anything apart from a vague notion of coming to my hometown, turning up outside of my old house and collecting Jess, or at least seeing if she is okay and happy.

And now, as I plod down the cold and empty dark streets, I could clearly see that "my plan" wasn't even a plan. It was just another easy escape, afraid to make a decision.

Perpetually singing self-doubt has made the decision for me and now I've parked us here, miles away from my old house, in the middle of the night, in the middle of the empty town centre, without money or a place to sleep.

And just like that I'm angry again. I'm angry at myself, at Rafe, at Sam, at my parents and all the goddamned angels out there. Again I've screwed up, again I'm in trouble, on the run, but God knows, this time this wasn't any of my doing. I want to stamp my feet and scream, and my laboured breathing is now matching Rafe's.

I abruptly stop.

Rafe clearly didn't expect it, as if on autopilot, his feet carry him forward and with two large steps he almost ploughs into me, his large body around mine.

My large purple wings protectively shoot out high and wide around my back, between us and I can feel his breath stroking the top of my head. His clothing brushes over my feathers and the delicate and wispy tips of my wings are tingling, sending angry wind chimes into my head, demanding more space between us, as I practically leap forward, before spinning to face him.

"Listen Rafe, just go back, huh?" I snap. "I don't want you here. I don't need you here and I don't need your help. I'm just going to find my sister and get out of here. And I can do all of it on my own. I don't need a babysitter and I most definitely don't need you following behind me like a bloody prison guard."

I try so hard not to yell at him, but I can't keep the annoyance and irritation from singing in my voice.

His hair, wet from the constant drizzle, is brushed away from his face.

A fine November spray coats his face and when the droplets, burdened to the full gather together, they slide down his handsome face like a dozen small rivers.

But he doesn't wipe the water off his face; he lets it run its course as he stands there, looking down at me, resolute, his warm hazel eyes locked on me.

And his patient silence, his care and pity in his gaze are more than I can handle.

"Mate, what are you here for? What do you want?" I scream and my voice, carried by the mist and the wind, echoes off the dark buildings and a dog's bark answers me from somewhere in the night.

"What's in it for you, huh? Why won't you just bloody get lost?" I shriek and although he is calm and silent, I'm on a roll and can't stop myself.

"Or still trying to score here?" I hiss at him.

"*My soul mate, my soul mate*", I mimic him, clasping my hands over my chest, rolling my eyes upwards, pursuing my lips in a bow as if about to kiss, and the next second I snap back at him, roaring, "she is not here! *I am* here! *I am!* And I don't want *you!*"

"Ariel, we've been through this. I need to keep you safe, not because of the essence inside you, but because of the oath I swore, and I have told you that I'm not going anywhere. I have to protect you, and that will always be my job. You know that."

His calm and low voice is of a mature adult who's trying to reason with a tantrum of a toddler, and that winds me up even more. And before I have a chance to bite my tongue, to rethink or remember to breathe, the words fall out my stupid big mouth.

"What's a bloody useless cripple like you going to do? Broken, with one wing?" And the second the words echo and register in my mind, I immediately regret them and I want to kick myself.

I clamp my mouth shut, but it's too late. The damage has been done. I went too far and I can see it.

His beautiful hazel eyes are open wide in shock and hurt.

The pain and anger blanket his face for a second, before he forces his face back into the earlier stoic and neutral expression. Only the tightened and bulging muscles on his neck and suddenly even shallower breathing betray his rage, and I could swear I can hear his teeth grinding.

I'm mortified at what I've just done, at what I've said. I can't believe I have been *that* cruel.

I want to turn back time and take it all back, every single word.

I want to apologise. I want to explain myself. Explain how scared I feel, how out of my depth I am here and have been for a while. How my life is moving away from me and I feel like a leaf, ripped from a tree and at the mercy of the wind, which carries me deeper into the unknown.

I want to tell him that his missing wing is my fault and I know it, and that the guilt will be with me forever.

I want to ask, *no!* – I want to *beg* for his forgiveness. I want to explain that I didn't mean any of it, that I'm scared and the fear spoke for me, before me.

I want to cry and I want to let him comfort me and tell me what to do and make all the decisions for me from now on and forever. I want someone, just for once, to look after me, take care of me and just let me be.

But instead of telling him all of this, I turn around and walk away.

With every step I take away from Rafe, the darkness swallows me deeper. Rafe's warm glow is left behind and I can feel my large wings fold tighter against my back, wrapping my shoulders, cocooning me. And for a while all I can hear is the night's quiet and the swishing of the wind with a heavy drum of the drizzle, which has now upgraded to a freezing November rain.

But then in the distance, the familiar heavy footsteps resume the pace again, their echo resonating off the asphalt.

Rafe catches up with me in a few long strides, but the distance between us is wider than it was before, and my wings detect a new emotion coming off him, and as if punched in the gut, I suddenly realise that it is hate.

That serves you bloody right! You totally deserve it and you've got no one else to blame for that but yourself and your stupid mouth. You wanted him gone, have it! Now you're truly on your own!

My feet keep their numb pace as these words slowly sink in and my tears start and spill, and I don't try to stop them now.

Chapter 2

*M*y hometown is small and compact.

Once grandeur, and now run-down and greying, five-storey tall Victorian buildings line up the central promenade, leading tourists to the beach.

The ground floors in these buildings were always occupied by businesses.

In the last two centuries they were bursting with tea rooms and sweets shops, traditional fish and chip shops and the obligatory pubs. But for the last few years, as shops were closing down one by one, the boarded up windows of the closed down shops begun to interrupt the promenade like a hiccup. And the last few standing businesses now sell the touristy junk to an annual ebbing flock of summer visitors.

The rest of the businesses in the town centre are mainly takeaways, betting shops and newsagents selling cheap beer and sweets to the locals. Even pubs are having a hard time surviving here.

The buildings get shorter and smaller as we leave the town centre. The five storey high, centuries old decaying splendour vanishes, giving way to the red brick of small two storey town houses from the same era. It's like the entire town was built under the watchful eye of Queen Victoria.

The council estate, in which I spent most of my life, is just a few miles away, erected forty years ago on the outskirts of the then busy seaside town and strategically tucked away from the gazes of happy tourists.

I have never made this trip on foot, always using a bus, but it would be stupid to wait for a bus at this hour.

In the thick darkness of an autumnal early morning, my estate's shadowy form looks the same as it did years ago.

My estate is still asleep and snoring, and only an occasional dog bark rips the somnolent silence.

The lights are due to be switched on in a few hours, but I know that they will not come on in here.

There never was a single working street lamp in my small estate for as long as I remember. Most of them were smashed for sport by local boys as soon as the broken ones were replaced, so eventually the council gave up on the lights. And on the people who lived there.

Only the morning sun will break darkness in the place of the forgotten people.

The rain had stopped somewhere along the way, leaving behind black puddles on the asphalt.

I know better than to step in these. The unexpected depth of these seemingly shallow puddles can surprise you, leaving not just the shoes wet.

A cold wind picked up, gushing down the streets and between the houses, raising tiny ripples on the puddles, rustling bared trees and whistling between the branches.

Rafe is still behind me and stayed there all the way here.

We didn't say a word to each other. I know very well that it is my job now, after all that I've said and done, to pick up the pieces of our broken friendship and to mend the shattered trust, but I can't deal with it right now.

Anxiety and apprehension, fear and joy, hope and the dark doubt are pulling at me, tugging me in every direction, making me dizzy and light-headed.

The dread pulls heavy at my stomach only for a moment later to be replaced by a tender whisper of hope, which later is washed away by fear. My mouth is dry and my heart is pounding at my ribcage.

Every step takes me closer to the estate, closer to my street, closer to my house. I can't think of anything but the moment I'll see my sister, for the first time in over a year. My sister and my mum.

And as I am about to turn the corner onto my street and to see for the first time in years, the fourth house from the end, the house where I used to live, the pit of my stomach squeezes and I stop.

With the last two steps I will round the corner and I will be on my street, the street on which I played with my sister as a child, drawing hopscotch on asphalt and running, playing "It" with my sister and neighbours' kids. The street on which I learnt how to ride a bike, on which my neighbours live and my sister still lives.

Our street was always loud, filled with loud laughter and chatter, and occasional dramas and arguments just like any large dysfunctional family.

I know that with these last two steps I will see my house, the house in which I suffered so much, but in which I was also so happy as a little girl, the house which held more of my memories and of my emotions than any building in this world.

I take a lungful of the night wet air and force myself to turn the corner.

The dark shadows of the street, the outlines of the familiar buildings along the street against the backdrop of the grey shadows of the morning are the same as years ago. Nothing has changed since I left.

My house is still asleep. It is dark just like all the houses next to it and my sister and my mum are asleep in there.

The heart is thumping in my chest and my hands are clammy and cold. I wipe them on my dirty and wet jeans.

I'm petrified. I'm finally here but I don't know how I'll be greeted. I don't know if I'd be wanted and with every step closer, I decide that I can't brave my house in the dark.

I shouldn't just bang on the door and wake them up and disturb them, I reason with myself. Or maybe I'm just trying to postpone the inevitable.

And just before I reach the dark and sleepy house of mine, I dart to the right, away from the house, across the road and the lawn, looking for the bench which I know should be here. My mum used to sit on it, watching us play tag or doing cartwheels.

The bench is wet, but it doesn't matter by this point: my clothes are so soaked that I doubt I'd feel any extra moisture.

My emotions are a tangled mess. I desperately want to be inside that house, to ring the doorbell and see their faces, but I'm too afraid to go in.

How is it possible for two such polarised wishes to coexist inside me?

So I sit there, consuming the dark quiet silhouette of my house with my eyes.

Rafe is behind me, still on his feet. He hovers for a bit behind the bench and then settles into quietness. He doesn't try to sit next to me and I'm surprised by the stab of hurt I feel.

My wings wrap tighter around me as if consoling me or maybe just simply trying to keep me warm.

∞ ∞ ∞

I wake up with a jolt.

The dribble pools in the corner of my mouth. I fell asleep, sitting on the bench.

It's now a few hours later and a weak grey dawn, misted by a morning haze, is trying to break through the blanket of the night, but so far only managing to turn everything grey, like in a black and white movie.

I wipe my mouth with my sleeve, scanning the street.

In the hazed light of the morning my council estate looks the same as it was years ago, when I was taken from here, driven away in the social worker's car, which held the smell of a new car and an overbearing synthetic smell of cherries. Even now, so many years later, I still remember the packet of a cherry air freshener bouncing on the elastic string off the rear-view mirror.

I scan the surrounding area, taking in the familiar sights and smells. The estate hasn't changed in the few years of my absence.

The broken and caved in places short fences surround the identical two storey grey council homes. These wrecked fences are like decayed mouths of old men in the estate, pitiful and sad. The cement panels on the houses are covered in chipped stone, giving the houses the resemblance of a bizarre box, gift-wrapped in grey sand paper. Net curtains are inside almost every window on the estate. It was chic then and it is still chic now. Most of the windows along the street still have curtains drawn, protecting the sleep of the people inside.

Carried by the earlier wind, rubbish is stuck in the branches of the trees and inside the bushes like weird Christmas decorations, adorning the November-bare branches of the estate. A carrier bag, caught at the top in the nearby tall tree, flaps loudly in a wind like a ship's standard.

Litter is strewn across the pavements and the mess of the plastic wrappers has faded and begun to break and crumble, and the little hills of rubbish have formed under the bushes, fences and under the curbs.

A few front lawns in front of a few homes sport the small armies of weathered gnomes. I remember local boys jumping into these gardens after dark, re-arranging the gnomes into all-sorts of disturbing and incriminating positions to the displeasure of the elderly residents.

The grass in the front lawn of my house is neatly cut and colourful plastic toys are scattered over the yellowed grass. A little yellow and red ride-along car is parked proudly amongst this child's heaven. I don't remember any of these toys being here and they are too young to belong to my sister.

Maybe my mum had another baby?

The door of the house next to mine opens and an old lady in pink fluffy sleepers, a thick brown and red tartan coat over a fleecy pink housecoat comes out, dragging a protesting dog on the leash with her. The overweight old dog pulls at the leash and shakes his head, he is peeved as he'd rather be inside and sleeping on the sofa, than standing outside and bracing the cold November wind.

"Come on, Georgie", the old woman yells to the dog and her high-pitched, crackling voice travels around the block. "Come on, do a wee-wee."

The dog, ignoring her instructions completely, turns back and tries to climb up the two small steps back into the house but she yanks at his leash again.

"Come on, Georgie, do a wee-wee."

I can easily recognise this woman and her signature call to Georgie is unmistakable. She was our neighbour for as long as I could remember. Every morning instead of the alarm bell, I'd be woken by her calls to Georgie. Even when I was very young, she was already very old, and she hasn't changed a single bit since then. Even her thick tartan coat and pink housecoat are the same.

The resigned dog paddles down the steps and squats down in the middle of the lawn to do his business.

I could swear he did it on purpose, as some sort of payment for dragging him out at this early hour. I expect the woman to tell him off, but she just stretches her thin pale lips in a wide smile, yelling down the wind: "Good boy, Georgie, good boy." For an old lady she has a decent pair of lungs on her.

The sudden wave of memories engulfs me. The sudden call of my childhood is so strong and welcoming that tears gather and spill from my eyes and I feel as if I am back home.

I'm back to where I ran from. I'm back to where I've run to. I'm back to where I want to be. But I'm afraid if I may be no longer wanted.

And without a clear reason in my head, I get up and cross the lawn and the road, stopping in front of the wrought iron short gate of my neighbour's house, which hangs closed just by a single hinge.

"Excuse me", I croak but even I can barely hear myself.

I clear my throat.

"Excuse me? Auntie Pat?" I call louder.

The dog notices me first.

He turns his head, staring at me with his sad, wet olives eyes, then he gets up and trots to the gate, dragging his owner after him. Georgie is a chunky grey staffie. He was always on a lazy side, so jumping over a fence or even barking was always too much of an ask of him.

Auntie Pat follows him, coming closer to the gate. Her face is now only a few inches away from mine. She never had great eyesight to begin with, but now I think it has disappeared completely. Up close, she smells of "Dove" soap, baby talcum powder and her never changing, unmistakable perfume, which must have soaked into her pores by now, always smelling too strong when mixed with her sweat. This morning she smells of porridge too.

I remember, every Friday after picking up her pension from the local post office, she would walk to the small estate's corner shop, buy a few sweets and then would call me and my sister to her gate and give us either a small packet of "Haribo" each, or a tight roll of "Love hearts" and for me, that was the best thing about Fridays.

"Hello? Who is it?" she yells into my face.

Her unseeing eyes and lips smile, and the deeper wrinkles form around her eyes. She is pleased at the prospect of a visitor and a nice long chat.

"Auntie Pat, it's me, Ariel. Do you remember me? I used to live here with my family. My family still lives here", and I point to the dark house next door.

Auntie Pat is still looking at me and not following my hand. She really can't see.

"Davies. Your next door neighbours? I'm Ariel Davies." My name sounds like a question out of my lips as if I'm asking her.

"Oh, yes", she urgently nods, as fast as her old neck would allow her. "I remember Davies's. They had these two lovely beautiful girls, such lovely girls. They used to play so nicely together, just over there."

She points to the lawn behind me.

"I used to watch them play. Even Georgie liked them."

She smiles towards the end of the leash.

"Such the lovely girls. Shame what happened to Davies's eldest girl."

She leans in closer to share the secret, but she doesn't reduce the volume even a single bit as she adds, shouting so close to my ear, "the social services took her away. Just came one day and took her away. Just like that." She loosely waves her hand.

"I heard the mum and the girl rowing a lot, but who doesn't row? Especially here. Every evening is like an episode of 'Eastenders'. But the girl was always so polite, always would stop and say hello."

She goes into one, suspended in her own memories.

"I know, auntie Pat", I edge into a gap of her memories, leaning in and yelling a bit louder. "I am Ariel Davies, from the next door."

I glance at my house and at the windows, draped in lacy net curtains.

They are about to hear me, about to come out following my voice.

I expect it now. I want it. I think I would prefer them to open the door and come out, rather than me knocking on the closed door and not to be allowed in.

"Ariel? Is it you?" she yells and her lips stretch into an even wider smile. "How have you been, pet? It's so wonderful of you to stop by. Come on in, come on in. I have fresh porridge on the stove and I'll put the kettle on. I got some fresh Digestives the other day. We'll sit down and you'll tell me all about yourself", and she makes a move to open the gate.

But "open" would imply that it was closed to begin with. The gate sits ajar, hanging on the top hinge, resting its weight on the ground. Auntie Pat would need to drag the gate along the grass to create a gap wide enough for me to slide in.

"That's okay auntie Pat", I yell back, leaning to her. "I'm here to see my family."

"What family?" she yells back, lifting her head at me, pausing her futile attempts to move the gate.

Oh dear, she has lost her marbles as well. Vision, hearing and now that. Poor woman.

"My family – Davies's. Next door", I yell.

"There are no Davies's next door no more, dear. They've moved."

"What do you mean 'moved'? How? When?"

Baffled, I forgot to yell.

Not hearing me, she clutches the side of the gate with her frail, creased fingers, now actively trying to move it, even if for an inch, but the gate wouldn't budge, stuck in the soggy ground.

"What do you mean 'moved', auntie Pat?" I yell to the old woman.

My mind is reeling, uncomprehending her words.

Rafe told me that his man is watching my sister. He told me that he is next to her, looking after her. He promised me that he'll keep her safe. He said that his man is nearby, and that nothing is going to happen to her under his man's watch, that if anything, anything at all *is to happen, we would know and we will be there at a moment's notice. I don't understand.*

I turn, looking for Rafe by the bench across the lawn. But he is already here, standing not far behind me, listening to our conversation, and then our gazes meet.

His concerned hazel eyes are on me, under his drawn eyebrows. Two perfectly parallel deep wrinkles cut across his forehead and his lips are pursed into a thin line and through all of it, I can't read him.

And at that second I wonder if this news is only news to me. I wonder if maybe now he is desperately scraping in his mind, trying to figure out his way out, looking for an explanation of something plausible that gullible old me would believe.

"Oh, yes, moved", auntie Pat shouts and with a rod stiff neck I turn back to look at her. She happily nods her head, pleased to have the information that someone else doesn't.

"Last summer. After the littl'un was out of the hospital. They all packed up and left, littl'un, mum and that fella of hers. Packed up and left in just two days. Police with the social services' lady came after a fortnight, looking for them, asking me all these questions, but how would I know where they went? Nobody says nowt to me anymore. Not like in olden days", she yells, but her voice zooms out in my head and the words fuzz out, replaced by the dull ringing.

Gone. Moved. My sister. Alone, with no one to protect her. Taken away by my mother and stepfather.

Nobody now will be there to protect her, nobody will be there for her.

My sister's face rises in front of my eyes: her cheeky cute dolly face with big rosy cheeks, wide unguarded smile and big innocent eyes of a happy, protected by me, child.

But the next second her face morphs into a fearful mask. Her scared, confused, startled eyes are pleading for forgiveness just the moment before the fist with a heavy cheap gold ring, that I know so well, drives into her soft bones.

I sway on my feet.

Why did the social worker let her go? How? She said they would keep her. She said they wouldn't let her go. But now I don't know where she is and no one does. Rafe told me to come with him. He promised me he'll look after her. He promised he would keep her safe. He swore. He promised.

But he lied, just like all of them. He just lied, lied to get what he wanted.

My confused head is ringing.

Why would he let me come here if he knew they had moved? Did I upset him that much that he would let me walk to my house for miles through the rain, whilst worrying about meeting them and get my hopes up only for it all be for nothing?

I whirl to face Rafe. Auntie Pat is still yelling down the wind, saying something but I can't make out a single word. Rafe's gaze meets mine.

Anger and betrayal rake through me.

I'm livid. I'm scared. Hopelessness and fear are screaming at me.

And the next second a loud piercing noise of a slap rings in the morning air, followed by a single terse Georgie's bark, which echoes down the street, as Rafe's cheek grows red under my gaze and my right hand itches and burns.

"You, lying bastard! You promised! You told me you were looking after her, but you lied and now she's gone. You promised me that she will be okay and now she is certainly not. Do you understand that?! She has no one with her now! *No one!* And I don't know where she is. All that she has is my mother and step-father, and I don't know who is worse! It's all your fault! All of it!"

We stand there and stare at each other – accusation in my glare and stoic silence in Rafe's.

But that is not enough. Rage is waking, flooding me. Tears are burning my eyes.

I turn away from him – I'm afraid of what else I might do.

"Thank you auntie Pat", I yell and I can hear spikes and drops in my voice, as the words catch in my throat on unshed tears. I'm afraid to come undone right here and right now.

"I have to go. Thank you for everything."

And as I bend over to kiss the top of the old lady's head, the warmth, softness and smell of her is so welcoming and reassuring, that it floods me and I can't any longer hold my tears as I feel them falling, round and fat like pearls, falling on top of this old lady's hair.

I so desperately want to hold on to her, to turn back time and take myself back to the childhood I had once. But I know that none of it will ever happen.

The past is no longer alive, it's no longer there. It's gone, and I will never step back in it, and the earlier rage evaporates just as fast as it came, replaced by the throbbing emptiness of grief.

And before I start balling my eyes out, before I break down completely, I try to let go of my old neighbour and I am startled to realise, that she is holding me now, responding to my hug, softly stroking my cold back just under my wings. And I'm so afraid of losing it, to rip the last stitch right here in the middle of the street, for everyone to see and hear, that I nudge away from her and she lets go.

The chill seeps into me, replacing her caring warmth.

"Why don't you come inside, dear? You're so cold", auntie Pat calls.

Hearing the word "inside", Georgie behind her turns and paddles back to the door and the unmanned leash drags after him – he doesn't need a second invitation to get back into the warmth of the house.

"Thank you, auntie Pat", I start, but I forgot how hard it is to speak up when you're holding back tears. "But I have to go. Thank you", and I give the last fleeting hug to the warm woman in front of me and on the leaden legs, I force myself to turn and walk, as tears now freely flowing down my cheeks.

But I can't stop myself and I look at my home one last time.

I glance over my shoulder at its quiet and peaceful shape. It's now the home to another child and I hope that this child would have a happier childhood in it, a childhood filled with laughter and hugs and with millions of kisses. I hope that this child will always be loved and happy in this home – happier than I've ever been.

I've lost something else today. Again.

I thought I had nothing more to lose. I was sure that I was alone at the empty and lonely rock bottom, but as it turned out, there was still something for me to lose and I didn't even know that I had it with me until I had lost it just now.

I didn't realise and never admitted to myself, but I always had a flicker of hope living inside me, the hope to find my way back home.

But finally I have no home to come back to.

This home is no longer mine. My home is gone, taken away from me. I have nowhere to go.

The lies that I was telling myself are now shattered against the reality of it all. There's no way back for me. I'm no longer wanted.

Nobody is waiting for me and I am no one's child. I am unwanted and unloved, left behind on the street like a forgotten plastic toy, discarded and abandoned.

The weak November sun rises at the bottom of my street, lighting up with its orange glow the dark rooftops of the peaceful buildings around me.

It revives the ashen grey clouds above, illuminating their bellies with a reddish copper glow. It wakes up the sky with a tangerine glimmer, turning the wet pavement under my feet into a soft polished bronze, reflecting the light of the sky above.

And at this precise moment I feel as if the sun is calling to me, asking me to come to it, to come with it.

Offering a way out.

I can't see anything but the calling sun.

It is here, rising for me. It hasn't left me and after a few stumbling steps, my walk becomes rushed, urgent and before I know it, I'm running down the illuminated bronze runway of my empty street, running like I'm being chased.

Tears are rolling down my face, dripping off my chin and stealing my sight.

Ugly, heart-wrenching wails and screams surround me and with a surprise I realise that it's me who is screaming. I howl and I can't stop.

I want to run away, to hide, do anything I can to stop the pain that rips at my heart and slices at my gut, pounding in my head. I want it all to be done, all to be gone.

Why me?

How much more?

These two questions are on an unending loop shuffle in my head, and like a colourful glass in a kaleidoscope they shift and fall off only to form into the same questions over and over again.

Waves of misery and pain cover me, whispering that it never gets better. It presses inside, constricting my lungs and chest, pressing heavily like a concrete slab, pushing, punishing, crushing and I struggle to breathe.

It never does and never will, not for me, that's for sure. Life only gets worse, always had and always will.

Misery whispers the helpful reminders that I've been here before, just like that, running down this street, kicked out of my own home, told never to come back, told to forget that I even had a family.

And with the last step, I push at the ground with my foot and my glorious purple wings open wide around me, lifting me up to the sky. My wings beat around me and my ears are filled with their loud swishing.

Birds are silent in the trees and in the skies around me. They're probably scared of me, scared of a monster, abomination, freak or maybe because they know what I can do to the whole world.

I always thought that animals are smarter than humans. I guess the size of one's brain is never an indicator of one's ability to think and understand.

I'm flying on my large purple wings and for the first time I'm not scared or afraid of flying. Something weak inside my head pleads for me to be careful but I don't have any space left for anything, apart from this gruelling pain of rejection and loss. With every push of the wings, with every new beat, I get closer to the sun. I get higher.

I fly under the cotton wool of clouds, through the lace of fog and moisture, over and then above them. My neck strains, my rigid body calling me to push forward, and my wings can't take me up fast enough.

The sunlight grows stronger and brighter above the clouds. It blinds me, so I slam my eyes shut, beating my wings faster, all rationale gone, wanting, no! – *needing* to see the sun and its promise of escape.

And as I get higher, leaving the curly morning clouds of an orange candyfloss carpet below, the air temperature drops and my warm breath leaves my mouth in a white, warm cloud of smoke.

My black jeans and sweatshirt are crusting over under my gaze. A layer of prickly frost crystals grows over me and their millions of facets catch the sun, and small fleeting rainbows wink and shine around me.

My mind drifts off again, bringing the memories of my life to shore, but these memories are just a rotting carcass of an empty vessel, battered for a long time by the raging waves of a turbulent life.

It never gets better.

Never does and never will...

And with it something changes in me.

This shift is more of a snap: ragged and irreparable, subtle and yet profound.

I can't catch it, can't name it, but it is there. It is spreading the nocuous numbness within, fuzzing my head, disconnecting my heart and I know it's here to stay.

It's like the frost crept inside and now freezing everything within. I feel numb, empty, spent.

I am bereft of life.

The air is silent and I'm silent with it.

The piercing numbness echoes in the void inside me. I *become* the empty void. It is as if everything that I had there before was scooped out, leaving the dark and mute shell behind, filled with emptiness and desolation.

Even the tears have abandoned me.

The icy blanket of frost covers me. Like a white thick layer of moss, it covers my clothes and my shoes, spreading over my hair and the first flake of frost sprouts over my wings.

I'm struggling to move my legs and my arms now, and every time they move, the crunching sounds of breaking ice over my clothes cut through the silent air.

Frozen, my wings are no longer flexing as the wings should. They turn rigid and stiff, and a memory from my childhood suddenly rushes in, when I tried to fly off the top of the shed on my cut out cardboard wings.

But today I have real wings and I keep pushing them as if it's the only motion I remember how to do. I force the beating of my wings. I want them to take me higher.

My heart rate has been increasing for a while, and now it hammers at my ribcage as its rhythm changed from the frightened pumping of emotions of when I was running down the street, to the deafening drumming of survival.

I can't feel my toes or my fingers anymore.

With every new push, my wings slow their beating. As if in slow motion, they take longer to rise and fall, and with it my ascent is slowing.

My stifled wings can barely move, and now and again, when the wings lose their pace and freeze, I'd feel the sharp jerk of a second short fall, sudden like a hiccup, before my wings would regain their pathetic mobility again.

And after one of these falls, with a sudden clarity I can see why I flew up this high, why I'm here.

The sharp stab of this thought surprises and calms me.

Unexpectedly, I feel clear and at peace, I feel like this is what I meant to do.

I feel like I am finally in charge, like I am making a decision and for the first time I know, that I am making the right one for a change. And I know that it would be the last decision I'll have to make, so I relax and settle into the promised peace of it.

"That's it. That's the end", and with that thought, I take in a deep steadying breath and turn my head, taking in a blue silent world around me with a blinding bright light above.

The beauty of this world startles me.

It will be safer without me.

I take another clearing breath.

I've made up my mind.

I close my eyes. I drop my arms to the sides, forcing my wings to stop their beating, forcing them to shut down their protective survival.

Then a sudden jerk and then... a fall like a cannonball jump into a pool off a diving board.

A wind rushes past me. It picks up pace, wheezing past, whistling in my ears. The air tugs and pushes at me, pulling at my clothing, at my hair and I start to tumble, spinning like a forgotten sock in a drier.

I'm losing control and I can no longer see where's up and where's down.

I'm in the clouds now, falling through a haze of fog and moisture, and the warmth of the cloud is defrosting my clothes and my wings.

Blood rushes back to the surface of my skin and I feel hot and flushed, with an unsettling feeling of hundreds of needles prickling at my face.

The next second, a high pitched scream rings in my ears. It's distant and metallic, as if badly tuned radio just caught a rogue transmission.

I cover my ears with my hands and shut my eyes, but that piercing noise is not going anywhere. It rings in my head with such a nerve-twitching noise and with such force, that I'm sure that my ears are about to bleed.

My nerves feel open and raw under its call.

Suddenly, this static interference finds the pounding rhythm and as the sound deepens, fading in and out, I can hear a low guttural chant behind that screech.

And with this chant I feel the presence with me, *inside me.*

That presence is angry with me. It wants something from me and I know it's something I'm not prepared to give.

Of its own accord, the essence twists, unfurls, waking inside me. It stretches like a sleeping lion which had just heard the beating of gazelles' hooves and is about to give a chase, and with it my wings wake up.

Fuelled by that weird chant and by the warm power of my essence, my wings, no longer frozen, open wide around me in their full glory. They feel alive and awake, they are singing with joy and power.

The chanting stops and with it stops the piercing screech.

I open my eyes.

Revitalised, my wings want to show me what they can do. They want to take me on the fly, they demand to protect me.

They try to open and close, looking for the lost rhythm and every time they find even a shred of old mobility, they would open wide and my tumbling would stop, my fall would slow down and I would float for a bit, but not by much and not for long.

But I'm not interested. I'm not willing to give up.

I reach around myself, yanking at my feathers, pulling at them. I want to hurt them. I want to push them into submission.

"I said 'no'. Damn it! It's my life. I'm making the decisions here", I screech into the blue silence but I'm being ignored and now I'm angry.

How pathetic am I? Not even strong enough to do this right!

I'm disgusted with myself. The self-loathing is so strong and deep, that I rush to get this thing over with, to relieve that pain within.

I reach around, grab fists full of feathers and tug at my wings, wrapping them around me.

A lot can be sorted with blunt crude force!

The power inside is maybe angry with me, but so am I. For once I want to do what I want, for once I need to control my life.

The battle of wills over my life has begun, and I'll be damned if I lose my life again.

So I hold on tight to my restricted wings and as we fight, while tumbling and soaring, past the curly morning grey clouds, I can finally see a patchwork carpet of the fields below, outlined with the black thick marker of a dense dark line of bare November trees.

It's here. Now it's not far. Not long left at all.

The restricted wings can do very little now. They pull from my hold but I'm not prepared to let go.

The smell and feel of the air has changed. Now it is wetter with a fine drizzle knitted in it, and it has an earthy muddy smell of rotting leaves.

It's not going to be long now.

I close my eyes.

I take in the last lungful of November air. I breathe out.

As I'm falling through the last layers of clouds, expecting the crashing impact of collapsed ribs and punctured lungs, a hard missile collides with me, kicking the breath out and disorienting me.

But it comes from an unexpected angle.

Surprised by the impact, I release my wings.

Using that moment, my wings take over control. They open wide and I'm soaring again and once I regain my balance and orientation, I realise that two familiar arms encircle my waist and the November wet air unexpectedly smells of tropical fruits.

"What the hell do you think you're doing?" Rafe's angry voice roars next to my head.

What is he doing here? How has he ended up here? I thought he couldn't fly anymore.

Why am I still in the air?

Why am I still alive?

One after another, these thoughts rush through in my surprised frozen mind like a bullet train, before the final thought arrives at the platform, announcing in a nasal voice that it is its final destination and it's not going any further.

"*He!*" my mind roars.

"*Again! It's none of his business. It's my life. Whatever is left of it, it's mine!*"

"Let go of me! Let go!" I thrash in his embrace, screaming over the settled wind. The air is still and quiet around us as we float only a few yards above the tree tops.

His remaining two wings swing and flap as he hangs under a weird angle, like a puppet pulled up by two strings on a side. His left side is pulled upwards, keeping his body almost horizontal, pulling mine along with his.

My wings are pleased to have an accomplice on their side, happy to have freedom and power to float, dance and keep me up.

I'm no longer falling. I'm not allowed.

"Get off of me", I wail.

I claw at his arms around me, at his hands. He needs to let go. He must let go.

But he doesn't. Instead he squeezes me tighter in his grip, pulling me closer to him.

"For Arllu sake, would you bloody stop with all this drama? I'm so sick of it all", he bellows and I feel him shaking next to me, and his hold tightens on me as if he's trying to strangle my waist. "I'm sick of your childishness, sick of your whining, of your constant drama. Do you think you are the only one who has lost? Do you think you're the only one who is hurting?"

We have stopped falling completely, and now floating on the airstreams as I continue to thrash in his embrace.

For a fleeting second, I wonder how ridiculous we might look to anyone who might be watching from the ground. The two bodies aligned and seemingly snuggled in a warm embrace. Only me, shaking in his hold, disturbs that perfect image.

But that's if anyone would've bothered to look up. Nobody would. People tend to watch their feet far more than the sky.

"Selfish little child", he seethes through his teeth, "always with her own needs and everyone else can be damned. Everyone can go to Hell as far as you're concerned, can't they?"

I can't see his face but his voice behind me bellows, shaking with anger, spiking now and again and I can feel his anger pulsating off him and something tells me, that I should be afraid, but my mind can't process any of it right now.

"Let me go", I screech. "It has nothing to do with you. Sod off."

"You always have to be melodramatic, don't you? Like a ridiculous child you're always making assumptions, decisions all by yourself, thinking you know better. Have you ever thought to stop and think for a second? Maybe talk to me? To ask me? Haven't I proven myself to you? Haven't I proven my loyalty to you?" he bellows, as he shakes me and like a rag doll, I flop from side to side in his hands.

"Yet I still haven't earned your trust, but *he* did. After everything I have done for you", he fumes behind me, his voice rising with every word and dull fear finally begins to mutter something, still incoherent, at the back of my mind.

But even that tiny spark of fear can't compete with the insatiable, overbearing need to finish what I've started. And right now he is keeping me away from it. He is keeping me away from the promised peace.

And with it my hate spikes in return.

It's all his fault.

Everything is his fault. It's his fault I'm here, his fault that I've been taken away. It's his fault that I lost my sister and now he's not letting me to do the only thing I need. He is here just to ruin my life.

I reach behind and he is right there.

I'm livid. I want to hurt him, just as badly as I am hurting.

I can feel the soft skin of his face under my fingers and, as my anger seeps into my fingertips, my nails sink into his skin.

Rafe's agonising roar echoes in the misty air, the hold of his arms loosens, and he lets go of me.

It's unexpected and I drop for a few seconds before my wings open up again, lifting me.

But I'm pleased. This drop brings me closer to the ground.

I feel as if I can touch the tree tops with my feet now. I probably can skip from tree top to the tree top and for a fleeting moment I wonder how that might feel like.

I lost everything. I need to do it now. I must.

I try to take another calming breath, but the air coming in is chopped and ragged. I'm desperate to finish what I have started, but I'm unsettled now, my peace and resoluteness are replaced with urgency and need, fear and doubt.

But as I grab hold of my wings, stifling them once again, I'm rammed at full speed by the warm solid body, with Rafe's voice bellowing in my ear and I'm engulfed by him again.

I'm no longer surprised and I can't take it anymore.

I jam my elbow somewhere behind me and it makes contact. As my elbow sinks into something soft, I then kick. I'm twisting and turning, wiggling to give myself room to push him away from me. I throw blind punches behind me, screaming, and in this mess of tangled bodies and limbs, we drop the last few yards and our bodies catch on the tops of trees.

And suddenly, we are swallowed by the trees.

Once through the first branches, my wings can no longer open.

Obstructed by the serrated tree limbs, which are slicing at my face and my wings, ripping at my clothes, the wings can't open or lift me up, leaving my body to the mercy of the woods, while gravity pulls me down towards thicker branches at the base.

The branches are dense now. I'm surrounded by the deafening cacophony of loud snaps of tree limbs, sharp tearing sounds of the fabric and my pained and surprised cries. Somewhere in the distance, Rafe's groans with sudden pierced screams answer me.

38

The branches are thicker now and although they're slowing my fall, they hurt more. I'm tumbling from one thick branch to the next, even thicker one. I cry out in surprise and the air leaves my lungs when I land backwards across another one.

I can hear a deep crunch of bone and instantly the blinding pain slices through my wing and my lower back.

My body balances for a second before it rolls over and drops again.

I swing my arms, desperately grabbing empty air, trying to stop the fall before I spot a small branch in front of me. I close my hand over it but it snaps with a celery like crunch under my fingers and I plummet again, bouncing off the tree's thick branches and my cries turn into painful whimpers. The feelings and senses dim, but not before I see a tree limb, as thick as the tree itself, coming at me with a promise of impending doom.

Chapter 3

I awaken lying on the damp padded forest floor.

Wet leaves and moss under me seep with moisture and my cheek rests on the cushioning slush of brown decaying leaves, and my nose is filled with the stench of a bog or a compost heap. I'm on my front and the stagnant water, covering the ground is soaking through my clothes, coating my belly and my legs.

I try to open my eyes, but my eyelids are refusing to lift.

I'm hurting all over.

I try to move, to move my arms, to raise myself up, but my body doesn't obey me, shooting a burning rod of pain down my back and I cry out.

Or so I thought.

A pitiful whimpering sound escapes my throat instead.

And I don't move anymore, I can't and I don't want to, finally the pain inside my soul has a mate in the agony of my body.

A solitary magpie in the branches above swears into a deaf silence like a lonely machine gun. She is too busy with her birdy life to pay attention to a half dead human on the ground.

A freezing November wind rushes past the bare tree trunks and branches.

Without the protection of a leafy canopy, the free wind can travel anywhere it wants, nothing can restrict its freedom. The wind whistles through the tree tops, it rustles up the last dry leaves on the ground or, when it wishes, it can pick up the pace and push an unexpected walker off his feet.

Its cold gentle hand strokes my hair like a gentle hand of a parent.

The wind is soft and sympathetic. It knows me. It'd seen my pain before. It can hear my soft cries now.

I cry and I can't stop nor do I want to.

I feel bone raw and drained, as if everything was scraped out of me with a blunt rusty knife, leaving the raggedy wounds and an exhausted shell behind.

The grinding guilt of what I've tried to do is weaved with a weak relief that I have failed. The anger and the self-loathing are back with a vengeance, sniggering at me, whispering "helpful" reminders of how truly useless I am.

Embarrassment and shame, guilt and relief, anger and disappointment are spinning in me. It's like a morbid rollercoaster, a gruesome thrill ride, which stops at the barrier of disbelief at what I just tried to do.

My defeat is the last and final. Even death is out of my reach.

I no longer know what to do. What to do with my life, with myself. I have no more moves left.

And the desperate resignation floods in.

The misery, endless misery and pain will be mine forever. They will move in, swallowing my heart and my soul, and there will be nothing else left of me. I might as well stay here and wait for the rain to come, for the stagnant water to rise and bury me in.

The wind picks up again.

Now it pushes at me. Maybe it wants me to get to my feet or maybe it's trying to push me deeper into the rotting slush, I just don't know.

Still swearing into the quiet, the magpie takes flight, taking her grievances away with her. She is a bird on a mission and judging by her earlier angry rant, someone is going to pay.

With her gone, it's only me and the wind left.

Carefully I open my eyes.

I must've been out for a while as the light in the forest has changed: it's milkier and duller somehow. It feels like evening. It's as if the sun had enough of its pointless task of lighting up the world, even the sun is tired and sick of life.

Brown leaves, in different stages of decomposing fill my vision. I have never looked at old autumnal leaves that close-up before. Their bodies are weathered, paper-thin with leafy veins running underneath. These leaves are so frail that they can be crushed to a grey powder between my fingers. They are food to the last autumnal worms and starving beetles. They are the building material for insects' homes.

The rotting leaves are almost the soil itself. The decomposing leaves are no longer the juice-bursting green lustrous canopy above. They are no longer the strong army of a million.

The end of life is ugly and unattractive. Everything eventually turns into dirt.

Even me.

Brown should be the colour of death, not black.

A few inches away from my nose, a small spider is weaving his small flimsy web, balancing it precariously between two fallen thin twigs, standing upright in the bogged slush of the ground.

His black latex glossy body is moving around and his eight brown legs, as if dressed in a shimmering lycra, are busy spinning and anchoring new strands of the web to the old ones. When even the slightest gust of wind would come, the spider would stop, holding tight onto his pitiful web, but once the wind would die, the little spider with the same enthusiasm would resume his work. The tiny spider is methodical and relentless. It's like he hadn't been told how pitiful and meaningless his task is, that he's not going to achieve anything with it, and that when the destruction would eventually come, it will be devastating against the possible gain of a few malnourished pre-winter insects.

But he is busy, working, constructing his weightless web to catch non-existent flies, which are already fast asleep in the ground for the winter or dead.

What a pointless work. One strong gust of wind and these twigs will collapse under him, breaking his web and him with it.

But the minuscule spider doesn't concern himself with November wind or what it might do to him, nor does he question insects' sleeping habits in late autumn. He is engrossed in his work, running circles, filling in his web.

I'm mesmerised by the tiny spider. There's something magical in the measured creation of his web, in the methodical movements of his body. There's something soothing in his rhythmic moves. It is robotic and artistic at the same time, precise and flowing.

Through the haze of unblinking eyes, I watch the spider, suspended in my own thoughts, when the soft moans come through to me.

I blink myself awake. I stop and listen, but I hear nothing. Only the wind whistles in the trees.

Must be my imagination. Maybe it's concussion. I hit my head on that branch pretty hard.

But that thought doesn't alarm or scare me, it doesn't call me to get up and find help. It's just a passing detached observation.

So I lay there listening to the quiet when another wave of moans is brought to me by the wind. Now I can hear my name in those. Someone is calling for me.

Shit! What is it? Is it concussion? Could I be imagining things? Or maybe I'm having some sort of passed out dream, like they say people in a coma might have.

But what if it's not? What if I'm not in a coma and someone is really calling for me?

Who'll be calling my name then?

And a moment later, the memory brings one clear thought: *Rafe!*

It must be Rafe! Oh my god, he needs help!

He probably hurt himself during the fall!

Nobody asked him to butt in there! Nobody asked for his help! Bloody hero! Macho!

But what if he will die? He didn't ask for it either. Unlike some...

But what if it's not him? What if it's a trap?

And what? What are they going to do to you that you haven't tried to do to yourself just now...

While I lay there, having a full on argument with myself, the helpful November wind brings my name to me and I know this time for sure that it is Rafe's voice is calling.

I try to get up.

I have more mobility than I had earlier and the pain is more bearable, but it still twists at my muscles and bones as I draw my arms underneath myself.

Slowly and precariously, I manoeuvre one arm at a time, one leg at a time and after what feels like a century, I manage to lift myself up on all fours. But I'm unsteady. I swing like a drunken pub patron after a good night in his favourite establishment.

My knees and hands sink into the muddy ground, giving me some stability. While I'm swinging from side to side, my vision tilts as if the sky and ground have agreed to swap places. And suddenly, surprising even myself, I throw up, loudly, wrenching, exhausting.

Maybe my strength is back or maybe the fear of falling face forward in my own mess is greater, keeping me up, but I manage to lock my arms underneath me and stay up. I wipe the corner of my mouth on my shoulder. How I wish I could have some water to wash out my mouth, but for now, the vile aftertaste is here to stay.

Another set of moans and calls of my name descend upon me.

I have made up my mind to get up and go, however pathetic the execution of that plan might be, so I better get on with it.

And like a clumsy baby that is still learning how to crawl, I manoeuvre myself around, around my mess, toward the direction of the calls. I'm careful to not disturb the spider, not to knock over his pitiful twigs and his web.

Good luck, buddy.

With countless stops to catch my breath, and collapsing on the wet bogged ground, I make my way forward.

When the air becomes silent and still, I'm petrified that I might be going in the wrong direction. But every time I hear my name called through the pain, and I can hear the voice a bit louder, I'm relieved that I'm moving in the right direction.

I'm out of breath. I can't be far now. I wasn't to begin with, but with the shearing pain, I have been crawling for what feels like hours, and my hands are scratched by the brown fallen pine needles.

"Ariel."

The call is clear now and I can hear a breath of pain in it. It's Rafe's voice without a doubt.

The large scaly pine tree trunk in front of me obstructs my vision, and in the murky darkness of the forest I wait for my vision to adjust, before I spot the corner of a black boot with a thick thread, just behind the centuries old pine tree.

Breath catches in my throat.

It wasn't my imagination after all.

I exhale, continuing on my laborious crawl around the tree trunk. My eyes are glued to that boot, and as I continue around the tree, more of the boot comes into view.

Under my gaze and with every inch I cover, the boot sprouts more of the leg attached to it. The leg grows into a hip and eventually the full body comes into the view.

It's Rafe. I still can't see his face but its Rafe's clothes underneath that layer of mud and Rafe's two wings squashed underneath his body, spread over the muddy ground.

"Oh no, oh no, oh no."

Oh, no; oh, no", I chant under my breath and I can't seem to push past these words or formulate my thoughts and fears, as I rock myself.

My gaze is glued to his lifeless form. He lies on his back and the entire front of his body is covered in mud, peppered with thin twigs and frail leaves. His face is covered in mud as well, and an 'out of place' thought shoves at me, that he looks like a client in a spa retreat, having a cleansing mud face mask, but I push that ridiculous thought out of my head.

"Oh no, oh no, oh no." My broken record is still going strong.

Eventually, I push past the shock, and as fast as my searing muscles allow me, I crawl towards Rafe. But my attempts at speeding the crawl only result in more faffing about rather than producing any results.

Suddenly my hand slips in the puddle of a slimy mud. It slides sideways, away from me as if it had enough of my shenanigans and now ready to look for a new owner. The sharp pain sears at my shoulder as I fall, clumsily, with all my weight into the bogged rotting ground.

"Argh!"

The heavy fall knocks the air out of my lungs.

My face hits the edge of a puddle, sending broken brown leaves surfing the tiny waves, as the echo of my cries bounces off and fades into the forest.

Damn!

I want to say it out loud, I want to swear some more, but I'm afraid to open my mouth and swallow any of the stale water.

Inwardly, I roll my eyes at myself, cursing my clumsiness in my head.

I pull myself up again. With every passing minute the hot rod in my back cools down, the joints and muscle find their old mobility. But I don't want to risk the fall again, so I'm back to my crawl, desperate to cover the last inches between me and Rafe.

His eyes are closed and I can hear his ragged breathing from here.

And the closer I get to him, the deeper the panic sinks its claws into me.

I am next to him. I just stare at him, afraid to touch him, afraid to hurt him even more, when his eyelids flutter just ever so slightly and he calls my name.

"Ariel."

It's a weak plea rather than a call. His chest rises as he takes in some air.

"Ariel."

This one is louder and stronger but still belongs to a person in pain.

"I'm here, Rafe, I'm here", I busy around him, scooting closer to his head. I want to wipe his face, I want to lift his head onto my lap but I'm too afraid to hurt him.

"I'm right here, Rafe. I'm here with you."

I don't know if he can hear me as he doesn't answer, so I brave to stroke the top of his head.

His hair is caked in mud. He doesn't cry out in pain under my touch, so I pull down the sleeve of my shirt and softly wipe the mud off his face.

"Rafe, can you hear me? Are you alright? Are you hurt?"

Duh! Of course he is hurt. What a stupid question!

It's quiet for a while and I wonder if he even heard me when he finally answers.

"A bit", he admits. His coarse breathing catches in this throat between his words. "How are you? Are you hurt?"

"I'm fine, Rafe. Don't worry about me", I rush as I wipe the mud off his face. With each of my strokes, more of his pale skin is revealed and by its ashen colour, matched by his laboured breathing, I know that he is in a bigger pain than he is admitting.

"I'm okay, I'm okay", I gush.

The guilt creeps over like a tide. At first its waters just lick at my toes, but it's slowly rising to my knees and it is not long before I'm engulfed by remorse.

All my fault! All my fault. As usual. Always.

The last thought as a mallet pounds at my head.

I grab my head. I want to force that thought out, all the memories out of my head as I hold it in my hands, and I begin to rock, sitting on my knees deep in the murky mud.

But the stubborn and poisonous guilt just won't budge.

The tears come next and I begin to cry, sobbing my heart out, bringing with it a minor relief.

Me. Always me. Everything because of me.

And I rock there as the heart-wrenching sobs and wails come out of me, when I feel the warm hand on my back, unsteadily stroking me.

"Shh, shh, Ariel, it's okay. Everything's okay", he groans, "I'm okay and I'll be alright. It just might take a bit of time to heal, but I will be alright. Nobody died. We're both okay, we'll be okay. You're already healing and will be like new in a few hours."

He tries to reassure me but it's not what I want to hear, it's not what I need.

I need him to yell at me. I need him to swear at me and tell me, that all of it is my fault. I want him to be angry with me just as much as I am angry with myself.

His warm words are like a lighthouse beacon, but their light is too weak and small to get through the thick fog of guilt and grief.

Rafe has now stopped talking. He doesn't say a word, doesn't make a sound, he just silently keeps stroking my back. Slumped over his chest, I ball my eyes out as the stress of the last few hours is riding me hard.

So much for the decisive way out. Oh god. I can't bloody stop crying now. I need to stop. I MUST.

Now I literally have no choice. No way out. I'm inside that perverted game where no normal rules apply and there is no way out. Not the normal way that is.

$$\infty \quad \infty \quad \infty$$

Hours later the light is gone from the sky. The last of it has vanished as if sucked out by a giant through a straw, leaving dark emptiness behind.

The wind is now colder and the earlier rain has turned to sleet.

It is pitch black in the woods and as always, Rafe's body is like a beacon, radiating the light, encasing us in his pearly, glowing bubble.

I get off Rafe.

"Rafe? Rafe?" I call, carefully stroking his chest but the sudden irrational fear that he might be dead underneath me, blankets me and I begin to hyperventilate.

"Rafe?!" The panicked urgency rings in my voice.

"I'm okay, Ariel", he utters through his teeth, "I'm already better than I was before. How are you doing?"

I exhale and slump back on my heels with relief. Then I carefully move, stretching my neck and my back, gently rotating my shoulders.

I feel just as flexible as I was before. The rod in my back is extinguished without a trace. My wings open wide behind my back of their own volition, sweeping brown leaves and mud with the bottom ones.

"I'm okay."

I have to admit, physically I feel as fine as when I was walking down the street only a few hours ago, but mentally I have covered new ground. I'm in new and unchartered territory, and the Hell that Taby dragged me through, comes to mind.

Another dumb arse idea. Brought to you courtesy of my screwed up brain! Welcome to the fudging Wonderland, ladies and gentlemen! Enjoy the ride!

Anger rises within and hot on its heels Rage makes her past due appearance, asking me what the hell have I done now and what dodgy shit I've got myself into this time.

But she is a smart girl and catches up in no time.

She folds her arms at me, tapping her blood red Doc Martens, asking with a challenge why I am trying to make everyone's life easier for them.

"They want it? They had better come and get it. Make them work for it! Mik'hael wants you dead? Let him try. Since when are you working for him?"

The logic on this one is strong and I can't argue with any of it.

"So they've moved. Billy big shit! They didn't die, and neither did your sister. Use your wings to find your sister, or something. They must be useful for something, or are they here just to look pretty? Did you ask Rafe why his man just took off? Was any of it Rafe's making? Did you talk to him?"

Rage has always been the bossy one, and very often she does make sense, so it's no wonder that we've been mates for years.

"He will probably lie", I argue with her.

"Maybe. But you'll see it in his eyes. You'll feel it."

I'm not convinced, but exasperated Rage just rolls her eyes at me and that's the end of the discussion.

"How are you feeling, Rafe? Can you move?"

I don't really know where I want us to go but to lay here overnight is definitely not the plan I'd like to follow.

"I think I can", he pauses, "if you don't mind helping me a bit."

"Of course", I rush. I lean over and freeze a few inches above him. I don't know where he is hurt so I don't even know how to start with him.

How am I going to lift him up? Hold him by his hand and yank him up or do I roll him over to a side?

The school's "First Aid" lesson comes to my mind with its "recovery position" technique. It's called "recovery" for a reason, right? I probably better to start "recover" him that way.

But first things first.

I practically imagine myself as an old fashioned doctor with a leather bag, stethoscope and a monocle, leaning over the ill one, asking: *"Well, well, what do have here? Why don't you tell the good doctor where it hurts?"* And out to the relatives: *"Let's start by examining the patient".*

"Well... um, well", I start, "where does it hurt, Rafe?"

Rafe turns his head giving me an odd look. The mud mask had crusted over his face by now, and begun to crack and chip off.

"My back", he grunts. "I think the earlier wounds have opened up."

"Would you like to roll over?" I'm solid in my role of a 19th century doctor, paying a visit to a patient. I bet if I had a goatee beard, I'd be stroking it by now.

Probably it's my tone, but Rafe gives me another quizzical look, which draws his brows together, cracking the layer of mud on his forehead and some of it falls off.

"You need to help me", he answers.

Okay, the recovery position it is then. I need to roll him onto his left side.

I raise myself off my heels, anchoring my feet into the muddy ground.

Awkwardly I grab hold of his jacket, then changing my mind and releasing it again. I slide my hands under his side but I don't think it will work either.

"When you're quite ready", he bites off with sarcasm.

"Excuse me. I'm trying here." And fuelled by annoyance, I lay my hands over his shoulder and his arm and push, with all my body weight and strength, without giving him any warning.

Rafe's breath leaves him in a short and surprised puff and I can hear his teeth grind next to my ear. Maybe I should've warned him.

"Sorry", I mumble.

"That's okay", he grunts.

His scent assaults me.

That is the strongest smell of fruits, ocean and breeze I've ever experienced next to him. I close my eyes and inhale, and I could swear I can hear seagulls squawking in the bright blue sky, where busy tropical insects buzz next to my ear and the ocean waves lap at the sandy shore, dragging the sand in the water behind with them.

I swear, I can even hear each grain of sand rub against each other as they are leaving the shore.

In a daze, I open my sticky eyes.

Rafe is on his left side. His mud covered wings are spread over the ground under his body. His back is covered with a jacket and I can't see the wounds, but I don't risk taking the clothes off him, especially here – in the middle of nowhere, especially when I don't know what I'm doing.

The puddle of mud under his body, Illuminated by the glum light of his body, looks thicker and stickier than the mud around us, and when I narrow my eyes at it, looking closer, I notice a large autumnal leaf, flat on the ground, just where his shoulder was only a moment ago. This large leaf is still intact and pliable, probably spending its first night on the ground.

But the leaf is not what interests and surprises me.

The leaf is smothered in burgundy red blood mixed with dirt. Only a small corner of it is clean from the mess of life, showing off its glossy yellow skin.

The ground under Rafe is covered in blood, in his blood.

"I think you are bleeding", my pathetic small voice squeaks in the darkness.

"I know. You need to help me to get up", he bites off.

I'm still holding him rolled to the side and I'm afraid to let go.

"How?" I squeak at him.

"Urbat Manzazu", he spits under his breath and I don't understand what he's saying, but the tone of someone swearing at me hasn't changed.

"Stop yelling at me", I scream. "I'm trying, okay?"

"Right now, you are the one who's yelling", he points out between his heavy breathing. "Just carefully, push me a bit forward, then help me to sit up and then I should be able to stand up with your help."

I can't see his face and as I say nothing, he adds, "as long as you don't touch my back, I'll be fine."

"Okay." My small voice is shaking.

I rise up further on my feet, straightening my legs, pushing his body further forward. Carefully, with the agonising breaks he pulls his knees closer to his abdomen, securing himself in this position and then gingerly, he pushes his arm away from his body, anchoring himself.

"Can I let go?"

"Yes, that's fine."

But it takes me extra two minutes before I could risk it and let go of his body.

And as I let go, he moves his arms in front of himself.

He raises himself up on his arms, pushing his body up, and his heavy breathing and grunts are suddenly cut by his agonising cry.

But it doesn't ring in the woods long before he clamps his mouth shut again, manoeuvring himself on all fours and I can hear his soft suppressed cries. My heart is breaking for him.

"Rafe, please let me help", I rush to him. But before I have a chance to touch him, he cuts me off, "No. Stay there. I'll do it."

It takes forever, the careful manoeuvring peppered with weak whimpers and cries, before he manages to stand up. I rush to him to pull him up, helping him to stand upright.

He is finally up, weakly swinging on his feet.

His eyes are closed and his breathing is choppy. I hold on to him but I don't know if he feels my hands.

He opens his eyes and looks at me. The whites of his eyes are glowing in the dark against his muddy face.

"We need to go somewhere to rest, sleep and clean ourselves."

"Where?" I whisper.

"You know this area better than me, you tell me. Where can we get a room and bed in here?"

"I don't know", I mumble thinking out loud. "There's nowhere I can go now." *I will not think about it now.*

"There are few B&Bs along the seafront, but you'd need money to stay in one of those", I look at him, explaining how things work in this world.

"How much money? Will three million British pounds be enough to cover the night?"

"What? Do you have three mills? Where?" I stare at him as if suddenly he sprouted a tail and an extra head.

"Here." He pulls a small plastic card out of his back pocket.

"Where did you get this?"

"For Arllu sake", he weakly bawls into the silence, rolling his eyes skywards, "you, with your never-ending questions. Can we get a bed with this money or not?"

"Well, if it's *real* money", I snap at him, demonstrating that I think his money is probably pretend nonsense from a play set, but if he is ready to stake his rest on it then so be it. Who am I to stop him from playing with pretend papers and plastic coins?

"We can probably get a few years in B&B for this money. But we need to get there first."

He turns his head, looking pointedly at me.

"Earlier, you demonstrated how well you can use your wings now, and your aerobatics skills were truly excellent, so I'm sure you wouldn't mind to take us there on your wings. It's the middle of the night, very dark and the chance of us being seen is very slim."

"Me?" I'm so surprised and taken aback, that I take a small step back to add extra space between us.

"Yes, you!" he barks at me. "Or is there someone else I might be talking to?"

Wow! Talk about temper! And I'm the one who's always in trouble for that? Wow.

He takes two unsteady steps of a blind person to the nearby tree and rests his arm on it, leaning into it with his weight.

"Okay, okay", I surrender. I can't stand seeing him in so much pain. "I'll take us there."

I step closer to Rafe. His back is to me, I'm petrified touching or brushing his back even by mistake.

I walk around him.

His cheek rests on the rough of the tree bark. With his face to me, I can see beads of sweat dotting his forehead, and the laboured breathing of his has the unspoken words of pain.

I'm trying to think how to hold on to him, if I'm to fly the two of us out of here.

I take another decisive step closer, but change my mind and step away.

I take a few steps around and take a glance at his back, then change my mind again and shuffle around the tree, returning to where I have started from.

Again, I brave moving closer to Rafe only to walk away the next second.

I circle around his frozen in pain form and another 'out-of-place', inappropriate thought pops into my head and I want to giggle.

I imagine how ridiculous I must look. It's like I'm dancing the Black Nag around him, the one I had to do at the school summer fete when I was little. Only the jolly fiddle music and the skipping on my part are missing to complete my stupid moves: *"two steps closer, two steps back, around each other and clap your hands"*.

I clamp my mouth shut before the nervous giggles have a chance to escape. Talk about an inappropriate response to the situation. It must be all the stress.

I firmly plant my feet on the ground, deciding to come up with a plan to transport him before resorting to any more of the dance moves.

But nothing comes into my head.

Apart from him sitting on my shoulders, I can't see any other way to hold on to him, while avoiding touching his back completely.

"Rafe", I quietly say, "do you want to sit on my shoulders?"

I'm not going to tell him, how vividly I can see myself toppling forward during the flight, throwing him off my shoulders and him plunging to the ground, becoming nothing more than a wet splat on the pavement.

He lifts his head at me, bug eyed, when the first gurgling sounds escape him and before I can start to panic about his imminent death, the gurgling sound changes pitch and volume, turning into a thunderous laughter.

He throws his head back and laughs and it's a loud, cathartic and carefree sound.

He folds again, rests his forehead on the tree, but his laughing doesn't stop and I wonder if it's the hysteria that is now talking.

But I love that sound. It's a wonderful sound of freedom and happiness, and surprising myself, my lips stretch, forming a smile.

Rafe is still going as I watch and listen, mesmerised by his release and seeing him like that makes me happy. It elevates me, it empowers me.

I can feel his energy move around me, seeping into me, tingling inside me. It wakes, brightens and enlightens me and before long, my lips stretch further and the little bells of laughter jingle, and like the bubbles in a can of fizz, they rush upwards, bubbling at the top, bursting, escaping my mouth, producing the light and carefree sound I haven't heard from myself in a very long while.

I feel free and light. I feel weightless as if I can float even without my wings.

I had forgotten how wonderful it is to smile and laugh, how uplifting it is to share a laugh with someone, to feel that tingling, deep connection, and at this moment I don't know if it's my essence talking or me.

Now, like two wallies, we stand in the dark silence of the night forest and laugh, scaring the sleepy nightlife and any lost human.

But my laughs do not last long before the bubbles of happiness die down, pushed out by the bitter flat taste of rejection, as my mind reminds me how I've ended up in here, bringing the "helpful" memories of how I used to laugh at night in the dark room with my sister, after mum would say her restricted goodbyes and would shut the door.

That was mine and my sister's connection, a connection which is now lost.

The happy bubbles die in my throat, before seamlessly turning into cries. I can hear it but I can't stop it.

"Come." Rafe grabs at my sleeve, pulling me closer to him.

I take a step and the next second I'm swallowed by his embrace. The wet smell of rotting leaves is deeply woven with the smell of Caribbean sunshine, and that weird combination makes me feel even more confused.

I make the move to throw my arms around him, but he cuts me off.

"Careful, my back." He takes my hands and places them just below his waist. I can feel his belt under my hands.

"There. If you keep your hand right here, we should be alright and we should be able to fly. And I'll just hold on to you."

"I'm sorry", I mumble through tears and snot, which is pooling at my nose, "I'm sorry for everything, Rafe. I'm sorry you've lost your wings because of me and I'm so sorry that you're hurt today again because of me. It's all because of me and I know that. I never meant for any of it and never meant for you to get hurt."

I look into his warm brown eyes and I really want him to know how truly sorry I am.

"I never really told you how sorry I am that you've lost your soul mate and how sorry I am that out of all people in the world the essence ended up with me. I can only imagine how disappointed you must have been when you found it was *me*, a useless, damaged good for nothing girl, rejected by everyone and everybody, even her own family. How ashamed you must feel, knowing that this pure and clean soul of your mate is in someone like me. How disappointing that must be for you! How embarrassing! Everybody is probably laughing and pointing their fingers at me. Out of all the people in the world, who could've had it, out of all nice girls, it ended up with me. *In me!*"

I scream.

The tears stream down my cheeks and I want him to know how sorry I am for everything that I am and for everything that I'm not. How much I wish I could make it all better for him, for myself, for my sister, for everybody.

Right here and right now, I'm trying to tell him that it what I was trying to do. I was trying to make things better, *I was trying to fix things.*

"You are stuck with me. With a big useless screw up! And yet you are still here, following me, trying to make it better for your soul mate's soul and her legacy, still trying to protect her, still following me, still helping me. You are probably hating me as well.

And why wouldn't you. Look at what I have done to you! Look at the mess I've made. I'm an embarrassment!"

I can hear the hysteria setting in and I can't stop it or maybe I don't want to stop it. Maybe finally I need to say it all out loud.

"And you are right to be disappointed! Everything about me is disappointing! You probably hate me now for everything I've done to you! For what I said to you yesterday! And you're right! You should! I'm a monster! A horrible monster and that's why nobody wants to be around me! That's why nobody wants me! I'm just a monster!"

A sharp sound of a slap suddenly rings in my ears and my cheek grows red, burning as if it's on fire.

"Ow!" I put my hand over the stinging skin, trying to calm the burn.

We now glare at each other. I am shocked and surprised, looking at Rafe through the mist of tears, and Rafe stoic and serene.

"That's to calm you", he says, shrugging his shoulder. "And for the other day", he adds, the challenge in his eyes is supported by his smirk.

"Feel better? Calmer?" he enquires with a cool detachment.

But I just stare at him, unable to say a word and now afraid to say anything else.

"I'm sorry that I slapped you", he continues, "but you just wouldn't stop and we don't have any time left for your dramas. If you ever wanted to know how I feel about you, if I'm embarrassed or disappointed, you should've asked me instead of assuming things in your head on my behalf. I would have told you that I don't feel disappointed or ashamed. You are a human and that says it all, and explains things. It would be ludicrous of me to expect something from you that you can't deliver. It would be as ludicrous as to expect this tree to grow legs and a tongue and start walking and talking. You are a *human*", he repeats, his gaze bores into mine.

"Just that, a human, with flaws, desires, weaknesses, stupid ideas and mistakes. That's what you are."

He drops his voice as if sharing a secret, "And I have to say, I doubt you'll ever change, essence or not."

He gives me that resigned look as he shakes his head at me.

"But at the same time you are strong, resilient, loyal and very brave. You are like a small ant, very easy to kill, even if by mistake. One careless step and it's crushed on the ground under a shoe. Yet this ant just keeps on going with his life. Determined and focused, the ant builds his home and builds his life. This ant is not scared of what might happen to him nor does he wait to die every second of his short life. The ant gets on with his life, every moment of it. He just keeps going, just like you."

"I am... an ant?" I mumble, taken aback, staring at Rafe in disbelief. I don't know if I should take it as a compliment or an insult. I think he means it as a compliment but, oh boy, he does need a lesson in the art of compliments.

But I bet that's exactly how angels see us: a pathetic army of small ants, easy to destroy.

"You are", he answers, nodding his head in confirmation, "the brave little ant, who keeps going, busy building the nest for his family, even when the family doesn't thank him. You are the strongest ant I've ever see."

He lifts my chin to him as he drops his voice.

"I don't expect miracles from you. I don't expect you to do more than you can. But I do expect you to keep fighting. In your life you've made it this far and I know that you have it in you to go further. I was pleased it was you, who got the essence, because I know that you're not going to give up. I know that you are very strong and I know you will make the right choice when it comes to humanity, because you have a big heart, one which can forgive."

A small smile pulls at his lips before he sobers once more.

"I am sorry that I have failed you in keeping your sister safe. I know how much she means to you and I should have done better, but for what it's worth, I know that she loves you and I promise you, we will find her", he vows.

And as I say nothing he pleads with me in a soft whisper, "Please."

I just nod.

"Thank you", he pulls me closer. He leans his cheek over the top of my head, holding me close, as he strokes my arm.

A few minutes crawl by in the dark silence before he speaks again.

"Are you okay to fly?"

I sniff and wipe my nose and face on my poor, grimy sleeve.

"I suppose. Like I have a choice" I huff, shrugging my shoulders at him, "it's not like you can walk there."

"And I don't know which way we would walk anyway", I add to myself.

I inhale and exhale to steady myself.

"Okay", I say, all business-like, flexing my shoulders and my neck like a boxer in the ring. "I'm ready. Hop on", I outstretch my arms in front of myself, ready to catch him and carry him in my arms as if he is a bride. I can practically imagine Rafe running towards me, jumping up into my arms and then me, spinning with him, while holding him close. I'm the leading partner in our unorthodox waltz, but who cares?

"Strictly", eat your heart out!

But Rafe doesn't jump into my arms. Gingerly he comes closer, takes my hands in his, spreading my arms wide and steps into the circle of my arms, smiling softly down at me.

"Like that", he says, bringing my hands around and placing them on his waist. "Just here. Don't go any higher."

Keeping my hands in place, I step closer. Rafe circles his arms over my waist and the weight of his arms around me makes my heart race.

But is it him or the fear of taking to the sky on my new wings with a wounded person?

"Ready?" he softly asks.

All I can do is weakly nod.

As we are still on the ground a few moments later, Rafe raises his eyebrows at me, a mute question of "why the delay"?

"Okay. Here we go." And adopting the refined and upbeat pronunciation of a flight attendant I add, "hold on tight, ladies and gentlemen, and remember, in the event of a crash landing the oxygen masks will fall out, pull it over your face, take the brace position and kiss your arse goodbye."

"Funny", Rafe rebuffs with a stoic, unamused expression.

I stick my tongue out at him and the next second my wings open wide around us and I grab hold of his waist and take to sky.

Rafe's hold on me tightens and the moment we are airborne, I can see a twinge of fear in his eyes. He is not sure if I can do it without killing him and quite frankly, neither am I.

You told me to trust you in Hinnom. Now it's your turn to trust. Difficult, huh?

My wings are taking us higher and higher, folding slightly around obstructing branches, opening wider later. My wings know what to do and the extra weight doesn't bother them, they are free, strong and singing with power.

It's as if they are illuminated from within. The purple of the wings is vibrant and the golden shimmer glisten in Rafe's glow and slowly I am learning how to trust them.

Trusting the wings... I wonder how long before they betray me too?

Or maybe they are more like animals and haven't learned how to betray as people do?

Once above the line of trees, I can finally get my bearings to where we are and where we need to go.

At this altitude the strong November wind and rain are ruling the roost. No longer under the protection of dense canopy of pine trees, I am cold and wet in no time and I spin on the spot, looking into horizon.

A few miles away in the distance, in otherwise engulfing darkness of the night, a tight throng of dim lights is sprinkled, glistening like a swarm of fireflies in the grass.

This swarm congregates in the centre, gradually thinning and dispersing into the darkness to the North, while the opposite side of the throng is clearly cut as if pressed against an invisible black wall. The consuming darkness beyond that wall is so vast that only two explanations come to my mind. It's either Baza has managed to open the Hell without my assistance and has begun his "world take over", or it is the consuming blackness of a sea at night.

The logical thinking is all that is left in this crazy illogical world of flying human beings, and tonight I will hope it's just the shore line of the sea ahead, illuminated on one side by the lights of the promenade.

My wings open and close behind me, adopting a faster tempo and with it they pull me forward, towards the cluster of lights, carrying Rafe with me.

The tempo is increasing with every new beat of my wings, now tilting me and Rafe forward, until we both hang horizontally.

I glance at Rafe below me and he wraps his legs around mine.

My wings beat a strong rhythm above us, as they take us closer to the twinkling lights of the town.

Chapter 4

*T*he night promenade, basking in the golden glow of the street lamps, comes into view.

This time of night it is deserted and quiet.

I can see the clear outline of the shore and can hear whooshing waves crashing over pebbles on the beach, and the air coming into my lungs is saturated with sea salt.

The spidery network of lit roads snakes away from the promenade in every direction inland. The yellow glow of the roads dissipates the further inland they go, like tendrils of smoke disappearing into the sky.

The promenade is the only area of the town which stays lit throughout the night, dimly illuminating the entrance onto the pier which is shut at this time of the night.

The pier is dark and invisible amongst the pitch black sea, but I know it is there. I've spent countless weekends there as a child with my family, before dad left, playing in an arcade or eating donuts, chips or candyfloss on the pier, chasing seagulls or throwing pebbles into the water.

I always loved the bustling happy rush of the pier as a child.

It was filled with magic, happiness and fun. It was filled with carnival music, laughter of children, screams of thrill seekers on the rides. It was filled with the smell of burning sugar of candyfloss and the aroma of cooking donuts, all laced with the scent of a sea breeze.

The pier was a place, where families who love each other would go. The pier became a symbol of family love for me.

But since dad left, I have visited the pier only twice, each time taking my sister there, wanting to take her away from the acidic air of obsession and hate, violence and blame.

She needed to be a child, even if I couldn't be one.

Our flight up to this point wasn't long or tiring. Surprising me, my wings took on extra weight without trouble, steadily swishing behind my back, and his body wrapped around mine was the only uncomfortable strain.

My town's promenade is just like every seafront of every English seaside destination, with the only difference being that our town was a holiday destination about a hundred years ago, but desolate and forgotten now.

The promenade flaunts the only hotel in town. This hotel was built in the second half of the nineteenth century to welcome British aristocrats and wealthy industrialists into relaxing and breezy Northern resorts, away from the black smog and poverty of crowded London. Now this four storey red brick building with tall windows and two tall turrets under the "onion" roofs is like a forgotten grandma, visited only on special commemorative occasions.

The promenade is like a glitzy facade of a bankrupt widow, parading the last of her jewellery and furs.

The traditional candy shops, a couple of fish and chip shops, ice cream parlours and gift shops tightly fill the promenade. A few B&Bs hold the prime real estate spots along the seafront and I hope that this late in November they will have vacancies.

"Rafe", I call to him.

His arms are still tight around me and I take it as a good sign that I'm not carrying a corpse.

"Would you be able to walk?"

I don't think it will be prudent of me to land right in the middle of the road, under the exposing lights of the street lamps, right outside the door of an unfortunate B&B.

"Depends how far", he hisses through his teeth.

"Okay, I hear you. I'll land just outside the pier. It's darker there and then we'll walk across the street and hopefully we'll be able to find an open B&B."

He doesn't answer me. Maybe he is too weak or maybe just letting me make a decision and take control.

We are almost above the promenade and I can make out individual buildings and the shop signs.

A few cars are parked along the promenade, probably belonging to the local business owners and a few unseasonal visitors.

My wings slow their beating, suspending us above the dark and locked entrance to the pier. We are still high above the street lights, hidden in the darkness.

Okay. I need to move fast now. The less my wings are flopping under the street lights, the better.

Suspended mid-air, our joint bodies slowly turn vertically and, as if following an unspoken instruction, Rafe unwraps his legs from around me, and I take it as the signal he is ready to land.

Our feet touch the ground simultaneously and I feel the impact of the landing push through my feet and legs, and I feel Rafe's body shudder in my arms, as a weak cry leaves his lips.

His fingers are digging into my skin and I want to scream next to him, but a second later, his hold on me loosens, and he lets go, taking a weak stumbling step back, keeping his hand on my arm to balance himself.

"Sorry for the bumpy landing", I mumble.

"I'm sorry", he breathes. "Did I hurt you?"

"No, that's fine", I dismiss. My pain is probably nowhere near as bad as his agony.

"Can you walk?" I ask him.

"Just give me a second."

His breathing is choppy and with a sudden clarity I realise that this flight took more out of him than he lets on, and the next moment, I need to stamp out an irrational panic, which helpfully reminds me how much harder it would be for me to find my way out of this mess and find my sister, if anything ever happens to him.

Across from us, the promenade's front is packed with now closed shops behind metal shutters.

The colourful signs above the shops are urging seaside visitors to try the best fudge in town or the award-winning sausage, or local mussels, competing for the wavering tourists' pound.

I scan the row of businesses, looking for a B&B sign. I don't know why, but I don't feel like going into the "Grand Hotel".

Maybe I worry about the documents they'd want from us, maybe I fear that his money in fact are a toy set after all and the embarrassment in a B&B will be less severe than in the hotel for aristocrats, or maybe because I feel like a fraud myself – I don't know. But I know for sure it will be B&B for us tonight.

A few yards down the street to the right, a large yellow neon sign in the window winks with a cheerful announcement on the "vacancies".

"Rafe, we need to walk over there", I point towards the yellow sign. "It's not far, but... Can you make it?"

He lifts his head, turning it to the direction of my hand.

"Yeah."

With pauses and breaks of a frail man, he straightens his back.

"Let's go", he rasps, holding on to my arm and taking the first step.

"The Driftwood B&B and Guest House" a dark red sign with chipped paint announces above the door. The sign is lit up by a few lights.

We stop just at the bottom of the set of steep steps, leading up to the closed at this late hour B&B doors.

"Okay, Rafe, you stay here. I'll go and call the bell."

Carefully I lean and prop Rafe against the steps' railing like a bike, and once I'm convinced that he is not going to slide off, I sprint up the stairs to the B&B's closed front door and press the bell.

The house is dark inside. The building softly groans and squeaks, as if it's breathing, asleep and snoring like a living creature.

I press the bell once more and eventually I can hear a light shuffle of feet behind the white Victorian front door, and a second later, light floods the entrance hall of the house, spilling into a weak puddle over the stairs where I stand, touching my toes.

A round female figure, wrapped in a robe with a messy bun pinned on top of her head, comes into a view, but I can't make out her face yet, until she comes closer, leaning against the glass, squirming into the outside darkness.

"Hi", I yell through the glass, taking a step closer, so she can see me. "I'm sorry for waking you and calling so late, but it says you have vacancies?" My question is more of a statement, as I point to the neon plaque in the window.

This Victorian building has tall and wide windows on each side of the front door. The windows are framed within white panes with chipped paint. At the top, each window is crowned with a colourful stained glass design of blue and red flowers, and some elements of the design have a feel of an Art Déco era.

The key turns in the door. The chain slides, released from the nest, and softly rattles as it brushes over the door.

The door opens and I slam my eyes shut, blinded for a moment by the bright white light flooding from the hall.

"Yes, we do have vacancies, but we usually take bookings online", a fairly young female voice, no older than the early thirties, stretches in response.

She sounds cautious and quite frankly, who wouldn't be if a random girl, caked in mud appeared at their doorstep past midnight, asking for a room.

"Our train was delayed and by the time we found the taxi and came here..." I apologetically spread my arms, keeping my upbeat friendly voice.

I gush, desperate to pour out as many words as possible, to delay the moment when this woman would decide that she doesn't want us here.

"We're visiting your seaside town. It's for my college project and I thought we'd have enough time to arrive, look around and then decide where to stay, but with the train arriving so late, we kinda got stuck for a place to sleep", I smile, bubbling like the happiest college girl alive.

I'm trying to copy these lucky girls in my school, who had a normal and happy life, trying to copy their smiles and giggles, their openness to the world.

With my eyes finally adjusted to the light, I can see inside the hall and I notice white, freshly painted walls, holding large, yellowed framed prints of the town's pier on the walls.

Silence hangs in the air as she looks past me.

I follow her gaze, glancing over my shoulder at Rafe behind me, who's still leaning on the railing.

Shit. I should've straightened him a bit more. I hope she wouldn't think he is drunk. If she does, we can kiss the room goodbye.

"And who's that?" I jump up at a deep male voice.

A large tall male now stands behind the woman, blocking out the light and taking the space inside the doorframe.

"I'm her brother", Rafe answers behind me in an even voice. "Sorry, that I'm not there with my sister, but I ate something on the train and really not feeling well now. You know, these sandwiches probably were out of a fridge for hours. I've promised myself never to buy one, but was too hungry and now I'm paying for it", he smiles with a sad steady smile and then, under my shocked gaze, he pushes himself off the railing and takes the steps to stand next to me.

He stretches his hand out to the man for a handshake, "Rafael. And that's my sister Ariel."

A polite smile is glued to Rafe's lips.

"I know", he shrugs apologetically, "Rafael and Ariel. We were paying for it at school, trust me. Our parents thought it would be a fine idea to rhyme their children's names."

My gaze shuttles between our hosts' faces and Rafe's outstretched hand.

I hold my breath, knowing full well that the decision is being made right now and we will either have a peaceful and comfortable night's sleep in here or we're back on the streets, looking for somewhere else. And if we don't find anything tonight, then we will have no choice, but to sleep on the beach under the stars and icy November wind and rain.

The man steps forward past his wife and shakes Rafe's hand.

I exhale.

"Our rooms start at eighty five pounds a night for this time of year", he says in a way of agreement. "We'll need a proof of identity for both of you and the payment in advance for all of the nights you're planning to stay", he warns, still holding Rafe's hand in his.

"That will not be a problem", Rafe assures him, giving his hand a light shake.

"Please come on in, come on in", the woman chimes with a smile, now a pure embodiment of excellent customer service. The doubt and suspicion has evaporated from her face with hubby's seal of approval of a handshake.

She steps back, pulling her husband with her, inviting us in, and as Rafe pushes in front, past me, I can see the thick beads of sweat covering his forehead. The tendons strain on his neck and his jaw is set tight.

I wonder how long will he last like this?

"Thank you", he politely responds.

"Ariel?" he looks back at me.

"Yes, brother, I'm coming." I can't resist it, and as the innuendo falls from my mouth, he glares back at me.

Oops, maybe over the top.

The hall of "The Driftwood B&B and Guest House" is bright and smells of mint, almond, with a faint tinge of cleaning products and disinfectant. It has been recently redecorated, now sporting a white minimalistic style of clean lines on the backdrop of the Victorian grandeur of a wide dark wood staircase, a white mantel of a large fireplace in the hall and original burnt orange tiles on the floor.

The woman is now behind the white tall reception desk, which looks more like a bar. She is in her late twenties, early thirties, slim, with long, dark, straight hair pinned up loosely on top of her head. She is wrapped in a fluffy white bathrobe with large pink spots all over it.

In the bright light of the hall, our grubby attire is fully noticed and appreciated, as both hosts are now eyeing us suspiciously. I'm afraid that maybe at this precise moment, we will be asked to leave.

"Sorry for arriving in such a state", Rafe utters, smiling apologetically, loosely waving his hand over himself. "It was so dark around the train station and as we were looking for a taxi park, we slipped over and fell. Really not our day today."

Oh my god. These excuses are wearing thin even for me. How much more of our crap will they buy?

"Okay", the woman stretches, keeping her professional smile in place. The man comes and stands next to his wife behind the reception, for moral support no doubt.

"We have a lovely large room available. Twin beds with a sea view and only ninety five pounds for a night." I inward wince at her "only". Ninety five quid is how much we used to live on as a family for a week.

"Yes, that's fine", Rafe meets her smile with his. "We'd like the room for a week please."

He reaches into his back pocket and produces the credit card, then fishes out two passports in burgundy covers from the breast pocket of his jacket.

He is stocked up! I wonder what else he has in there?

The second the burgundy covers touch the polished surface of the reception desk, the man of the house scoops them with his hand.

"No luggage?"

"No. We're travelling light."

It's like a car crash. I want to close my eyes and hide behind my hands, but I can't stop watching Rafe's conversation with this guy, to see how it will unfold. It's like a ticking bomb and I'm waiting for it to explode into our faces.

For a split second the guy and Rafe lock their gazes, but the owner says nothing, dropping his gaze to our passports and I hear the rustling of passports' pages.

Another glance to each of us from the man, checking our passport pictures no doubt, while his wife chirps next to him: "You will like your room. We've preserved all the rooms in the B&B just as they were when we bought it three years ago. The whole place has such a wonderful, undeniable charm, don't you think? Even the town is so cute and quaint."

I nod along to her words, keeping the polite smile in place, hoping that Rafe is doing the same next to me. I'm so tired. I can't wait to have a shower and lay down, but I am afraid to sabotage the promised luxury of a room with hot water and a soft bed with my uncaring words or the lack of interest, so I stand there, waiting to get the keys, while playing the role of the interested guest.

"We have completely redecorated only this hall and the breakfast room, leaving the guest rooms as they were. Of course, in some rooms we had to take old wallpaper down and re-plaster completely, the wallpaper was just falling off the walls", the woman bulges her eyes at me, shaking her head in shock.

I guess different things are shocking to different people. For some it's the old wallpaper, falling off the walls, and for some, it is the hordes of naked, crying and dying humans in Hell.

I keep my smile in place, nodding my head in time with her story. Now and again, I pull my mouth to form a surprised "O", or when the story calls, I draw my eyebrows, sharing the woman's concerns about the undertaken work.

"In all rooms we had to update pipes", she resumes her chit-chat, "but we've managed to preserve the original bathroom suites in most of them. Your room is one of those. Isn't it so much nicer when the hotel and room has character? Don't you think?"

I eagerly nod.

She places the two slips of paper on the reception desk.

"If you don't mind signing here, Mr Watson. Miss Watson, one for you to sign too", she pushes the small sheet of paper my way.

"The breakfast is served between seven and ten in the breakfast room. And we don't offer room service, so if you miss breakfast, you only will be able to get food in the pub down the road or maybe something in a fish and chip shop."

"That's fine, thank you", Rafe answers next to me, scribbling on his piece of paper.

"Okay, it will be six hundred sixty five pounds", the guy interjects into our pleasantries.

Rafe puts his finger on the credit card, still on top of the counter, and pushes it towards the man.

The pleasant soft beep of a card reader tells me that I am now even closer to a warm bed and a shower.

"Here you are."

The man hands our passports and the card back to Rafe, locking his gaze to Rafe's.

The way the both of them are eyeing each other, I can swear I can hear the unspoken conversation between these two: *"I hope we won't have any problems. There will not be a problem, sir."*

"If you follow me please, I'll take you to your room", the woman says and I and Rafe follow her up the stairs.

Chapter 5

S he wasn't lying, the hall is the only room the owners had redecorated.

Our room is wide and I'm relieved at the sight of two old single beds separated by a night stand.

I like this room. It's old-fashioned but cosy. The walls are covered in yellowing floral wallpaper with large blue flowers all over it, and matching drapes hanging on the each side to the window.

The furniture in the room is so old and out-dated, that at some point it went up in value and came back into fashion as an "antique". The decorator was trying to give the room a nautical vibe by mounting a wall mirror within an old and cracked ship wheel, and hanging it on the wall between two old prints of seagulls above raging sea waves.

"Where did you get passports? And money?" I ask Rafe, just to say something and fill the silence while we scan our room.

Rafe turns his head and glances at me with a pity that one might reserve for a sick dog.

"How do you think we blend in here?" he shrugs his shoulders. "There are more of us here than you think. Different ones..." he pointedly stares at me. "And if these kind of papers make you, humans, think that you are somewhat in charge of your lives, it is certainly not a problem for us."

He turns away again.

Okay. More information.

I wonder if I will ever catch up with it all.

"Do you want to go in the shower first?" I ask just to change the subject.

"No, that's alright. I can wait."

Once we are alone, he no longer hides his pain.

This little "easy" performance took a lot out of him. He plods heavily across the carpet and sits on the edge of a bed. Suddenly, in the warm and weak yellow light of the room, he looks old, very old. Looking at him now, I can easily believe that he is an ancient archangel and as old as the universe itself.

"Rafe", I start and once he lifts his eyes to me, I brave to say something he should've heard from me earlier, and probably more than once.

"Thank you for everything", I whisper. I drop my eyes to my feet, "thank you for earlier and thank you for getting us here."

'Thank you's taste alien on my tongue. I can't remember the last time I thanked or even wanted to thank anyone. Not just a fleeting "Ta", but the deep gratitude that comes from depths of your heart. I don't remember if I ever thanked anyone. Maybe because nobody ever did anything for me, not without expecting something in return, usually demanding more from me that I was willing to give.

In the silence of the room I dare to look back at him. I don't know how this should go now.

Rafe's steady gaze is on me, before he gives a short small nod. "That's fine."

It's all too uncomfortable for me.

Okay, I think we're done here.

"Okay", I rub my hands, looking around. "Where are the towels? Oh, here they are", and with that I grab a towel and head for the bathroom.

The old fashioned bathroom compliments our old fashioned room perfectly. A pink ceramic bath tub, a pink sink and even a pink toilet stand out in the room. I bet in the days of steady money and a constant stream of tourists, these ugly beauties were the pride and joy of B&B owners. The bathroom floor is laid with old and now worn, ochre brown tiles, giving the room a chilling resemblance to the bathrooms in the mental institutions at the turn of the 20th century that I've seen in old photographs in the local museum.

The pink bathroom is clean and smells heavily with disinfectant, but I don't mind it.

Cream tiles cover the bottom half of the walls in the room. Some of the tiles have very retro pictures of woodlands flowers, bluebells, cowslip, honeysuckle and... lily of the valley.

I turn away.

I can't wait to take my dirty clothes off and stand in the shower, letting the dozens of hot jets beat at my skin. I grab my sweatshirt, about to pull it off my head, when a new thought hits me.

Shit! Wings! How do I take these off?

I throw my head skywards, cursing angels, wings and the general lack of manuals.

I release the sweatshirt, open the door and walk barefoot across the room to where Rafe lies on his front on the bed. His eyes are closed and his left wings are spread to the side, weirdly offsetting his body.

"Rafe", I call softly, "Rafe."

He opens his eyes and turns his head to me.

"Sorry", I start, "how do I take the wings off to have shower? You know, so I can take off my clothes?"

The silent and confused stare is all that I get from him in response.

"Do I like, I don't know... press a button somewhere? Or maybe I have to say a prayer? Like 'Hail Mary' three times or something?"

I sound ridiculous or deluded, and my annoyance spikes when I see Rafe's puzzled eyes rake over me, probably questioning the fact.

"What?" he finally asks, baffled. "No. Just take it off and that's it."

He doesn't get my question. Well, neither do I. I've never had to ask anyone how to remove angel's wings to take off the clothes.

"Just take your shirt off, as you always do, and the fabric will slide over your wings."

Looking at my confused expression, he continues, "The wings will just seep through the fabric, just like water would. Or smoke", he waves his hand to help himself along with the explanation.

"Thank you", I cut, turn and walk back into the bathroom.

It's getting really old now, playing catch up with all information and being a complete buffoon at every turn. How the hell, do the solid and material substance that I am able to touch and stroke, and that lifts me and Rafe in the air, can get through fabric like smoke or water?

I strip fast. I toss Mia's swords in the farthest corner, next to the toilet seat. They hit the floor with a light conker knock, which is so disproportionate to the size and the weight of them, I would've expected more of a bang. As Rafe predicted, the wings slide through the fabric unobstructed, not leaving a rip or even a small feather behind.

I climb over the edge of the pink bath tab, behind the glass shower screen, dragging my wings behind me.

With every day and every passing hour, I notice my wings less and less. They are weightless, and although they take space around me, I began to adjust to the area I need to move in with them. It's like with arms, they are there, you learn how to move them and how they move, and you learn not to swing them too wildly when you're snaking through a crowd, unless you want to hit something unpleasant.

I open the tap and water begins to roar in old Victorian pipes, spitting, increasing the pressure and then suddenly easing off.

That capricious system reminds me of one we used to have back at home. Our gas heater was on its last leg, so we used to turn on the tap for about 10 minutes before having a shower, wait for the water to warm up and have a fast shower, knowing full well that the light will go out in the heater soon, leaving us with only cold water for the rest of the day.

But for all the noise and roar in the pipes, the water is steady and hot, so I stand there, daydreaming, not thinking about anything in particular, letting the water run over my back and my wings. My wings are warm and tingly now, and their happiness flows into me as I stand, mindlessly turning my body left then right, left then right.

Finally, I'm done. Not that I had enough of standing under the water, but the thought of Rafe sitting in the room, waiting for me to finish, kicks me out of the bath.

Wrapped in a towel, I look at the dirty pile of my clothes on the floor, with disgust realising that for no money in the world I would put these back on.

I grab the only bathrobe off the back of the door and kick the clothes against the farthest wall. I'll deal with it later.

I walk with my bare feet across the weathered old carpet. Rafe is still sprawled over the bed where I had left him. He looks peaceful when asleep.

"Rafe", I whisper. "I've finished. The bathroom is all yours if you still want to have a shower."

"Okay", he answers with his eyes closed.

He inhales deeply before he softly grunts. He raises himself up and without further word, heavily plods into the bathroom, slamming the door shut behind him.

I had already made my bed for the night and begin drifting off to sleep, when an hour later, the latch finally clicks behind the door and Rafe steps out into the room, bringing fog and mist of a hot shower with him.

A cream towel is wrapped around his waist.

His hair and wings are dark with water. Like a drowsy old man, he shuffles blindly to his bed and falls forward, across it and I have to bite on my lip and try not to cry out at the sight of the wounds all over his back.

His wounds have gotten worse. What I saw in the angelic hospital were the horrifying wounds of a burnt victim: they were raw and horrific, but at least they were clean, surrounded by the clean gauze and they were clear of blood.

Now his wounds have raw and torn edges of a burnt victim mauled by an animal. His back is raw and ugly. I'm surprised that he managed to stand and walk until now.

I can't take my eyes away from his back. And I begin to cry.

The quiet soft tears roll down my cheeks and I hold my jaw shut to stop even a single whimper to escape me and betray the turmoil within.

I don't need to be told again that it's my fault. I know it. I can see it. I don't want to see his face, his kind eyes and him telling me, that it's okay. I wish he would yell at me, would tell me that it's all my fault. I wish he would just get up and leave. Damn sure I deserve it.

I weep softly. My hands clasped over my mouth, but my nose is blocked up, so I sniff and wipe at it, throwing the quilt over and scurry to the bathroom, closing the door behind.

The bathroom is still stuffy and warm from our showers. I slide down the wall next to the toilet, clasp my head between my hands and softly weep, keeping my sobs as quiet as I could.

Seeing my old house and my neighbour today has brought to the forefront the memories of my mother. Her accusing voice now dances in my head, like a tolling bell, echoing her constant reminders that I'm an abomination under the light of God and should never have been born, that demons in Hell and the Devil himself are speaking though me and everything I touch is tainted by their wicked power.

Her high voice rings in my head. It's a voice of a preacher in church, boosted by the dome above and his righteousness.

If only she knew what I could do now. If only she knew I could end them all, she would have a field trip of preaching.

But she is right. Everything I touch turns to shit.

I'm crying with my hands clasped over my mouth. The tears roll down my cheeks and the sobs rake my body. I sit there and cry, letting myself go.

Hours later, I feel dehydrated and sore, exhausted and drained, but I have the first non-negotiable point in my action plan. I need to find my sister. That's what I came here for.

I need to keep her safe and for that I need her with me, and the only way to do that, is to find her.

I get up and splash water on my face.

Rage stirs inside, huffing at me with her eyebrows raised high: *"If you want something done, do it yourself!"*

Fair enough, it's not like I can argue with that.

Having a plan, no matter how small, makes me feel in control again and I like it. And what if the rest of the plan is unknown? I'll come up with it later.

I tiptoe to my bed. While I was hiding in the bathroom, Rafe turned off the main light, leaving a night lamp for me. He lies on his front and he looks asleep.

I turn off the light and slide into my bed, wrapping myself into the quilt like a cocoon. The therapist gave me a lecture on it once, pointing out how I cover myself as if trying to protect myself from an outside world. I didn't argue with her then and I wouldn't argue now. Maybe she wasn't wrong.

"Are you okay?" Rafe's soft whisper brushes the quiet of the room.

"Yeah, fine", I mutter.

"Are you ready to talk? About your sister?" He asks into the darkness.

"Are *you* up for it? Because I'm ready if you are." I'm ready to roll.

"Let's start with you explaining to me where she is now and how she vanished on your watch and why you are none the wiser?" I keep myself as composed as I can, but I can feel my control beginning to slip, as Rage pokes her head through an ajar door.

"First of all, you need to know that I had nothing to do with her disappearance." I hear a rustle of sheets under him, as he lifts himself up, "but of course, that's not an excuse. I have failed you when you trusted me with her safekeeping."

He stops, clearly expecting me to say something, but so far he didn't say anything that I wanted to disagree with.

He draws in a breath.

"When you were talking to that old lady with a dog, I spoke to my kyriote and according to him, he received the order to return to

Uras and suspend the guardianship of your sister, and the monitoring of the immediate area."

"So who had issued this *order*?" I practically spit out the last word.

Order-shmorder. Do all of them do what they are told? If my mum knew, she would love angels even more, as if it was even possible...

He clearly doesn't want to say as the silence stretches for longer than required.

"Chamuel."

I'm not even surprised to hear that name.

"Nice. I see the backstabbing in your Uras is blossoming."

He is quiet, not rebuffing my remark. Again... If the shoe fits...

"So, what now?" I'm happy to discuss it with him. He is the one who wanted to talk. "Do you know where I can find my sister? Did your guy tell you at what point he left her? Where she was? Or maybe he knows where she is now?"

"He was called back and suspended his watch when she was still at your home", he pushes slowly, clearly admitting defeat.

"But I was thinking about it", some liveliness comes into his voice, "we can try to track her with our kyriotes, maybe they will be able to help us to trace her. If you give me any inkling on her essence..."

"No", I cut him off. "No kyriotes, no Chamuel, none of that! I already told you that I'm not risking bringing Baza to my sister's door and I am most definitely not expanding this fantastic apocalyptic party to now include Chamuel and half of fluffing Heaven!"

"And quite frankly, I don't trust Chamuel as far as I can throw him, so we'll have to find her on our own. No! Let me rephrase it. *I* will find her. I'm not a hundred percent sure on how yet, but that's just details. There must be a way. I'll start later today by combing the streets. I'll go to my mum's church. I'll speak to more of our neighbours. I'll see if I can find anything through the social services... I don't know", I'm annoyed. "I'll start there and will make decisions as I go. I must be able to find something. People don't just vanish into a thin air."

Unless it's me.

I hope this disappearance has nothing to do with Baza's, because then I wouldn't know what to do... But I will think about that later.

"I still think we would do better if I contact Uras first and try to get a location on her"

"Rafe, no offence", I cut him off again, "but I'm done with all this angelic bullshit. I can't trust a single person on either side there. Up or down, it doesn't mean squat anymore. I will still lose. I will do it myself now, and from now on, however I want, or can. Okay?"

This is not open for negotiations. I'm not asking him, I'm telling him and he had better get on board. Otherwise, hit the road, Jack!

He says nothing. Good!

"Good night Rafe", I reach out and push the switch on the night lamp, then turn on my side, away from Rafe, settling deeper in my bed.

The soft light seeps through my eyelids, slowly waking me.

I yawn and stretch in my warm bed, waiting for the usual morning school call from the staff, before realising, after a few long heartbeats, that it was a lifetime ago.

I turn my head and look at Rafe's sleeping form.

He is spread like a starfish on top of his covers. I drop my gaze down his body.

His back is still raw and angry-looking, but overnight, the blood pooled in his wounds, has dried and crusted over in a bumpy layer like an uneven volcanic landscape, coating his wounds.

At least he isn't bleeding anymore.

The cream bath towel is still secure over his hips.

I turn left to the window. November sunshine is always weak and sporadic and I'm unable to tell what time it is. It could be morning or afternoon, but either way I need to get up and start looking for my sister.

I throw the bathrobe over myself and plod to the bathroom.

The stinky pile of my clothes is still against the wall where I kicked it over last night. The thought of dragging those filthy jeans and sweatshirt over my body repulse me but I have no choice if I want to go out.

At least my underwear is nice and clean. There are some blessings.

As I pick up my jeans, dried mud falls off, hitting the tiled floor of the bathroom with dry shallow clanks. The jeans smell of the rotting leaves and the bogged ground of the forest and the reminder of what I was trying to do yesterday, punches at my gut, leaving me breathless, squeezing my stomach.

"Yesterday is yesterday. Today is a new day", I mumble to myself, starting my recovery chant that I used to repeat daily. I never thought I would be saying these words again. "Yesterday is yesterday. Today is a new, better day."

I take a few uneven breaths in, trying to regain my composure.

"Okay. Quit whining! No big deal", I reprimand myself. *"Since when is stinky, dirty fabric that much of a big deal? Yeah, a bit stinky, a bit grubby – just put it on and go!"*

I'm not ready to acknowledge the real reason for my stress right now. If I don't say it, I could always pretend that it's not real and it's not happening to me.

But I'm angry with myself right now so I get dressed, yanking the door open, stepping into the room.

Rafe is already up, standing by the window with his towel around his hips, watching the day outside.

Excellent, saves me the bother of waiting for him to wake up.

"Ah, you're up. Excellent", I bristle at his back.

Rafe slightly turns, giving me a sideway glance. "Morning to you too."

He carefully manoeuvres himself to face me.

"What's up with you this morning?" he narrows his eyes at me.

"Nothing. I just don't have the luxury of lying around and sleeping in, when I have my sister to find, that's all", I snap back. "Listen, Rafe, I remember yesterday you said you that you have three mills on your magic bounty card. Can I have the card please?"

"What for?" he draws his brows at me.

"Listen, quit parenting me", I rebuff, "It's not like you're going to miss a few quid. But if you really want to know, I need new clothes so I'm going to pop into a Primark at pick up a few things. 'Cause you know, this rip on my butt is rather chilly this time of the year. And on the way back, I'll pop into a corner shop and get myself some pick & mix."

What is he thinking I'm going to do? Go on a drinking or smoking spree?

"What is a 'pick and mix'?"

"It's just sweets, okay? Or is there some angelic reason why I can't have sweets now?" I'm picking a fight and even I can hear it, but he really annoys me with this checking and double checking on me like I'm a child.

"No, no angelic reason, and no problem at all", he tries to diffuse the situation, "I just thought you might want to know, that since you became a full angel, you don't need any food."

"What do you mean?" I huff.

Now what?

"Once the transformation was complete, you've lost the need for nourishment in the form of human food to sustain you. Your essence does the job for you. The essence nourishes you now", he says.

"What does that mean? Will I die if I eat food? How come all these angels in Baza's place were eating food?"

"All that I'm saying is that you don't *need* it. Of course if you want to eat, nobody is going to stop you and most definitely, you're not going to die if you eat something. I am just saying that you don't need the human food to survive", he snaps.

"And with the regards to the angels in Baza's place? Well, sometimes even angels like to feel human. But in the case of Baza's malakhims, eating food, consuming resources, what could be more human than that, yet so ultimately Baza? To consume, to use, to drain, to eat up, to ravage?"

And right on time another lecture!

"Okay", I bristle at him, "I hear you. I don't need food, yet I'm not going to die if I eat a bit of "Refreshers" or some "Strawberry laces". So I'm gonna go now, get myself some clothes, get some sweets, then come back, get changed and start looking for my sister. Is that okay with you?"

He rakes me with an exasperated and mildly peeved gaze and I'm glaring back at him.

His righteousness is getting on my nerves.

"Can I have the card please?" I outstretch my hand.

"If you wish", he grunts through his teeth.

He paddles across the room, scoops his jeans off the floor and fishes the card out of the back pocket.

He turns to me and I think he is about to toss it at me, but instead, he just stands there with a card in his outstretched hand.

"Thanks."

I snatch the card out of his hand on my way out.

Chapter 6

*T*hree hours later I'm walking back to our B&B under the light of the promenade's street lamps.

As it turns out, we've slept through the day and the grey light, which was seeping into the room, was the first glimmer of the evening.

Two large "Primark" brown paper bags and a medium size white and pink stripy paper bag, jammed to the brim with Pick & Mix, are pulling at my hands, but I don't mind.

The earlier extra large strawberry milkshake still sits heavily on my stomach.

I just made it to Primark in time before it closed for the night. With only half an hour to spare, I was scooping clothing off the shelves and throwing them into my shopping basket under the watchful eye of a security guard and impatient glares of staff.

But I've got the main things I needed. Now I am the proud owner of two pairs of jeans, two pairs of clean socks and a set of underwear, a couple of T-shirts, a hoodie and a pair of "cheap and cheerful" black plimsolls.

Unexpectedly, this little impromptu shopping spree did cheer me up.

As I approach our B&B, humming to myself and swinging my heavy bags with my steps, while chewing on a long red string of

"Strawberry laces", a young family emerges through the doors of our B&B.

The "picture perfect" family of a strong dad in jeans, jumper and petticoat over, a young and happy mum in an elegant beige coat with just an inch of skirt showing from underneath, and an adorable little girl, a cute, rosy cheeked toddler with the shiny wet eyes of a puppy, in a dress up princess outfit with a plastic crown lost in her jet-black curls.

The adorable family are in their "Sunday finest". The three of them stop at the top of the stairs, as mum smiles, bending over, telling something to the little princess, more than likely negotiating seaside treats in exchange for good behaviour. As much as it's odd to see a child without a coat at this time of the year, I could only imagine the grief she gave her mum in order to wear this princess dress, of which she is rather proud.

I stop at the bottom of the steps and step to the side, waiting for the family to clear off before I barge through with my bags.

The dad notices me first. He smiles and tugs the little princess down by the hand.

And the next second, as the little princess lifts her shiny brown eyes to me, her gaze travels over my body, taking in everything, and when our gazes meet, her sweet face lights up. Her eyes and pink pouty mouth open wide and, as if in a slow motion, she raises her small hand, points at me and declares in a bright lisping toddler lull, "Angel. Pretty angel, pretty wings."

The air leaves my lungs in a puff as if I've been punched.

I have only ever read about "when the world had stopped spinning", but with her words, the world slows down around me and then freezes. Everything goes still as I look at her and she looks at me and she *sees* me.

Her gaze travels over my face. It jumps behind my back, taking in the length of each wing in turn, even the bottom ones. Her gaze lingers there, inspecting my wings behind me.

She sees who I am, she sees my wings and to make things worse, she is telling all of that to her parents.

I stand frozen to the spot, afraid to move, childishly hoping that if I don't move, they won't see me or maybe I'll become invisible.

But unfortunately, I'm not invisible.

Unsatisfied with the silence, the girl tugs side of her mother's coat, demanding attention, as she announces once again, and louder this time: "Pretty angel", pointing squarely at my chest.

Her mum lifts her eyes at me and for a long moment the entire happy family looks deeply at me, the parents in search of an angel and the girl in awe of one.

I push a pathetic lopsided smile out.

Rafe said they can't see my wings! They can't see my wings. They can't see my wings!

A rhythmic affirmation plays on a loop in my head and I hope he is right.

My wings, as if sensing my fear, shoot open around me, taking me by surprise, and the moment it happens, the girl yanks her hand out of her parent's hold, and squealing with delight, rushes at me.

If I was scared before, now I'm petrified.

I want to run. But before I can make up my mind and decide what to do, two small warm arms encircle my legs just above my knees and her warm body presses against mine.

"Oh, dear", the mother gushes, running down the stairs after her child, "I'm so sorry."

"Juliet", the father's deep voice calls after the toddler, "you can't just come over and hug people."

The mother runs at the toddler and scoops her in her arms, while I stand there, giving a fantastic performance of a silent rooted tree.

"I'm so sorry. She doesn't usually do anything like that", the mother continues apologising. "Sweetie, you can't do that and you shouldn't have done it to this nice young lady. That's not nice. You need to ask first if you want a hug. Mummy and daddy will always hug you, but you need to ask before hugging other people", she softly chastises her child.

But the girl is not interested in any of it.

She twists and wriggles in her mother's arms, reaching her hands to me, swinging her legs. Her gaze is locked on my wings.

"Pretty angel!" she cries. The disappointed wail fills the street.

Finally I managed to find my voice.

"That's okay", I croak.

With the entire family now down at the bottom of the stairs, the stairs are finally clear.

Now it's my turn to scoop up my baggage in my hands and dash up the stairs under the accompaniment of the girl's howls about the "pretty angel" and "pretty wings", and exasperated and dismayed reasoning from her parents.

I launch up the stairs, jumping over two stairs at a time, and only once the door to our room slams behind my back and is propped with my body, can I breathe again.

Our room is lit with both nightlights and the desk lamp. The TV is mumbling something incoherent in the background like a drunk.

Rafe sits on the corner of his bed, gazing into the blue twinkling screen with unseeing eyes. His black combat trousers are back over his legs, but his torso is bare.

I say nothing to him, breathing like a marathon runner as I gather my mojo.

Rafe turns to me.

"Are you alright?" he furrows his brow, studying my sweaty face.

"A little girl just saw me!" I mumble in a terrified whisper.

"Of course she saw you", he turns his attention back to the TV, "I can see you too."

"No!" I rush, "you don't understand. Like *seen* seen."

My dramatic whisper and bulging eyes bring his attention back to me, as he is giving me a once over.

"Well, I warned you that it might happen", he answers, impatiently, blowing a strand of hair from his eyes.

"Interesting, though", he mumbles again, this time more to himself.

"Interesting?" I roar, shocked by his chilled attitude. "A girl just pointed her finger at me and called me an angel, pretty angel. In front of everyone! I thought you might want to know, in case if you need to clean it up somehow or do something!"

"How old is this girl?" He is calm and unflustered, unlike me.

"I don't know, small. Maybe three–four years old."

"I wouldn't worry about it. You'll be fine", he is bored with our conversation already. "Think about it for a moment. Who is going to believe a child that young, when a child says that she has seen an angel?"

Of course he is right and I'm probably overreacting, but I can still taste that electric panic of exposure on my tongue and I still can hear my heart beating in my ears.

"Anyway", I mumble, swallowing past that metallic taste, "I need to get changed and I will go out again. I need to speak to my neighbours, see if anyone knows anything about my sister."

I drop my sweets on the bed and take my new clothes to the bathroom with me.

The new clothes fit surprisingly well. The fabric is not as soft and luxurious against my skin as the designer gear from Sam's wardrobe was, but the clean and dusty smell of a new garment is better than the rotting, decomposing stench of my current ones on any day of the week.

Mia's white swords are still where I had left them.

Their silvery blades are dim and subdued, and the surfaces are smooth and clear as they rest on the floor.

Probably better to take these. Just in case...

But the second my hands wrap over their intricately carved hilts, the swords wake up and their blades illuminate from within with a bright light. Their surfaces begin to ripple again just as I remember they did before, when I held them.

Ignoring this angelic wakening of the bloodthirsty swords, with a practiced move, I tuck them at the belt at the back of my new jeans.

Rafe is still engrossed in the late evening news broadcast, read on the screen by a young woman with annoying nasal voice.

"And now for the local news, where you are", she chirps, signing off at the end of her segment.

The picture changes, transporting us into a local TV studio and after the familiar, past eight o'clock evening intro jingle, the camera zooms on a local TV presenter, a stout middle aged woman in a suit, with short dark hair.

She turns her head toward the camera. Her gaze is serious and grave.

"In early hours of this morning, after a series of raids on four gang controlled premises, police apprehended the leaders of a notorious local gang that has been thriving in Yorkshire for the last five years. The gang is suspected to be involved in the illegal firearms trade, 'Class A' drugs distributions in the North East, along with an organised human trafficking, slavery and exploitation ring. The operation lasted only a few minutes and was the result of six months of careful planning by the Yorkshire Police force, The National Crime Agency and anti-gang Trident unit. Three gang leaders were arrested during that raid. A submachine gun, along with a handgun, forty rounds of ammunition, cash and the suspected "Class A" drugs were seized in the raid."

I turn to the screen in time to see the photographs of the three familiar faces magnified over the TV screen.

My legs buck underneath me and I sink to the floor, unable to draw my gaze away from the TV.

In shock I scan the arrogant faces with shaved heads, and a wicked fat chavvy round pendant on a thick chain around the fat neck of one of them, and an involuntary spasm squeezes my stomach.

Them! How?!

Baza said he killed them!

How are they here, out again?

My head spins in shock and fear hammers at my gut. My dried out lungs demand some air but I can't seem to remember how to breathe.

The world around me fuzzes out and disappears down a long tunnel, and some weird buzz spreads inside my head as if a beehive full of bees moved in there.

My gaze is still locked to the screen.

And the next second, the last breath leaves me, when the two grainy black and white pictures of me and Rafe come onto the screen.

"Ariel", Rafe's shocked whisper pulls at me, but I don't need to be told. I'm already watching. I was watching the screen all along.

Rafe reaches out to the remote and puts up the volume.

"... The two gang leaders still remain at large and a nationwide manhunt has been issued. Police asks members of public to call immediately on 999 if they have any information on the whereabouts of the suspects. Police warn that they are both dangerous and may be armed, and that members of public should not approach them."

The bees fled my head, leaving the dull vacuum behind.

I stare at mine and Rafe's faces looking back at me from the TV screen, and I can't and don't know what to think.

It feels so incredibly surreal, like a bad dream. Or a joke.

I almost expect the TV lady any second now, to look back into the camera, give me a wink, a big smile and say "gotcha".

"The plans for the UK biggest wind farm off the Yorkshire coast were given a 'go-ahead'..."

The female presenter is much happier now, delivering to the local electorate the wonderful news of a big and shiny new government venture, that will bring new jobs and money into the region, but I've stopped listening by now.

The mug shots of mine and Rafe's faces are frozen in front of my eyes. It's like they are carved into my cornea, and no amount of blinking will be able to remove them. I can't see anything but my pale scared face staring back at me from the TV screen.

Me? Wanted? With them?! How? Why?

The picture from my passport... Where did they get it?

I can't formulate or finish a single question.

The sudden piercing buzz of static slices through the room, pulling me away from my shredded thoughts, making me jump.

Chapter 7

The smiling TV presenter vanished from the screen, replaced with the black and white pixelated noise of the static.

Rafe outstretches his arm with the remote towards the TV, but before he has a chance to change the channel or to turn the volume down on this ear bleeding noise, the static disappears, just as unexpectedly as it came, giving way to Baza's soft and smiling "Father Christmas" face.

"Gil-im si nunus", Rafe spits at the TV and hurls the remote to the floor.

I am completely confused now. I don't understand...

"Good evening Ariel", Baza's soft warm baritone fills the room.

His signature kind open smile stretches his lips, deepening the wrinkles around his eyes.

"Rafe", he adds in a curt greeting, easing off the force of his charm.

"It's nice to see you again and it is a relief to find you in a good health, Ariel. I hope that Apkallu treats you well and that you're not *too* disappointed with people over there, even after such a short stay", he lifts his eyebrow and I can swear I can hear an undercurrent in his voice, but I don't understand where he's going with it. I just simply don't understand what's going on.

"I have to say, Ariel, your departure was rather unexpected and left me very confused. I thought we had an agreement", he draws his brows at me through the screen. "I was hoping that maybe, finally, you understood the opportunities that were presented to you, understood what I was offering."

He shakes his head.

"I was very disappointed with you, child", the sadness in his voice is so tangible that for a fleeting second I really feel bad for my earlier "dump and run" tricks.

"Especially, when you left for the second time and decamped in such a rude manner without even a 'goodbye'. And that's after all my offerings, after my warm welcome to you into my family, after all the gifts and hospitality I have bestowed upon you? I thought at the gates of Uras that you had agreed to my proposal..." he shakes his head, confused, his bushy eyebrows are drawn together.

"I was offering you everything that is mine. I was offering you my glorious army."

A soft grandfatherly outrage, shock and hurt play on his face and I have to push the rising apology down my throat.

I have to give myself an internal shake, to remind myself of the instructions he had given to Sam, which I have heard with my own ears.

He is good! I need to learn a thing or two from this man...

"So can you imagine my surprise when I was advised that you were here?" he continues.

And the next second, his face lights up, leaving no trace of the grave disappointment of a second ago.

Wow, we have ourselves a seasoned Shakespearian actor here! The "Globe" is looking for you, mate!

A small smile tugs at his lips, "but then I thought to myself, Ariel was so concerned over her sister's wellbeing, negotiating a better life for her kindred with me so hard, that without a doubt, the worry for her kindred is what beckoned Ariel to leave. This concern is probably what made Ariel abandon our agreement.

"And then, I find that your sister is indeed lost to you and you are here perilously searching for her, living through such heartache and worry, so..." he tilts his head, pausing, the deeper smile sets in.

Drumroll please!

"I've decided to aid you with your quandary, and I'm happy to say that I have uncovered your sister's whereabouts."

My heart stops.

He found her! He probably has her!

After all I did to keep him away from her.

The home cinema footage of my sister comes on the screen next.

She is older than I remember, taller and lankier, but she is still small and scrawny for her eleven years. Her long stringy hair hangs lifelessly to the sides of her face, hiding it, as she keeps her head down, looking at her feet. Her old, worn out blue plaid dress is too short and small on her.

She stands outside an old yellowing caravan, facing my mother who is yelling at her, reprimanding her. And as my sister says nothing, my mother pinches my sister's chin, yanking it up, as she continues admonishing her, screaming right into my sister's face.

There's no noise to the picture, just the silence of my B&B room and maybe because of that, but my sister's misery, pain and sadness are so profound and tangible that I can't watch it any longer. I can feel her hurt and pain. I can feel them as my own.

Maybe because it was me once, maybe because all that pain was mine.

My sister is no longer the child I remember and the tears swell up in my eyes.

The TV gives a dry click and the picture returns to Baza.

He leans in closer to the screen and I can make out individual hairs in his glossy, neatly trimmed silver beard and moustache.

"Just more evidence of my infinite powers, Ariel, if you ever needed it", he winks at me with a gleeful smile. This "Father Christmas" manages to look arrogant and humble at the same time!

"You go and collect your sister, Ariel. Go! Ease the pain in your heart. And that little piece of the local evening news earlier", he nods his head to the side, clearly talking about the country-wide manhunt on my head, "is just a little guarantee to make sure that you don't extend your stay in Apkallu any longer than required. Honestly, child, what possibly would you want in there that I can't provide? What is it in there that you are so eager to keep? Questionable people? Suffering? Gluttony and starvation, poverty and greed? Sub-standard enjoyment, if you ask me."

He shakes his head again.

"Here's her address."

A slim B&B notepad on the nightstand lights up with an orangey red glow, and slowly under my gaze, the writing begins to seep through the pages like a coffee stain, growing clearer and bolder, forming the letters and words. The ink is brownish red, carmine colour, the colour of the dried blood.

Hypnotised, I'm watching it.

"Go, my child, collect your precious kindred and I shall see you soon."

With his last spoken word, the TV in front of us goes silent and black. It went off.

My mind is spinning and I wish I could turn it off just like a TV, with the push of a button.

Wow! Now that's the way to make me move!

Rafe breaks the silence first.

"Ariel, you can't go there. You know it's a trap, right?"

"Ariel!" he barks, as I don't acknowledge him, still sitting silent and immobile like a piece of furniture.

I turn my gaze to him.

"You can't go there! Do you hear me? I forbid it!"

I pull back, glaring at him from my carpet spot in disbelief.

What? He didn't just say that!

"What did you just say? You *forbid* it?!"

I'm gobsmacked and it takes me a while to remember how to breathe and to push the anger down.

"You ain't the bloody boss of me! You can't forbid shit!"

I am up to my feet.

I'm livid and my Rage is doing energetic "Macarena" dance in my head, warming up her muscles.

I am between a rock and a hard place. I'm played, twisted and pulled in every direction and he has audacity to tell me he *"forbids it"*?

"I know it's a trap, okay? Give me some credit", I huff, "but you listen to me too. It's the only solid lead I have on my sister and I don't think Baza is lying here. And if we're to assume that he isn't, then it means that now Baza knows exactly where she is and he is just swapping her for me, the trade, which I'm willing to make by the way. I'm not prepared to see how far he'd be willing to take this game if I don't show up."

I'm getting wound up with every word I say, and I'm yelling at Rafe now.

"And what exactly do *you* propose? Call on Chamuel and have the two backstabbing slime balls to deal with? Or maybe you'd like to call on your men? But will they come? Do you know where their loyalty lies nowadays?"

He doesn't say a word and I see that he can't object to any of it.

"And what am I supposed to do? Ignore this chance and run away? Hide and keep my fingers crossed for another, better chance to find her?"

I take a breath in.

"You know, sometimes there are no better chances and no pleasant choices. Sometimes all choices are shit, with one as bad as the next, and sometimes the best person for the job is yourself!"

I turn away from him, already thinking about what I might need with me when I go to that mysterious address.

"I can go there", he offers quietly, "I will go, check on everything and I will bring her back."

I peer at him over my shoulder, as I'm about to put on my plimsolls.

"Come on, Rafe. Even you, deep down know that you are not going to help here. You can't fix this situation for me. Baza had set it up all for me, for *me* to deal with it. He wants me and, quite frankly, he will get me."

I pause for a second, "And I think he knows it."

My mind is set. There's really nothing more to discuss.

"At least in this little assets exchange, for all this hassle, I will get Jess", I mumble, more to myself than answering Rafe.

At least I hope so.

"What I do want from you though, what I want to ask of you", I sit down on the bed next to Rafe and look up at him, "is to look after Jess for me. I want you to promise me that you'll keep Jess with you at all times and keep her safe when I'm not around."

I meet his gaze.

"Remember the promise you made to me when I came with you? You promised that nothing will happen to her. You promised that she will be safe. Well, I want that promise back, only this time I want *you* to keep her safe. No more asking your minions to do your job, no more mucking about. I want you to take care of her. I want her to be your sole responsibility if anything happens to me."

He could tell me to get lost right now and there would be nothing I could do, but because he hasn't done it so far, I seriously hope that he is not going to start now.

I need him now. He is all that I have left. He is the last one I can ask for help.

But Rafe says nothing as he glares at me. His lips are set in a thin hard line.

I take in a deep breath ready to beg, to plead.

"Rafe, please."

And as he says nothing I continue, "Rafael, please, can you understand me here? I will do it. I will go there because I need to find her. I need her with me, I need to protect her. Just like you had to protect this essence", I jab at my chest.

"I need her to be happier than me", I whisper, "Otherwise, nothing makes sense anymore. Do you understand what I mean?" I don't know how to explain it any better. I don't know how else to explain it to him so that he understands me. "And I will do it, no matter what it takes. But it would be much easier if you were with me."

Asking another person for help feels weird. It feels awkward and alien. My pleas grind on my teeth and come falling out of my mouth like clumps of dirt.

But I have no choice.

I don't know what I will find there, but I think I know Baza well enough to know that my trip wouldn't be that simple. I only hope that my sister is there, and that she is well.

"What do you want me to do?"

I sigh in relief at Rafe's question, he is on board.

"We'll go there. You hide somewhere nearby. I'll go in and get my sister and then we'll meet up and get out of there. I think it would be best if we meet a few yards away as I don't want anyone to know that you're there, just in case."

"Okay."

Strangely, he's not arguing with me and I hope it's not because he's given up trying to reason with me, but rather because my plan is so excellent and "thought through", that he has nothing more to add.

"Okay", I echo.

"Shall we get ready and go?" I ask.

"I suggest we wait until darkness falls, ideally after midnight. If our pictures have already been transmitted to your people, I think it would be more prudent not to risk exposure beforehand."

"Sounds good", I pipe in, nodding my head like it was the part of my plan as well.

"And we should stay inside this room", I add.

"That is very wise, Ariel", he utters and I swear I can hear sarcasm.

Chapter 8

*L*ocked in the room and waiting for midnight, I can't do anything but pace.

The "Refreshers" and "Strawberry laces" are all gone, chewed up like finger nails – not for the enjoyment but to fill the nervous void.

The tips of my bottom wings brush over the aged carpet with a light rhythmic swish as I walk.

I'm terrified of the possibility of the B&B owners, watching the exciting segment of the evening news, recognising us in those chalky mug shots and calling the police, who are already en route. Or worse, already behind the closed door, the entire team with weapons and in masks, ready to break down the door and arrest us.

I tried to switch the TV back on, but I'm too jumpy and scared to watch it. I prefer the clock ticking silence. At least in that silence I'd be able to hear the breathing of crouching police outside.

Rafe is nowhere near as skittish as me. After agreeing to help me, he sat comatose on the bed, with unseeing, wide-open eyes staring into space like a yogi, who had reached the inner peace and enlightenment.

We haven't said a word to each other since our agreement.

I don't know how else to prepare for what I've decided to do.

With the swords glistening on the top of the dresser, I don't know what else I might need. I don't know what other weapons to take, and more to the point, if any weapons will help me there at all.

"We had better get ready."

Rafe rises off the bed, gingerly stretching and twisting at the waist.

"I'm ready." The mousy noise coming out of me is not a convincing call of a warrior, ready for battle.

I clear my throat and want to say something battle worthy but I shut my mouth, changing my mind.

What's the point?

"Make sure to bring your swords. Are you sure you want to do it?"

He offers me a way out. He is probably hoping for that.

"No. But I'm not leaving my sister again."

I'm pleased how decisive and strong my voice sounded this time.

"Okay", he nods. "I still think it would be better if I went there on my own."

"I would love nothing more, but we both know that if I don't turn up there, my sister would vanish again."

With that said if she is there.

But something tells me that Baza wouldn't lie to me about her location. I'm not stupid or naïve enough to expect this gift from the kindness of his heart. I know that some crap is coming my way, but what I have learnt after dealing with Baza so far, is that his traps and schemes are not blunt and obvious. He plans in advance, playing a "long game". There's always a bit of truth and kept promises woven within his deceit. He usually delivers what he promises, taking something unexpected in return.

"Do you still want me to hide in the bushes?" A lopsided smirk tugs at the corner of Rafe's lips.

"Yes. In case it's a trap, in case if my sister is not there or if something happens to me. Basically, if the shit hits the fan."

"I understand", he nods. "So if the proverbial 'shit' hits the proverbial 'fan', I am to run in and turn the fan off, right?"

Bless him. He tries to lighten the mood and I'm so grateful to him at this moment that I take two large steps towards him, crossing the distance between us and hug him tight, wrapping my arms around his waist.

I lean my head against his chest and the smell of sunshine, ocean and fruits rush forefront, doing a little happy dance in my head. I breathe in and out.

This embrace confuses me.

I don't know what I want. I don't know what I want to say, but I'm so tired and scared. I am tired of being brave, and grown-up and in charge. I'm tired of distrusting, and constantly suspecting everyone.

I'm tired of being strong and rescuing others. *I* want to be rescued for once.

I wish I was rescued back *then* and I wish I would be rescued now, rescued from all the mess, saved from all pain and tough decisions. But I wonder if it is simply too late, too late for regrets, too late for empty wishes and hopes. It is what it is now.

His arms come around me, hesitantly hugging me back.

"Right", I whisper.

I step back and he lets me go.

"Please promise to take care of Jess for me", I whisper, "I have nothing else left." I gaze into his eyes, willing for him to understand.

He just nods.

I walk to the dresser and scoop up my short swords.

When the swords hilts are not touched by a hand, the white fire of the blades is calm and smooth like a mirror surface. But when the swords sense my hands closing over the hilts, the cold yet blistering flames of the blades ignite, and the surfaces of the blades begin to ripple and move.

I can practically feel the swords' excitement. These swords are bloodthirsty, just as Mia was.

But I push back these disturbing thoughts. I have no time left for any of it either.

I have a job to do now.

I had a look at the address that bled over the page of the notebook earlier.

It's a caravan site about five miles up North from the town. The site is surrounded by farmlands and fields, and the earlier TV image of my sister and my mum, standing outside of a yellowing caravan, comes back to mind. This address feels like proof that my sister is in there.

I take a deep breath in. I breathe out.

I shove my shaking hands into the pockets of my jeans.

"I guess I'll fly us there", I say.

"If you want to be there tonight..." Rafe answers.

Rafe is already suited and booted for our late night gander with the appropriateness of the crowd we might be meeting.

He has less lethal gear on him than he had back in Hell, and his "plastic" tactical breastplate and pauldrons are missing, but he is still packing plenty, ready to fight should he need to.

Seeing him so fearless and strong, the anticipation and excitement spike in me.

I look forward to seeing my sister again, crushing her small body against mine, and never letting go again.

I look forward to giving everyone their dues, if needed, and taking back what is mine.

I throw the door open, leading the way. I don't look back at the room. I don't bring anything unnecessary with me. I have a feeling that with either outcome, I will not be coming back here again.

Rafe's steps behind me are less weary than they were earlier, but I still can hear the tired shuffle in his limping rhythm.

"Are you sure you'll be okay?" I glance at him over my shoulder.

I need him to be okay, I'm about to trust him with the last important thing left in my life.

"Yeah, fine", he snaps, clearly tired of my constant checking on him.

"Wow, stroppy. Don't get your knickers in a twist. I'm just asking."

We're through the B&B's dark empty hallway and out of the door. The entrance door closes behind us with a soft click.

The weather had turned again.

The heavy black sky above rests on our shoulders, preceding the storm. The gale wind pushes us off our feet and the raging sea screams and roars against the shore.

My wings wrap around me.

"What you reckon? Take off from the same place where we landed?" I call to Rafe over the wind. With weak whimpers and squeaks, lamp posts sway with the wind along the street.

"Yes, that will be fine", he barks.

With every new step that takes us closer to our destination, Rafe gets crabbier.

It's darker and windier under the closed gates of the pier.

I'm nervous of flying in this wind, when even standing still on the ground is a job, but damn sure I'm not planning on telling that to Rafe, who would only be happy to pull the plug on this whole idea.

I turn to him, spreading my arms wide to him like a long lost relative eager for an embrace.

I know how to hold onto him now, so he just steps closer and grabs hold of my waist.

My wings flash open and the next second we are thrown up into the air like a kite on a windy day.

I scream, holding tighter to Rafe, and close my eyes.

The wind rushes past me and I'm choking on the force of it, as my screams are shoved back into my open throat and I cough.

I slam my mouth shut and carefully open my eyes.

In these few short seconds we've been thrown miles high up in the air, and the lights of the promenade are nothing more than a thin golden thread.

"Are you okay?" I ask Rafe, embarrassed by my flimsy control over my wings and my emotions.

"Would it change anything if I'm not?" he jabs.

I roll my eyes at him, deciding not to respond. I seriously don't have time for his passive-aggressive games right now.

Okay. Okay, bloody breathe and let's move it.

I scan the horizon for a few seconds, getting my bearings.

There, to the left.

Away from the town, past the motorway, a few faintest lights twinkle in the night, surrounded by a wide ring of thick darkness.

My wings hear me and now they know our destination too. They slightly shift back and fold around my body and begin to beat, and with it, the trajectory of our bodies change and we move forward.

My wings are so confident and strong, that I'm sure if they could speak they would tell me to chill, that everything is under control and that flying with them is a piece of cake.

With every new flight, with every new height, the delirium of freedom sets deeper in me, infusing my blood, making my head light and bubbly with excitement. I want to fly more. I want to fly longer, fly faster, zigzagging through clouds, past the trees and do loop the loops like sleek military jets in aero shows.

Once I get my sister, I'll take her for a flight.

A stupid smile comes over my lips and warm happiness pools at my chest when I imagine my sister's little squashed face with eyes shut and her mouth wide open in a scream when I take her for a flight, before the freedom and fun sets in, with wonder igniting her eyes. I can't wait to show her what I can do now.

Half an hour later, we circle above quiet and dark caravan homes scattered in the dark clearing of a field. Only a few of the homes have lights in the windows.

It's dark and quiet, and only the wind whistles between the homes, bringing the wintery smell of a late autumn.

I can't see or hear anyone.

The clearing is silent and peaceful and my wings sense only our two essences in the area.

Maybe Baza is not here yet. I silently hope and pray that maybe just this once I'll catch a break.

"Ready?" I ask Rafe like he was asking me once in the cave. Now it's my turn to lead.

"I seriously wish you'd reconsider, Ariel. Never, in a million eons in Arllu, would Baza gift something so deeply coveted unless there was something in it for him. Do you realise that?"

"I know that", I bite back, "but tell me this, what would Baza do to someone who refuses to play his games? Is he just going to walk away with "Oh, well, I tried"? I don't think so, and you know it! He will find a way to make me play, and right now I want to at least clear out the play area, so no one gets hurt during his perverted "hide and seek" game! And you can't offer me any alternative solution apart from "wait". And it's not really a solution, is it?"

I'm sick and tired of having the same conversations with him over and over again. I'm done talking to him.

I scan the clearing and the fields around, looking for the best place to stash Rafe away, not visible but close enough for him to hear and see everything.

To the left of the caravan park and only two yards away from the farthest caravan, a thin grove of slim trees forms a weak divisive line between fields and the park.

"There", I point to the trees. "I'm going to drop you there and you'll hide and wait for me. I'll walk around the park and get into it from the opposite side, just in case. When I find my sister, I'll go towards the trees and meet you there."

The wings heard me. They fold around us and we both dive head forward towards the ground with incredible speed.

And just before I decide to scream, ruining my plan completely, mine and Rafe's wings simultaneously flash open, halting our descent, holding us just a few yards above the ground, before we are carefully lowered to the ground. The ground touches my feet and I want to drop to my knees and kiss the pressed earth.

Enjoy flying?! Scrap that!

"Okay", I try to think of something to say.

I'm not sure if I should thank Rafe again or maybe to give us both an energising pep talk, but I decide against either.

"Off I go", I mumble, but before I set off, I turn to Rafe, "Remember. You promised."

I don't like goodbyes. To me they always felt like a preparation for death, and had a sad and bitter taste of finality in it, and I'm not saying goodbye to him now.

"See you in a mo", I chime, giving him a small smile, before turning and walking down the road, along the line of trees, away from Rafe.

We agreed that I would fly, but I decided against it, taking this time to calm down and to remind myself why I'm here.

I'm about to see my sister, my mum. I'm excited to see one and apprehensive to see the other. I feel little again. I feel scared and lost, and this time I know that my mum and sister are not the only ones I might find in here.

If something happens to me tonight, I will not be the only one who will get hurt.

The perverted game fate plays with me now has more players, and the stakes have increased.

As I reach the line of the last caravans, I barge past the trees, walking inside the clearing. I can practically feel the trouble zooming in on me the moment I step on the packed ground.

My wings still can't sense any angelic essence in here. Rafe's essence faded a while back, with only a fine tendril still reaching out to me, and I can sense only myself in the clearing.

Glancing around, I come closer to the nearest home.

Again gnomes! The weather beaten gnomes with chipped green and red paint litter the area, and an old swing chair squeaks in the wind, as metal brushes over metal. It's an old couple's house. Nothing about it speaks of my family.

I take a few steps closer to the next home. The two large, and now bare, flowerbeds, framed by neatly laid stones, run on either side of the front door.

I don't know if that might the right caravan...

Oh god. How am I going to find her in here?

Suddenly the silence is ruptured by a scream.

A man bellows somewhere at the centre of the caravan park. His long, agonising scream rings in the air before it dies off, as if cut and just as suddenly as it began.

The chilling silence hangs heavy for two long seconds before dogs' barks echo from every corner, and the timid activity of hushed voices begins. Doors tentatively creak open, lights flick inside the homes and on the porches, the squeaks of the floorboards under people's feet.

The voices are quiet at first, but slowly rising as more of them join in, as if reassured by their growing number people feel braver.

Suddenly a female shriek pierces the clearing and everything stops again. Everyone is silent.

This shriek is sharp yet heavy. It hangs in the air for a while, and somehow in this animal howl I can recognise my mother's voice.

I sprint towards the sound, running past and around caravans, past the wandering and confused people, who are talking again, running deeper into the nucleus of the site.

My feet slide on the wet ground as I take corners.

I round another corner at full speed and stop as if smacked into an invisible glass wall.

A body lies on the ground, illuminated by the light, streaming from an open caravan door.

But all that I can see are the legs dressed in dark jeans and white male-size trainers on the feet. The rest of the body is obstructed by a body of a woman in floral flannel pyjamas, kneeling in the dirt, howling, swaying and rocking the fallen on her lap.

The door swings wider and the light falls on the side of her face.

I'm frozen, watching my mother mourning someone and I can't find it in me to move.

I want to come over and see who it is on the ground, but I'm too afraid of what I might find there. I want to come to her and console her, but I'm too scared to see her grief.

I want to come and hug her, tell her that I'm here but I'm terrified to be rejected again.

I lift my eyes to the wide open door.

My sister, just the way I saw her in the Baza's video, in the same navy plaid dress, stands in the doorframe. The light pools behind her, keeping her face in the shadow.

My sister is motionless. With a frozen detachment, she watches our mother on the ground, who is hailing to the sky.

There's no fear, no shock to my sister's indifferent face, no sadness, no pain. Her glazed over eyes sweep along the length of the fallen body, as she stands there with a cold and cruel disinterest of a broken child, who'd seen too much.

I feel as if I've been punched in the gut. Seeing her like this, It's like my own reflection is looking back at me, as if time turned back and it is me who is standing there.

My shocked gaze is all over my sister, searching for my sweet little "puppy", who always was so playful, sweet, trusting and loving, but I can't find her anywhere. Nothing is left of her.

The empty and broken shell stands there instead, like an abandoned house with dark windows: broken, used, abused, left there to rot and decompose.

My searching gaze sweeps over her before stopping at her arms and hands.

Her right arm is longer than her left, by at least ten inches, and much darker, as if my sister wearing a black elbow length glove.

And with another "sucker punch" at my gut, the penny drops.

The realisation sinks in as I watch black, sticky and slow drops fall thickly under my gaze from her "long" right hand.

I thought I had nothing left in me for surprises, for disappointment, fear.

But I was wrong. This is a new one and it is raw.

It feels like a second punch or a second kick, the one which steals the last oxygen and hope from you, while the fresh pain laces with the agony of the first and you know there is more pain to come.

Fear squeezes my stomach, throat and I feel sick. I have to swallow a few times hard before I can move or think again.

I want to join my mother's wail to mourn the memory of my sister.

I want to hide behind my mother *from* my sister.

I want to run away from them both.

The sirens come next.

Quiet and lost at first, their wails are growing, drowning my mothers.

The sirens wake me with a sobering slap, breaking through the fog of terror and shock.

I sprint around my mother, purposefully not looking at the body on the ground, up four steps to the caravan door, to my sister.

She doesn't notice me. Her gaze is glued to the body behind me. Her unblinking eyes are the glassy eyes of a zombie.

"Hi, sweetie", I softly start, lifting myself onto another step. Our eyes are on the same level now.

"Jessie-boo", I coo at her in a shaky whisper, willing for her to look at me.

A fat bloody drop falls to the porch with a grandfather clock's chime. Or is it just me imagining it?

"Jess?"

She doesn't hear me, doesn't look at me.

"*Under the Sky*

Here I lie", I quietly begin to sing.

I sing the rhyme that I came up with when we were little. This was the lullaby I used to sing to my sister when she would cry at night, scared by the noises of our mother and step father fighting, by his drunken angry slur and her terrified screams coming from downstairs.

This rhyme was our secret. It was our private language, which would convey a lot, yet understood only by us. This rhyme was the promise of our eternal bond and love.

"Under the Sky
Here I lie
Under the sky
My sister and I.
Trees above us and the bottomless sky
Here we'll live – my sister and I."

And slowly, as if guided by the light, her eyes sluggishly travel to mine, staring blankly at me for a minute, before she blinks through fog once, twice, recognising me and her soft face I used to know, comes to the fore and her eyes fly open. The moment later the glassy film falls off her eyes and her nose wrinkles, her face crumples as she shuts her eyes and begins to sob.

With a dull heavy clunk, the knife drops to the porch.

I feel my sister now. She is with me again. She came back and I am relieved.

In one jump I close the space between us, throwing myself at her, crushing her hard against my chest and wrapping her tight in my arms.

I want to squeeze all that craziness out of her, to wake her, to remember her and to remind her. I want to feel her and check that she is still here, that she is still my sister.

"Oh, Jessie-boo, Jessie-boo", I mutter, hugging her, rocking with her, "what are we gonna do?"

I used to say it to her all the time when she was little.

"*YOU!*" A female shriek screeches behind my back.

I feel the familiar pull in that noise but I can't recognise the animal that is howling it.

I let go off my sister and step around on the narrow porch, pushing my sister behind my back.

The knife, nipped by the toe of my shoe, clangs down the steps.

I am still scared of my sister.

I don't know who is behind me anymore, who she has become. I don't know who this new animal is, *a murderer*, or what it might do next. But the instinct, or maybe habit, speaks first, demanding to protect my little sister from everything and everyone, and most of all, from my mother's wrath.

My mother stares at me. Her bulging eyes are ablaze, her finger is pointing at me.

"Spawn of the devil!" my mother screeches.

The hate and fear swim in her eyes.

"The abomination, which was sent to tempt and test us! To take us to the depths of Hell, to serve the Lucifer and to take us away from the Almighty Lord and his righteous light!"

Her words and her hate are like a slap.

I swallow and take an involuntary step back, but I bump into my sister and spin around, jumping away.

Now I'm proper scared, scared of the fanatic in front of me and of the murderer behind me. The doubt comes over me, questioning what I'm doing here, why I'm here, what for, whispering with glaring prudence the benefits and ease of Baza's offer.

I face Jess, I face my mother. I spin from one to the next. I am torn and I am scared.

My mother is crazier than I remember.

"Is there anything left to save?" my doubt whispers. I glance at Jess still crying behind me.

No! No! She is my Jessie-boo!

With another glance at my mother, I take a step down, pulling my sister with me.

"The Lord is my shield! The Lord is my fortress! The Lord is my power", the eyes roll back inside my mother's head. She foams at the mouth, her spittle flying everywhere as she starts her preaching recitals.

"He will protect me from Evil. His power will guard me and his light will shine over me", the crazy monotonous chant begins and with it she begins to rock, her eyes are inside her head as the trance sets in.

With every new word she utters, she forgets about the body on her lap, now desperate to guard off the evil. She rises on her knees and the body rolls off her lap.

"The name of the Lord is the mighty tower and the righteous will run to it and they will be saved! I walk through the valley of shadows of death and I will fear no evil because the God said he is with me!" she proclaims.

She throws her arms and head to the sky, yelling it to the heaven, desperate to reach the skies.

Her grief is seeking support from her faith, while birthing the anger and hate. And all of it is now directed at me, as her livid gaze snaps back to me.

Down another step, while keeping my eyes on the madwoman on the ground, who is praying for the evil spirit within me dead and no longer differentiating between me and the "evil spirit".

"Righteous, I will dwell in the house of the Lord forever. Who can serve the Lord? Who can stand before the Lord? Only the righteous!"

She yells that at me. She warns me, and not for the first time.

Right now, she sounds like preachers on the religious TV she used to watch all the time, and another memory of my childhood slaps me, almost sending me to my knees and I have to fight the fear for my next breath.

As my mother is no longer sprawled over the body, I can see my mother's beloved, I can see who she mourns so fearlessly.

It's my stepfather.

The shock rams at me.

But behind it skips in a small satisfied glee, who rubs her hands in delight at the dark and wet patch over my stepfather's chest, soaking my stepfather's shirt and wetting my mother's knees.

My Rage wakes in my chest as fierce as my mother's.

Tapping her blood red boots at me, exasperated, she mouths: "*Told you. Bloody. So!*"

No one is pleased with me.

The dark puddle under my stepfather grows, as does the crowd surrounding us.

Only now I've noticed people with pale, shocked faces, hiding in the shadows around us. Horrified, they watch the freak show of the family that we are. The family once ruled by obsession, terror and fear, now meeting its predictable end.

My mother's hateful gaze follows me.

"No weapons formed against me shall prosper! The devil tongues should be condemned!" she screams at me.

She looks past me at Jess.

Her mad bulging eyes shuttle between me and my sister, before she screeches, pointing her finger at both of us: "I take authority in the name of Jesus and I rebuke you in the Jesus' name! All Satan's children should be sent back to Hell and the bridges should be burned behind them!"

Jess begins to whimper behind me.

In a numb stupor, my mother abandons her husband's body completely, crawling over and past him and once she is closer, with the mad eyes of an animal, she lunges herself towards us.

Jess squeals and dives behind me.

I take another step back, pushing Jess with me. I scoop the knife off the ground.

Everybody will be safer if I hold it for now.

The handle is sticky, and the smell of earth and iron hits my nose.

The sirens are almost upon us. Their urgent hollers drown my mother's.

She condemned me a long time ago. I've got used to her constant denouncements of me, I grew numb and calm about them as if they were a part of her caring for me. But watching her mad bulbous eyes now, I wonder if what had happened today pushed her over the edge and maybe it's my fault too.

"Mam", I nudge in between her monotonous preaching, taking a small step closer to her. "Mama?"

I can't leave her like that.

Maybe without having me for a daughter she wouldn't end up losing her mind. Maybe she wouldn't have lost her husband, beginning the search for peace in different religions, becoming that crazed lunatic in front of me. Maybe Jess and I wouldn't end up where we are.

I glance at the body on the ground. That is probably my fault too...

"Ariel!"

I jump up, startled at Rafe's voice roaring in my head. *"Damu Azeru! What are you doing?! Get out of there!"*

I scan the dark crowd of pale faces and spot the top of Rafe's wing in the darkness, behind the crowd, edged in the corner next to the trees.

"I can't leave her like that!" I scream at him in my head. *"Look at her! She has finally lost her mind. Completely! I can't just take off and abandon her!"*

"You can't leave your sister. You can't leave your mother. Maybe you want to round up the entire Earth population and take all of them with us too?" his exasperated low growl reverberates inside my skull.

"It's not the same and you know it! Just give me a minute. Let me try –", I'm interrupted by another prayer declamation from my mother.

The sirens are here.

A few yards away cars' doors repeatedly slam. There are at least two cars.

"Step aside", a male voice barks. "Sir, step aside."

"Madam, please step aside."

The demanding voices, one male and one female, call from behind the line of spectators, as they make their way through, pushing through the crowd.

"Get out now!" he roars in my head.

"Get your sister and go! NOW!"

"Don't worry", I brush him off, *"nothing is going to happen to me. I can always take myself and Jess back to Uras or to our B&B..."*

I drift off as two blue uniformed police officers come through the crowd and with a quick look at my stepfather on the ground, the pool of blood underneath him, my unfortunate decision to hold the knife, they yank theirs tasers out of their pockets, narrowing them on me.

"ON THE GROUND! ON THE GROUND!"

Their gazes dance between me and my sister. My mother received only a fleeting glance from them.

Their eyes are back on me.

"ON THE GROUND, I SAID!! ON THE GROUND!" the male police officer roars.

They are yelling at me.

They are yelling at *me*?

"Officers..." I start, lifting my hands up in the air, still holding that damn knife.

"DROP THE KNIFE! DROP THE KNIFE!"

I release the knife from my hand.

"Officers, if I please can explain..."

But once the knife hits the ground, the commotion erupts.

Both "blue uniformed" jump up at me, turning me, twisting my arms and pushing me face forward towards the ground.

My body crashes forward like a chopped down tree.

They are on top of me, pressing their bodies into my back, crushing me, grabbing my arms, twisting them behind my back. My face is jammed into the soft mud.

"Hey, what the hell!" I scream, but I don't think anyone can hear me through my mother's rambling and chanting wails, through my sister's screams, relieved and excited chatter of bystanders, through the officers' screams into their radios.

The irony of Rafe's face and now mine shoved into the mud, all within the last twenty four hours doesn't escape me.

"Irtu Etu Dalkhu! Damu Azeru! Happy now?!" Rafe roars inside my head but I'm too preoccupied to deal with him right now.

I need to get them off of me and need to get to my sister, grab her and – *"Bibbidi-Bobbidi-Boo"* – take us on a very magical tour, courtesy of my archangel wings, somewhere away from here.

But as I lay there, bewildered and reeling, trying to plan through the rowdy chaos, something shifts in the air.

It is a gradual yet noticeable, invisible but distinct. It's like a cold undercurrent at sea, a streak of a chilling cold in warm waters. And it grows stronger.

I can't name it, can't pin point it, but my wings demand my attention, calling for me to get away. They demand for me to split.

With the trepidation brought by my wings, I thrash, wanting to get free. I madly turn my head from side to side, looking for the source of this cold, but the officers lean heavier on me, now jamming their knees into my back.

Sleek dark brown brogues come into my view and my wings demand my attention and my immediate departure. NOW!

"Here you are, officers", a deep baritone says above me in a thick Scouse lull and my wings begin to cry, telling me that it's either now or never, telling me that I'm in a deep trouble.

But I need them to understand that I need my sister. I came here to get her and I can't leave her behind, especially, not now.

But the next second, while still thinking, desperately looking for a solution, the ice cold metal of handcuffs comes over, closing over my wrists, and everything changes with their "clack".

The handcuffs feel... numbing.

Suddenly, my wings are silenced, leaving the vast ringing vacuum in my head. It feels as if my head, still alive and well, was chopped off. As if I've been shut away from my wings, as if *they* were cut off, and I turn my head from side to side, desperate to see their purple and golden shimmer behind my back and afraid to find nothing.

I feel disconnected and mutilated. I feel alive and dead at the same time.

"I am arresting you on suspicion of murder and possession of an offensive weapon. You do not have to say anything. But, it may harm your defence if you do not mention when questioned, something which you later may rely on in court. Anything you say may be given in evidence against you. Do you understand?"

"Ariel! ARIEL!" Rafe's voice roars above the crowd.

I know it's him, who is now barging through the tight circle of onlookers, towards me.

I'm yanked up by my arms to my feet but I have barely any strength to stand.

"Ariel!"

He is here at the forefront of the crowd.

"Sir! Sir! You have to step back!" The officers yell at him, while pulling me away.

The Scouser is just a step away, watching my arrest with a supervisory interest of an assessor, appraising his staff at the end of the training period.

"Ariel!"

I'm scared! I'm scared! I'm so, so scared!

I want to tell him this.

I want to cry.

I want him to come over and make it all better, fix it for me. And as I open my mouth, about to call for him, a weak Jess's cry, almost a whimper, comes to me.

"Ariel?"

It's a scared apologetic mumble of a lost child in trouble and instantly my decision is made.

My eyes meet Rafe's and at that moment, all I can manage is to weakly shake my head, warning him off coming to me. I glance back at my sobbing sister, turn back to Rafe, mouthing: *"You promised."*

"ARGH!"

He throws his head to the sky and bawls where he stands, with all the power of his lungs and his essence.

Rage morphs his face and for the first time ever, I'm scared of him.

I take a step back.

The wrathful Archangel of the Old Testament is in front of me.

"The Hand of God". The Archangel that killed millions. The creature as ancient and powerful as the Universe itself.

People around him disperse like frightened pigeons in the park.

They scatter away, slipping in the mud, falling and crawling away, darting around caravans, hiding. Even my mother shuts her mouth, breaking off her rhythmic prayers' recitals.

The police officers stop their tugging and pulling, I can practically feel their feet itching to scatter with the crowd.

But the Scouser is unfazed. He strolls over to me, leans in and whispers: "How far do you think Baza will let you run?"

Chapter 9

*M*y head is numb.

I can't hear a thing as if suddenly I've gone deaf. Even the earlier ringing has fled.

I can't see anything apart from the metal bars of the cage in front of my eyes.

The metal bars are black and thick, a solid sense of the hopeless finality and irreversible changes. It's like taking a "one way" road, half way through realising that you're actually on the wrong track, but you can't jump off and leave this road. You need to go through it, until you've reached the end or at least a junction.

I still can't feel or hear my wings and even Rafe's voice has vanished from my head.

I feel lost and abandoned.

The car pulls to a stop outside a small, one storey building, housing a local police station. The building swims in a bright pool of light from working street lamps.

The building is rendered in grey cement panels, and only large glass double doors and a notice board interrupt the "concrete chic" on this side.

The notice board, framed by painted, and now chipped, wood, hangs to the right of the door, informing unlucky cuffed visitors on the importance of crime prevention, numbers of the local "Legal Aid" solicitors and substances abuse charities.

The earlier arresting officers get out of the car and come around to my side, yanking the door open.

"Okay, come out now", the male barks.

I fumble with my feet, shuffling my bum along the seat, closer to the door, trying to get out. I never realised how hard it is to get out of the car with arms bound behind the back.

"Hold on. Let me help you", a female voice cuts in and a hand encircles my arm, pulling me out.

Keeping her grip tight on me, the female officer leads me into the building, up a set of stairs and through the large glass double doors.

The male officer presses a buzzer on a black dial on the right, and the barred security door in front of us unlocks with an answering buzz and a metal click.

Through the door is a large room with a tall reception desk and two processing offices behind it.

Posters are plastered all over the opposite wall and a narrow bench with a padded plastic seat pushed against it.

One of the processing officers behind the desk, a beefy black guy with a military short haircut, openly yawns staring at a poster, while the smaller officer next to him says something to a petite woman on the other side of the reception desk.

The heavy security door slams shut behind me, pushed by a sure hand. Its metal echo rings in the room for a second and forever in my numb empty head.

"Please, you don't understand. I need to see him", the frail woman with a tired face pleads to the officer, and the tears roll down her face, riddled in wrinkles.

"He shouldn't be here. He hasn't done anything wrong. It's all a mistake. He has Asperger's and he'll get very stressed in here. He has asthma, he'll need his medications."

Her tired eyes are surprisingly younger than her face. Her frumpy clothes are bigger than her little body.

"Madam", the small processing officer interrupts the woman. He is bored and disinterested. The small pointy features of his face and black beady eyes give him a resemblance with a mouse or a rat. "Your son was arrested with almost a kilo of cannabis on him. He was arrested on possession with intent to distribute and he's not going anywhere until he's seen a judge."

"No, you don't understand", the woman rushes in, "someone must've given it to him to take somewhere. He's a good boy. He would never do anything like that. He helps me around the house, he is very kind boy. You can ask all of our neighbours. He wouldn't hurt anyone."

"Madam", the officer interrupts her, "feel free to contact a solicitor and seek legal advice. The phone numbers of the local solicitors are on the board outside."

He turns his head to his partner next to him and rolls his eyes at the woman.

"Hi", the processing officer, a big black guy, calls to the pair next to me, "what do you have?"

"Came on a domestic disturbance call", the male next to me starts to report and the processing officer begins to type. Keys click surprisingly fast under his fingers.

"On arrival, we found an injured man, waiting to hear from paramedics, but presumably dead, from what appears a stab wound to the mid-section and this one", he jerks his head at me, "at the scene, holding the suspected weapon, covered in blood."

The male officer lifts a clear bag with the bloodied knife.

The processing officer types in.

"Offence?" he asks the officers.

"Suspicion of murder. Possession of an offensive weapon", the male reports behind me.

"Time of arrest?"

"Three fourteen AM."

The officer lifts his eyes to me, for the first time addressing me: "What's your name?"

"Ariel Davies."

He types that in.

"Do you need help with reading or writing?" Again addressing me.

"No."

"Do have any medical conditions, allergies?"

"No."

"Any alcohol or drugs used today?"

"No."

"Do you understand the charges, Ariel Davies?"

"Yes, but I didn't do it –"

I start. I don't even know what I'm trying to say, as no way in Hell I will tell him *who* did it.

"I'm going to authorise your detention", he interjects, busy typing, not interested in anything I might have to say.

He raises his eyes to me, "later you will be interviewed regarding this information and that will give you the opportunity to give your explanation."

He might as well say: *"Ain't my problem, sister."*

All I can do is weakly nod.

"A picture of you will be taken, along with fingerprints, a DNA swab, then you will be escorted into a cell and interviewed later", the processing officer recites in an automated voice of an answer machine.

"Would you like to read the code of conduct?"

Bored, he raises his eyebrow at me.

I shake my head.

"Let's remove the handcuffs –"

"No. We better not", the familiar voice interrupts. "She is the one wanted in the connection with a gang activity and yesterday's raids. And we need to add the drug possession charges with intent to distribute, the possession of a firearm, involvement in an organised crime, human trafficking..."

I no longer listen.

How far do you think Baza will let you run?

The Scouser turns, looking deep at me and I meet his gaze. The Scouser is tall and large, like a six and a half feet tall double wardrobe. I need to crane my neck up to look at him.

A small smile tugs the corner of his mouth. It is crystal clear why I'm here and who had orchestrated it all. Talking and explaining myself to these people will achieve absolutely nothing.

The Scouser wears a crisp and freshly ironed, light blue shirt, tightly buttoned all the way up to his neck, black jeans and the polished brown brogues that I was "admiring" earlier from the ground.

He is handsome and attractive. The soft skin, full lips, brown eyes, glossy, neatly trimmed hair, every girl and boy would be swooning over him.

"I'll remove one cuff at a time", he instructs the processing officers, "and you can take her fingerprints."

He comes behind me and takes my bound wrist.

His touch freezes and burns my skin at the same time, as if a hot metal is melting my skin, while the liquid nitrogen freezes, numbing and then breaking it.

Tears pool in my eyes and I have to clench my teeth, to stop myself from crying out.

A key turns and the handcuff clicks behind me.

"And what do we have here?" The Scouser mutters behind me. His lips brush my ear and I'm shocked to smell a stench of decomposing flesh on his breath.

I feel sick as the memories of Hell flood my mind. The scenery of a bared abused landscape, the stench of a decomposing flesh and... the bright white light of the "lighthouse" and the agonising human screams, accompanying each of its piercing glows.

I have to breathe through my mouth to prevent myself from throwing up and to stop myself from crying out, but little traitorous whimpers still escapes my mouth.

He dives his hand under my sweatshirt, extracting one of my swords, then he reaches for the other.

"Stupid humans", he mumbles to himself, "everything needs to be done for them."

He leans in closer, whispering in my ear, "I'll hold on to these for now. For safekeeping." The quiet laughter rumbles his chest.

One hand at a time, my hands are released from the handcuffs and processed, and all that I can do to stop screams from escaping my mouth, is to grind my teeth against the pain of the Scouser's hold and his handcuffs.

"It's good to see you again", he murmurs above me, feeling chatty. "Funny how things turn out sometimes. Who would've thought that I would have the fearless, deific Uriel, the beyelai of my kind at my durance and mercy", he chuckles low and squeezes my wrist.

I have never been arrested before. Never have I been in police custody, never been in that kind of trouble, but listening to him now and smelling the stench of Hell on his breath, I'm more petrified of him and Baza than the human police.

Probably because I know what he and his mates do to humans.

They are a new, the superior level of predators, and humans are just a dumb food source to them... cattle.

Blinded by the flashlight of a camera, with the blackened fingertips and still bound by the metal handcuffs, I'm escorted into a cell.

After the Scouser's list of my additional "offences and charges", the attitude of the male arresting officer has changed.

Of course, we were not "besties" to begin with, but there was care and respect in the way I was treated.

Now however, he marches down the hall, dragging me along and I practically have to run, trying to keep up with him. I'm afraid that if I fall, he will not stop and will continue to drag me after him. Fleetingly, I wonder how stark the bruises from his hold on my upper arm would be tomorrow.

The Scouser and the female arresting officer stayed behind, in the reception, probably to finish off with the paperwork, or maybe she and the processing officers were due to receive more instructions and information about the dangerous crimes I have "committed".

We turn the corner and a long narrow corridor stretches in front of us with at least a dozen of locked metal doors to the right. The enclosed space of the corridor stinks of bleach, disinfectant, dust and mildew.

With the first boom of the officer's boots on the cement floor, the tight corridor erupts with noise.

"Oi! I want my breakfast!" A deep male voice yells behind the nearest, closed metal door.

"Oi, you!" I jump up, as a violent kick on the inside at the closed cell door next to me, vibrates the door and air. "Oi, pig!" Another violent kick at the locked door.

The officer keeps his pace, ignoring the outburst completely.

"Please, please, I need to call my mam", a younger voice cries behind the next door. "Please!" Fists drum a rapid beat at the metal door from inside.

Unfazed by the violence and disinterested in the pleas, the officer keeps strolling down the corridor – his steps are a measured monotonous beat.

"I know my rights!" A slurring male's voice calls from behind the next door. "Since when it's a crime to sleep on a bench? I've done nowt!"

I look at each closed door, scared, yet wanting to see the people behind these doors.

The officer's hold on my arm is still solid as he leads me towards the end of the corridor, stopping outside a cell's metal door. Finally he lets go of me.

The key in his hand turns in the lock, before the thick solid metal door swings open.

"In!" he barks.

Oh my god! Oh my god! Oh my god!!

I'm so scared. A fresh wave of panic covers me at the sight of a small room with one barred window up under the celling. The walls are smothered in a grey paint and the metal bed under a thin blue mattress, covered in a blue vinyl, is the only furniture in the cell.

Terror consumes me. I want to cry and run away. I want to plead with this man, tell him what is happening here. I want to tell him that I haven't killed my stepfather, my sister did. I want to tell him who the Scouser really is.

My back is wet with sweat under my clothes.

The sweat beads on my top lip, on my temples, under my hair and I can't move my legs. I don't want to. Like a child, I want to drop to the floor and refuse to move.

Dread, panic, shock. Rising high like killer waves in a storm, they surge through me, drowning me and I can't control them, or my breathing.

"In, I said!"

He is not playing games and the next second his hand comes over my arm, squeezing painfully, and I'm shoved into the cell.

The metal door slams shut behind me. Its heavy boom echoes inside the concrete cell.

I barely make to the silver metal toilet in the corner before I throw up.

My ribcage aches and I can't take a deep breath, as I kneel on the floor, wiping my mouth on my sleeve.

Weakly, I rise to my feet, standing in the middle of the cell, unsure of what to do now. The cell smells of sweat, B.O. and urine. It smells like human suffering and desperation.

My shoulders hurt in the sockets and my arms throb as my muscles twitch, locked in one position. I have lost the feeling in my hands and fingers under the handcuffs a while ago.

A few cells down the corridor, the earlier guy still demands his breakfast. Someone weakly cries in the cell next to mine, and this old man's wheezy sobs are desperate, mirroring my feeling perfectly. They are the perfect accompaniment to the finality of this situation.

My thoughts drift to Jess.

I wonder if Rafe got hold of Jess.

I hope she is okay, I hope she is not too scared.

I hope he kept his promise.

The last thought saddens me. Once again, I trusted someone completely and I'll have no way knowing if they have kept their promise, usually until it's too late.

I come over and sit on the plastic mattress.

I don't know what to do now. I don't know how I'm going to get out of this mess.

I'm not going to cry! I'm not going to cry!

I repeat it to myself over and over again, but my mantra is not working this time, as my nose itches, tears fill my eyes and as soon as the first one drops, the rest follow. They fall down my cheeks but with my hands bound, I can't hide myself in my hands or wipe away the tears.

I fall sideways on the blue vinyl mattress, burying my face in the itchy, smelly blue blanket, courtesy of HM prison services, and I cry, wondering, if maybe now it is the end.

Chapter 10

"Get up, Davies! Time to go!"

Groggy and dazed, I turn, trying to open my swollen eyes. I fell asleep on my front with my arms still bound behind my back.

I roll, awkwardly to the side, trying to rise but I can't push myself off the bed without the help of my arms. Like an upside-down beetle on the ground, I roll from side to side, rocking myself, kicking my legs, trying to get the momentum going to hoist myself up.

I guess, two minutes of watching my clumsy rocking is as long as the guard is willing to entertain, before he marches across the cell to my bed, yanking me up by my arm.

"Ow!" I cry out.

It feels as if my arm has left its shoulder socket and came out in his grip. This new guard likes me even less than the arresting officer did.

"Come on. Time to go", he barks.

"Where?"

A fresh gust of panic blows over my frightened heart.

"Interview time, sunshine." His sly cheerful smile says it for him, that he hopes I'll be nailed in there.

Down the same corridor, only just before reaching the processing area with the reception desk and a trill of telephones, we turn right and after a few yards down that hall, the custody officer stops in front of an office looking door of a light wood, with frosted glass panel in the middle.

The metal plaque "Interview room" confirms that I'm here to be interviewed.

The problem is that I have nothing or very little to tell them. I wouldn't be able to begin to explain what happened to me in the space of the last few months of my life, and even if I did – nobody would believe me.

He knocks and without waiting to be invited, opens the door.

The Scouser is already in the room, behind a basic desk on metal legs, pushed against the opposite wall. Four metal-framed chairs with plastic grey seats are set to the opposite sides of the desk. The two chairs on one side and the two on the other, clearly assigning the teams: for two inspectors to interrogate the suspect in the presence of his solicitor.

Scouser's crisp white shirt has replaced the yesterday's blue one, and the room smells thickly with his rich sandalwood aftershave.

I wonder if having a shower of aftershave is what takes to mask the decomposing stench on his breath.

He raises his eyes to me and his face blossoms with a wide smile, but the smile doesn't touch his eyes. In fact, the wider his smile gets, the thicker grows the layer of frost over his eyes. His smile is a wicked promise.

I don't want to go into that room with him. I don't want to be left alone with him there.

The guard waits behind me for a few seconds, before losing his patience with me, he shoves me forward into the room.

I push my feet at the ground, refusing to move.

The Scouser chuckles low, entertained by my disobedience.

"Don't worry. I'll take it from here."

For a second, his hand slides into a pocket of his black jeans.

The Scouser rises and in two large strides he reaches the door and me, just behind it. His arm reaches behind my back, but I can't step back or sideways, blocked by the guard.

The Scouser's hand comes over my wrist and suddenly, I feel as if I'm being electrocuted.

My teeth clunk together, my jaws spasming. The muscles all over my body contract and twist as if I'm a washcloth, being wrung out by a diligent housewife, and the blistering pain shoots and explodes in my head.

Losing the feeling in my limbs, my legs buckle underneath me like the stuffed legs of a floppy doll.

"Do come in, Ariel Davies." With his hold firmly on my arm, the Scouser drags me inside and pushes the door shut behind us, in front of the custody officer's face.

Imagining the stupefied face of the guard gives me a fleeting moment of satisfaction, before it is taken away by another wave of pain.

With the door shut, he lets go of me and I collapse on the floor in a sweaty and whimpering heap.

I barely manage to stop myself from crying.

Not in front of him! Not in front of him!

I command myself, or more accurately, begging.

I sit on the floor, gathering my strength and finding my breathing, while the Scouser strolls from corner to corner of the room, methodically flicking switches, turning off cameras, unplugging recorders.

The tiny room has no windows. There is a movie staple mirror in here, a wall wide double mirror to hide snooping inspectors behind. The walls and ceiling in this tiny room are covered in porous light grey plastic panels, and the cameras are hoisted under the ceiling in every corner.

He walks around me as one might walk around a desk or a sofa: calm, relaxed, disinterested.

After finishing, he sits and reclines in his chair, throwing his legs on the desk.

"Shall I call you Ariel or Uriel?"

Patiently, he waits for my answer.

"I don't care", I breathe through my teeth. What does it matter how he's going to call me when he kills me?

"Excellent", he nods in approval. "I like open-minded and adaptable people. I hope you are adaptable, Ariel."

I stay where I've been left, watching him, listening, wondering where he is planning to take it, or more precisely, how far?

"Please, take a seat", he gestures to the seat across from him, "we have a lot to discuss."

I look at him.

I want to throw a tantrum so much, tell him where he can shove his discussions, but I need to hear what this freak has to say. I need to understand who he is and what Baza wants from me now, and maybe I'll manage to find a way out or at least, persuade him not to kill me.

I fold my legs under myself, pushing myself up to my knees and then I stand up.

My hands are still bound behind my back in the handcuffs, and with every minute, every passing hour in these, I feel worse.

It's not only the physical pain that bothers me now, but the hollow emptiness that spreads like a virus inside me. Before, it was only Rafe's voice I couldn't hear in my head, but now, even human voices around me are zooming in and out like ships diving in and out of sea fog.

It is as if I'm slipping into... a painful unconsciousness.

And I know it has something to do with my wings. It feels as if my wings are dying and I'm dying with them, and I'm horrified to think that this may be the end.

For a fleeting moment, I wonder if maybe that's how Rafe feels after losing his two wings.

I stagger and flop onto the chair.

My two swords, Mia's swords, lay at the end of his desk, glowing dimly. The ripples are gone and the blades of the swords are like the glass surface of a lake on a windless day.

The Scouser looks at me, waiting for me to meet his gaze and when I do, he places his hand on the desk and opens his palm, revealing a thick, long metal plate, running across his palm, just under his fingers.

This plate is like a knuckleduster in reverse. It's barely visible on his hand, with most of the metal laying inside his palm. The darkened metal plate is covered with deeply carved, ancient hieroglyphs shining through, and I swallow.

I knew he wasn't the police.

"That is to encourage your cooperation", he answers my horrified gaze.

Then changing the subject "I'll get straight to it and save us some time."

He closes his palm and folds his hands on his stomach.

"You know how you've ended up here, don't you? And who set it all up?"

I nod, he told me.

"Good", he nods. "So you're not a complete imbecile. That's a good start."

Um... Thanks?

"But do you know what was your main mistake?" he leans in, pausing, maybe for dramatic effect or maybe waiting for me to figure it out. His decomposing breath brushes my face.

As I say nothing, he continues, "becoming invested with humans and allowing yourself to get trapped because of them."

"Which is incredibly stupid as far as I'm concerned", he adds after a second, gazing deep at me, challenging me.

Thank you very much for this vote of confidence. At least we are clear on this point, I guess.

He opens the cufflinks on his shirt and, leisurely, begins rolling up his sleeves.

Mesmerised, I watch him. I'm afraid that this might be in the preparation to hit me, so I brace myself.

"Humans are here to serve our needs. I would have thought you'd have figured it by now. They're inferior to us in every single way. By all means, keep one as a pet, but to risk your life and freedom for one?" he closes his eyes at me in exasperation, shaking his head.

Wow! I don't even know him and I've already managed to disappoint him. Go me!

"But you know what else that is?" he tilts his head at me. "Weak! Stupid and weak!"

With every extra inch of the fabric of his sleeves rolled, I can see more of his arms.

The skin on his muscly arms is covered with busy and colourful tattoo sleeves, which start from his wrists, disappearing up past the elbows, somewhere under his sleeves.

There is something familiar about his arms, something familiar about these tattoo designs like I've seen them before. Something tugs at the back of my mind, but I can't seem to place it.

He rolls his sleeves just above his elbows and turns his attention back to me.

"I have to say, I was really looking forward to this meeting. I've been anticipating this moment for quite some time and now I am... disappointed. We've been planning tirelessly for this day. I was planning to capture the Uriel. All my plans were built intricately around her indomitable strength and power, around her wisdom. I set so many traps, weaved so many lies. I was ready –" he stops and exhales, deflated.

"And I didn't use any of them apart from these two blunt body controlling tools", he pursues his lips at me.

"I was hoping to find the Uriel", he raises his arms and face upwards, "the most feared of Archangels, The Harbinger of Chaos, The Keeper of the Gates, The Begetter of Life, The Dam of The Ends."

His smile is a mix of awe and blood thirst. It's like he's looking forward to bathe in her blood.

In the next instant he sobers and snaps his gaze back to me.

"But instead I found *you*, a weak, pathetic, stupid human. Disappointment all around. Ariel, indeed!"

The sheer volume of Uriel's titles and the awe, with which he speaks of her, stabs at me.

"You need to speak to my mother. You two can have a fantastic chat over a cuppa, trashing me", I snap at him. What does he want from me after this speech? To argue with him, to fight him? The second one would be very tricky, taking into account my bound position.

No way am I going to tell him, how little and insignificant I feel most of the time, let alone right now.

He stares at me with a challenge.

"And because you are as pathetic as them, you should be treated like them!" he barks.

"But there's Baza", the Scouser rolls his eyes, "with his plans to court you, to earn your loyalty and cooperation. All these dinners, jewellery, persuasions... Urgh! What a waste of time!" he glares at me.

"Why would anyone try to communicate and reason with an animal, when all that an animal is capable of understanding, is crude blatant force?!"

"Incredible waste of time!" he huffs. "You lot, should only be spoken to in the only language you understand, force and fear!" he barks again.

Clearly, it's a very touchy subject for him.

He takes a breath, folding his tattooed arms over his chest.

"I'm sick and tired of running after you, Ariel. The possibilities and opportunities that were shown to you fell on deaf ears. You are lacking in imagination and sense to see them. Some of us think that the time for courting games came and went, although some of us think that it should have never begun. Some of us are no longer interested in persuading or encouraging you. You are clearly not hearing the voice of reason, so be it! I'm one of those, who think that we can achieve more and go further by working with you like one should with the animal."

He smiles at me with a promising confident smile and I swallow.

"Force and fear", he repeats in a low tone, stretching his words.

"And what does Baza think?" I squeak.

"He tried his way", the Scouser dismisses, "now it's time to try ours."

I swallow against my parched mouth. Who would've thought that I would be thinking fondly of Baza and wishing he was next to me right now?

"Do you remember those lovely companions of yours? The ones Baza brought in for the dinner entertainment? Well, they are still alive and well", he smiles at me and cocks his head, as if offering a treat in exchange for an early bedtime.

"Maybe not *well*", he stretches, correcting himself, "but certainly alive."

"And we thought that you might like to finish it off with them!" he offers, excitedly. "Or them with you... whatever might work. We are open to suggestions here."

They're alive...

My heart flies into my throat, hits my mouth and dies. My chest contracts and I can't draw breath.

Panic hammers its toll bells in my head. I'm flushed and hot, but then the next second, I am frozen cold.

"Or them with you..."

"No", I push out. My plea is barely audible.

My mind screams in my head, petrified. I want to beg him. I want to fall to my knees and beg him, promise him anything he wants, but to spare me this again.

But all that I manage is to sit up in my chair, the control over my body completely lost, as I feel the warm liquid spreading over the seat underneath me.

"No?" he asks with a smile, raising his eyebrows at me. "Nobody asks an animal's opinion and nobody is going to ask yours."

He brings his legs down and leans forward in his chair. He rests his tattooed arms on the desk, right in front of my eyes. The muscles are playing under his coloured skin, moving the tattooed drawings like fabric in a wind.

Washing line in the wind...

The field, filled to the horizon with stakes and the skins stretched over them, flapping lazily in a wind, and the skin on the stake at the front... *with intricately tattooed colourful empty arms.*

I jump up from my chair, run into the corner and fold over, retching loudly, bringing up some pink mess of sweets and milkshake and loads of bile.

"Urgh", he pushes with disgust behind me, and I can hear him sniffing the air. "The animal indeed", he grunts with revulsion.

"You've got a couple of hours to decide how you're going to work with us. Not *if* but *how*. I need to finish off a few things, and when I walk into your cell later on, you'll tell me how much you will love to do what we tell you", he instructs me.

I turn my head, looking at him.

He glares at me, narrowing his eyes, "And animals shouldn't be allowed to touch the deific weapons", he spits, then opens a drawer in his desk and sweeps both swords in, slamming the drawer shut.

He presses the button under his desk and a minute later, the door opens and the custody officer from earlier marches in. He sweeps his gaze over the Scouser, then over me, on the floor in a stinking heap.

"Please escort Ariel Davies back to her cell."

The guard takes a few strong steps towards me before he catches a whiff coming off me and his earlier eagerness to do the job instantly evaporates. He takes the last two steps as if his shoes are filled with iron.

"Up!" he barks above me.

His earlier desire for grabbing, pulling and yanking, has disappeared as well.

"Up!" he roars.

With a last glance at the smiling Scouser, who watches this shouting assault with open, sadistic pleasure, I rise wobbling to my feet.

I stagger through the open door and the Scouser doesn't say another word to me, busy shuffling papers on his desk.

Chapter 11

I never thought I would find myself at rock bottom, where I would welcome the chance to hide in my cell. I'm disgusted with myself. I'm embarrassed.

For the first time, the guard's and my wishes are in-sync. He can't wait to shut the door on me and I can't wait to be left alone.

"Can I please have fresh clothes?" I mumble, too embarrassed to look up at him.

"In", he commands. He still refuses to touch me, standing next to the open cell door.

Little blessings....

I step into the cell and turn, risking sneaking a peek at him.

"Can I please have clean clothes?"

But he ignores me completely, slamming the door in my face.

"Clothes! I need clothes!" I scream at the closed door, jamming my shoulder at the metal, kicking it, but only my echo in the cell answers me.

I slam my shoulder at the door over and over again.

"I need clothes", I yell, "I'm not an animal!"

I kick the door once, twice, again and again. I yell, but nobody answers me.

I fold and collapse where I stand, and I start wailing, hailing, rocking myself.

Animal... dirty, disgusting animal... I am an animal... Like he said...

The self-loathing is back, lashing at me with her iron whip, and even months of absence haven't weakened her.

The disgusting animal.

I'm struggling to pull myself out of this vortex of misery.

No. No! No!!

I hang on by the last ounce of hope and I refuse to give in.

I'm not! I'm not!!

I am Ariel!

I'm human and I matter! I matter! I do, I do!

I'm telling it to myself over and over again, rocking myself with the rhythm of these words.

I'm telling these words to him, to everyone before him and everyone who comes after.

Tears stream down my cheeks and an unchecked howl leaves me, bouncing off the walls.

I do matter! I am human and I am loved!

I have a sister and she loves me! She loves me, even when nobody else does! I'm not an animal!

I'm not an animal!

I want to wrap my arms around myself, to hold myself if no one else around would, but I can't even do that.

I'm not an animal! I'm not an animal!

I rock myself, repeating these words over and over again. The words bubble out of me. I find a numbing rhythm in the repetition, as my control begins to slip away, and with it, the walls of the cell begin to fade.

"I do matter! I do matter! I do matter!"

The vacuum echoes around me, bringing back only the animal howls. I can't make out a word in these screams.

"I matter! I matter! I matter!"

I rock myself, kneeling on the floor of the cell.

"I do! I do! I do!"

I fold and I rock. I collapse sideways, pulling the knees to my chest.

"I do! I do! I do!"

My right temple is ice cold.

The metal screeches somewhere above my head.

"What's going on in here?" A strict female voice demands from above.

"I do matter! I do matter! I do matter!" I whimper, "I'm not an animal. I'm Ariel. I'm not an animal."

And I bawl and cry, I whimper and blab. "I'm not an animal. I'm not an animal."

A warm blanket comes over me and I'm lifted up to stand on my feet, but my feet refuse to hold me up.

Through the fog, voices come and go, playing peek-a-boo.

I hear a voice one second, can even make out some words and sentences, but the next second I am dabbed into absolute silence.

"Help me to take her to showers, then to medical. Why the hell is she still handcuffed?"

I'm propped from each side and it feels as if I'm flying again. That makes me happy.

"It's okay, Ariel. It's okay. We're going to take a shower, then we'll find you something nice and clean to wear...."

The voice fades away again, and the next time I can hear or feel anything, the tingling pins of warm water brush over my naked skin and my hands, unbound, hang lifelessly by my sides.

The water hits the tiled floor with a swish.

My gaze zooms in on the beads of water, which are blossoming on green tiles in front of my eyes. The beads swell under my gaze and then run, racing each other down the moss green worn out tiles.

I blink the haze out of my eyes and take in a deep breath. The room smells of water, bleach and cheap soap.

The small stall I am in has a short, now closed, door on one side – a pitiful pretence of privacy and modesty.

"How are you feeling?"

I spin around.

The small but sturdy female custody officer in her fifties, sealed in a blue uniform comes closer to the stall.

"Okay, I think."

My voice is coarse and my throat hurts as if I've been screaming for hours.

I lift my arms, surprised again not being bound by the handcuffs. I close my eyes and smooth my hands over my hair, turning from side to side, letting the warm water cover me.

I push my shoulders back, stretch and I feel the weak tingling like zaps of energy over my shoulders and my spine. The timid zaps dance over my skin like prickles of warmth on the frost bitten skin. They are weak and shallow.

I do feel better.

"I'll go and get you some clean clothes from our 'Lost and Found' bin. Are you going to be okay?" Her deep accessing gaze sweeps over my face, evaluating me and her chances of getting me some clothes, and coming back without finding any trouble on her return.

"Yeah, I'll be fine", I mumble to her, closing my eyes again and taking a step towards the shower, so the water hits me directly on top of my head.

The short confident steps start and disappear, as the custody officer leaves the room.

The water is hot and burns my scalp, but I don't care.

I lift my arms: to my hair, smoothing away the water, raising my arms over my head, stretching. I fold my neck side to side and then I lean forward, resting my hands on the old tiles in front of me.

And as I stretch, arching my back, unexpectedly, I hit the stall's opposite wall as if I had grown a third arm out of my back, which hits the wall while stretching.

And the dumbfound moment is replaced with pure joy.

Wings!

I spin, craning my neck, trying to see behind my back.

But I don't need to stretch far. My wings are back, all four of them, just as big and shimmery as they were before.

They are the ones that sending the tingles over my skin. They're still sleepy and groggy, as if coming around from anaesthesia, they are still not as strong as they used to be, but I don't care.

I feel glorious again. Powerful, strong, capable, unstoppable.

Weirdly, now with wings, I feel myself.

I reach over my shoulder and stroke the top feathers of my wing.

"I thought you had left me too", I whisper to them.

The door to the shower room opens and the earlier female custody officer comes in, hugging to her chest a large wad of folded clothes.

She dumps the stack on the low bench against the wall.

"Here you are. Wasn't much to choose from, but it's something. I've picked the smallest sizes I could find, so hopefully something will fit."

Her gaze sweeps over my face.

"Do you want me to take you to medical? Do you need to speak to anyone?"

"No, I'm alright." I am feeling better and stronger with every minute I'm out of the handcuffs. There must be something in those, some Hell bound, Baza's magic that disconnects me from my wings, screwing up with my head.

"You do look a lot better", she agrees.

"You have ten minutes", she clips, "to finish the shower, get dressed and I'll take you back to your cell. You're being transferred to another custody facility in a few hours."

"Why?" I stammer.

"I don't know for sure", she softens again. "Maybe something to do with all these additional charges you were wanted under", she raises her eyebrow to me. She might as well give me a speech on the importance of the right choices and the connection between the committed crime and the following punishment.

"Okay", I sigh. I wouldn't be able to begin explaining to her, how little this situation has to do with my choices.

She leaves the room, locking the door on the outside.

Okay, ten minutes to think.

The Scouser is coming and I need to get out and get away from here as far as possible – that's a given.

Ideally "Abracadabra" and I'm with Jess and Rafe. So... Escape...

Running? I'll need open doors. Flying? I'll need open doors.

But I have my wings back and that's a huge plus, so... "The wing transportation".

Grant you, I've transported myself only twice, to Uras and back to Earth, and both times I had Rafe with me, so I don't know how much of it is in the wings and how much is in my head, but I did it nonetheless.

Kinda... I sombrely add.

I think the "wings transportation" is the only way out.

The sudden thought hits me.

Oh! That was probably the reason for the handcuffs. Or maybe for me, to lose my mind. Although quite possibly the second one might've been a lucky coincidence, like taking flu meds and acne dries out as a side effect.

But whatever that was...

"No" to the handcuffs and *"yes"* to the wings transporting! I throw a mental fist up in the air.

I feel better for having a plan.

I know that my plan is rough and as full of holes as a sea sponge, and almost as dead as a sea sponge on a beach on a sunny day, but at least now I have the plan, and with it a chance to get out of here.

Now down to details, I say to myself, a commander and a soldier, all in one, while pulling on a pair of stranger's black leggings. They fit okay, not without issues with some sagging at the back of my knees, but they stay on and that is all that matters. I fish out a large man's hoodie from the pile. It's large and cosy but mainly, it is clean and covering my butt, it looks like a dress. I'll take that.

I have decided to take off once I'm back in my cell.

Of course there is a danger that the Scouser is waiting for me in there and my escape can go pear shaped, but disappearing from the locked room would give me extra time to get my "wings transporting" right.

Then another thought comes in, adjusting my earlier plan.

I want my swords back. I don't have any other angelic weapons and don't know how or where to get these, so... stopping at the "interview room" has to be the first stop on my agenda. Grab swords and go.

With sleeves rolled up fat like Michelin man's waist, I feel comfortable enough to move. My plimsolls are here as well. They are clean enough to wear, despite my earlier "troubles".

The key turns in the door and the female officer appears again. She sweeps her gaze over me and is clearly pleased (or maybe relieved) to find me in one sane compliant piece.

"Ready?"

I nod.

"I'm not going to handcuff you", she lifts he stern gaze to me, "but no silly business", she warns.

I nod again.

She comes over and closes her hand over my arm. It's a solid hold but she's not squeezing or pulling, and her stride is adjusted to mine.

With every step closer to my cell, the chilling dread sets in, as if every step I take is a step deeper into frozen abyss, which prowls around me, waiting to pounce and gorge me.

I remember the Scouser's promise. I know what it means.

I remember how it went before. I remember *everything*.

I clench my teeth, forcing my feet to move. I've made my decision.

"I still can transport even if the Scouser is in there. He doesn't expect me to have no cuffs on", I reason with myself.

Down the corridors and after a few turns, we are in front of the solid metal door of my cell. The key turns and the door swings open.

The custody officer steps aside, waiting for me to walk in. She doesn't yell, command or push me. She gives me these last few seconds of freedom.

I take in a deep breath of the custody facility's rancid air. I hadn't noticed earlier that the air smells not only of the mildew and disinfectant, but it is laced with smells of stale alcohol, cooked pot noodles and freshly brewed tea. The air has an iron smell of metal and an unexpected, sweet tinge of the custody officer's cheap perfume, so heartbreakingly human in the world of the meat grinder of incarceration.

I take a small step closer and peer inside the cell. The cell is empty.

I breathe out. I'm about to leave this place and I can't wait.

I turn to her: "Thank you."

Something moves behind her eyes and for a second I think she is about to say something, but she just gives me a small nod and a sad smile.

"That's okay, pet."

I step inside the cell and the door shuts behind my back, the key turning again.

Okay.

"Your wings can take you anywhere you've been before", Rafe's words echo in my head.

I don't know if there are magic words I need to say or if the certain steps need to be completed for me to be transported, so I just do what I've done before when I dragged Rafe back to my town. I close my eyes, remembering the place I want to see.

Right now, I picture myself inside the interview room, wishing for this to work and for my gamble to pay off.

For a second I feel nothing. The cell's presence is heavy around me, but then I can feel a pull. At first, at my hair like a tight ponytail, then at my face, as if an annoying aunt at Christmas pinches my cheeks. The tingles to my skin come next, bringing with them a crisp buzz of a struck fine wine glass ringing in my ears, crawling up and into the centre of my skull.

Next, all the smells and sounds are gone, as if I've stopped breathing and gone deaf, and then comes a violent pull, a jerk, as if I've been grabbed by the shirt and yanked forward.

But I feel the resistance of the air around me, as if I am being dragged through mud.

And suddenly the ground pushes at my feet, my knees buckle and I slam at the floor.

Shit!

I open my eyes, scanning the room. The interview room is empty and quiet.

Should've checked first if the Scouser is in. Oh well... Fantastic planning as usual.

I get up and run around the desk, yanking the top drawer open.

The top drawer is full of papers. I shut it and throw the next one open. Empty. I slam it shut and open the last one, empty as well.

No, no! I saw him throw my swords into a drawer.

I open the top drawer again, rummaging through the papers, feeling at the back and the sides of the drawer, but I can't find my swords.

I desperately want to take off and run away from here, but I don't want to be left unarmed and defenceless again. More people and creatures are coming at me than ever before and I will not risk to be caught again.

I'd rather be dead.

I drop to my knees and crawl under the desk. There must be a secret compartment or something. I refuse to think that the Scouser pocketed my swords and I'm wasting my time here for nothing.

I fold into the tight space under the cheap MDF desk.

The metal plate with a "pound coin" sized black button is fixed in under the desk's lid. The button is just too obvious and intentional to be a release for a hidden compartment, or so I think.

I twist on the spot, feeling the walls of the desk, touching the cavities but I can't find anything else. I turn to face the side with the drawers, sliding closer. The internal MDF panels are porous and coarse, bare of pretentious glossy vinyl of the outside panels, but even they are free from any buttons, levers or hinges.

Only tiny wood splinters in my finger tips are coming with me today.

I crawl from under the desk.

I lost my weapons. The Scouser has them now.

He and his crew are better equipped than they were before, courtesy of my diabolical decision-making. I don't know what implications there may be of leaving divine weapons in hands of Baza's mates. All that is left for me now is to run back to Rafe and hide behind his back, and wait for the Scouser to come at me, now two angelic swords richer.

I'm angry and annoyed with myself. Again I've screwed up. This time I've been captured and lost my defences.

The loser and dropper.

Cursing myself, I swing my leg and kick at the drawers, hard.

The desk creaks weakly in response, faintly swinging on its metal legs for a second and then rattles to a stop. And after a second of silence, as if thinking on my latest persuasion, the desk groans one last time and the bottom of the last drawer swings open and my swords fall out of the desk with a crisp sound of metal knitting needles.

Who said, nothing can be achieved with brute force? All you need to know is where to kick.

Ecstatic, I bend down to pick up my swords.

Chapter 12

"*I* see the rat dug her way out."

The Scouser's rich lull echoes in the small room.

Startled, I snap my back up, hitting my head on a corner of the desk. The pain explodes at the side of my skull, stealing my hearing, while fear takes my breath, clouding my vision. I am now blind and deaf.

I whirl towards his voice, blinking through the trembling haze, throwing my hands with the swords in front of myself, while shaking my head, trying to subdue the pain and clear my vision, but the next second, the punch at the side of my head sends me flying across the room.

My body crashes to the floor, then skids over old laminate and slams into a wall.

The air leaves my lungs with a puff.

My head rings and my hands are now empty.

No!

I blink through the pain, raising my head up.

The Scouser's heavy footsteps reverberate through the floor, sending rhythmic quivers through my bones, and I can no longer tell if the shudder over my spine is the floor's vibration or my fear.

My swords are scattered over the floor.

The closest one shimmers in the corner, about a foot away, and the Scouser is just as close.

He strides closer, decisive, merciless and strong and I know that I'm about to pay for all my deeds. But I'm not leaving without my swords. I went too far for these.

I'll take at least one.

I roll to my front, swaying on my hands and knees as I rise.

I catch a glimpse of the Scouser's shoes in my peripheral vision, and the second I weakly dive towards my sword, the Scouser's foot sinks into my stomach, throwing me against the wall again.

The self-preservation screams at me to get away immediately.

But instead I flop onto my front, reaching out blindly, and exhale, when my hand closes over the familiar hilt.

I roll to the side, with my back pressed against the wall, and in a blind mad frenzy I sweep the sword in front of myself from side to side and again from side to side.

It is not planned or masterful, but clumsy and desperate. I try to protect myself with all the animal survival that is left in me.

Suddenly, the sword slows its flight to a sluggish drag of a blunt knife slicing through cold butter. And in that instance, an animal roar shakes the room, and a thick and cold liquid covers my hand, running down my arm like a melted ice cream, which would cover my hand on a warm sunny day when I was a kid.

But this one doesn't smell of vanilla.

This goo smells of rotting flesh, blood, with tinges of metal and earthy soil, and something else that I can't even name.

I wipe at my eyes with my clean hand.

The Scouser stands above me, swaying on his feet.

His head is thrown up to the ceiling and the tendons on his neck strain, turning blue as he sways his head from side to side, roaring, and his animal bellow rings, bouncing off the walls and ceiling.

I look down to the floor, to his feet, trying to figure out what I have done.

The thick, gooey, black puddle is growing under his right foot.

A two inch wide strip is cut off of the bottom of his black jeans and now lying on the ground encircling his shoe, revealing underneath a soft tanned skin with a thin black line drawn just above his ankle, with a black substance pumping out of that line in steady beats.

I drop my gaze to my hand. It's covered in that black thick mucus and revulsion wakes in me and I have to close my teeth tight to stop myself from retching.

I'm baffled and can't understand how the fabric came off of his jeans, while it's just a cut on his ankle, when with another roar, he snaps his head back to me and steps towards me... leaving his right foot behind.

I scream and scatter.

Slipping, tripping over my own feet and hands, I crawl along the wall, rise and stagger away from him, holding my sword tight in my grip.

But he is coming at me. Without a foot!

Oh god, oh god, oh god!

"You", he bellows, "the disgusting worm! How dare you thinking of disobeying me? Your kind is nothing more than food to me, mindless cattle, living in its own filth, that needs to be whipped daily to remind them how to obey and who is their master. You are nothing more but a goat for me to slaughter, and you think you have a chance against *me*?!" he roars.

His eyes are filled with rage.

He keeps his hateful gaze on me as he limps along the floor, leaving black, messy round marks in his wake, which are like black stamps on a postcard.

His foot is abandoned without a second glance.

"Your kind has been put here to serve us! To feed us! Your essence transference was a mistake! You are a mistake! You are a freak of an animal, who suddenly spoke! Nothing more and nothing will change it, not the essence or your little angelic toothpicks", he jerks his head to the sword in my hand.

He walks towards me with a bright click of the heel of his elegant shoe and a meaty thump of the black butchered stump.

"Are you really that dumb, worm?" he hisses at me, his narrowed eyes are just slits. "Why do you think I'm here? What do think all of us are doing here?"

"Do you think I'm the only one in Apkallu?" he bares his teeth at me like an animal himself. "Do you think you can run away from me and hide?"

I don't answer, but he doesn't expect an answer from me.

"There are more of us here and we are everywhere. *Everywhere!*" he roars, throwing his head up in gloating pleasure.

"Apkallu is ours, always was and always will be! We hold your plane in our hands!" he folds his fist to illustrate where he holds us. "We are everywhere!"

Click, thump; click, thump.

"Dumb animal", he spits, still following me, "how do you think I found you? How do you think Baza finds all these souls? How do you think we find so many souls to harvest?"

His eyes light up with challenge and with glee, as he is about to share his secret with me.

"We are *helping* you to choose us", he hisses, "We are making your animal existence so unbearable, so excruciating, that you sell your souls to us. Willingly! With pleasure! Selling anything you can, just to make your animal existence a bit better!"

He glares at me.

"Your leaders? It's us! Your police? It's us!!" he roars. "Everything in Apkallu, including you, belongs to us! Your children belong to us!" he howls.

He quietens for a moment, before unexpectedly, soft laughter begins to rumble in his chest.

"Have you ever thought *why* these two words are so similar? Apkallu – Arllu, Arllu – Apkallu. No?" he raises his eyebrows at me, mocking me.

"Maybe you should have!" he barks.

"You never thought of this because you are a simplistic, stupid animal!" he roars again. "All of you! You never think, never question, never see anything past your own basic animalistic needs and past your own front door!"

Click, thump; click, thump.

"You animals, are ours and forever will be! You serve us and we will have you either way! We are either going to have your miserable lives or your pathetic souls, but your kind is ours! We own you and you have nowhere to go now."

His mad bulging eyes are on me, and I begin to wonder if I'm talking to a mad man.

With every step forward he takes, I take one back, sliding along the office walls, ramming my back along the way into a metal filing cabinet, a coat hanger.

With every new step, the skin on his chopped off leg begins to fray and roll up from the wound. I don't know how much longer I'll be able to hold the bile down, as now I stare at a greenish-yellow reptile skin with overlapping scales, poking from underneath the fraying human flesh.

"Get away from me", I bleat, swinging my short sword in front of myself, but he ignores me as if I haven't spoken.

Finally, the "flight response" sufficiently kicks in, reminding me of my wings' transportation feature.

Keeping my gaze fixed on the hobbling Scouser, I ransack in my empty mind, trying to remember how to transport.

Where to?

Panic blankets my mind, stopping me from thinking clearly.

I hit another sharp corner with my shoulder, jamming the side of my wing.

The Scouser is just a few steps away from me and I am only a few steps away from the door.

I glance at the door, eyeing my chance to escape.

And that is when the Scouser reaches for the collar on his shirt, finds the shirt's top button and unbuttons it.

His fingers slide down to unbutton the next button, and the next after that like in some perverted strip show. He follows me under an accompaniment of a "click" of his shoe and a "thump" of his gory limp.

Keeping his eyes on me, he opens his shirt wider.

A thin black line encircles his throat, just above the clavicle like a drawn pen line or a tattoo.

My breath catches in my throat, when I notice a gold stamp, sitting heavily at the middle of that line, at the centre of the Scouser's throat.

The stamp is deeply carved with a familiar looking design of ancient hieroglyphs I've seen before. This gold stamp looks like a wax seal on a medieval letter, but it shines brightly like a polished button on the parade uniform of a new cadet.

Under my stunned gaze, the Scouser reaches to the line and sinks his fingers *into* the line, into his throat, under his skin and begins to pull the skin off his face as if it's a mask... or a balaclava.

He bends his neck backwards and I weakly wonder if I will hear the snap of his neck. And would it be a crispy sound of a snapped twig or a meaty crack of a chopped down tree?

Non-stop shrills ring in the air, ricocheting off the walls, as I watch him taking off his face, sluggishly realising with the last ounce of functioning and processing brain that these shrills are mine.

He pulls the human face off and tosses it into a corner, exposing an oblong bold lizard head, covered in large green pentagon scales.

His head is smothered in human blood and plasma like a newborn.

A set of small lizard horns encircle his skull like a Spring Equinox flower headband.

And then he looks at me. No! He turns his *blind* head *to* me.

I'm sure he can't see a thing as he doesn't have eyes in his blind and bold lizard head.

His sleek head has only one large hole in the centre of the head: a large hole with jutting, protruding, grey razor-sharp teeth around it, which are bent like lethal metal petals on top of a high security fence.

He is a lizard from the wasteland, a blind creature who was hoarding naked humans.

But those in the wasteland were scruffier and smaller, and more importantly, they couldn't see a human, or any other creature for that matter, that didn't have the carved mark on the chest.

But this one *can* see me. He is zoomed in on me.

Stunned, I stand against the wall, when his mouth opens and a thick anaconda tongue flies out towards me with a slap of a wet towel.

But I'm still where I was, standing paralysed, watching the dark green and red tongue, which flies at me with the incredible speed of a cricket ball.

The tongue is only an inch away from me, when finally awake, I take a flimsy step back, pressing myself into the wall, wishing to disappear through it.

But I can't walk through walls and the meaty tongue makes contact with my side.

Its teeth rip out a chunk of my sweatshirt and skin underneath, and with it an agonising pain explodes and it's now my turn to howl.

I press my hand to the gashing wound in my torn side, hoping to stash back that pouring blood, missing skin and muscle.

The gurgling noise comes out of his mouth, guarded by his narrow and tall grey teeth.

The golden button at his throat lights up as if it's an intercom connection and with a second's delay the lizard's gurgling garble is followed by human words, said in the Scouser's voice.

"I've decided to give them to you", the lizard hisses at me, "animals need to be reminded of their place."

It's a grisly sight of a blind lizard head, sitting proudly atop of a human body, dressed in a "smart-casual" of the "office best", limping around with a missing foot.

My head rings. Horror, shock, revulsion and fear are playing leapfrog in my mind.

"All worms need to know their place! And we better start them young. I'll make sure I pay special attention to your sister", and with the last roared word, his mouth opens wider, the tongue escaping its cage again.

His last sentence is a wake up kick my mate Rage needed.

"No, you didn't", she narrows her thickly outlined with black eyeliner eyes at him.

She is awake and ready to roll. She was absent for a while, but as a lifelong mate she always catches up in no time.

More on instinct rather than with a conscious decision, I take a small step sideways, opening my stance wider, balancing myself.

I am ready.

When the lizard's tongue whips out again next time, flying toward me, I drop into a low wide squat, throwing my arm with the sword above my shoulder. And once I can see the grainy bumps of the soft flesh of his tongue next to me, I slice with my sword in a wide arch above and around me, drawing a half moon shape with it, then bringing it down to the floor.

A black sticky shower opens above my head.

The chunk of meat hits the floor with a heavy thud in front of my feet, and the Scouser (or the lizard) screams again, only this time it is a shrill of a creature in pain.

Disjointed from the body, the tongue moves and wriggles, slithering along the floor and spaying the dark mucus all over my shoes.

The Scouser takes another limping stumbling step towards me, but I slide around him. It's my chance to get out of here.

The lizard throws his human hands towards me, reaching for me, but with his tongue missing, he is blind and powerless, and he grabs hold of the empty air.

I take a few rushed steps away from him, deeper into the room, pressing at my bleeding side. But as if attached to me by an invisible cord, he turns his head towards me and follows me blindly, stumbling like a zombie.

His throat gurgles again, followed by the Scouser's weak voice: "You, little rat. I'll get you."

But his promise is weak and unconvincing, and I don't stop to listen.

I wipe at my face, briefly scanning the room. My other sword is at the other side of the room, not far from the spot where I fell.

"Could've scooped both swords", Rage rolls her eyes at me.

Oh yeah, she is back alright.

Skirting along the walls, past the interrogation desk and around the chairs, I stagger to my sword, relieved when my hand closes over its hilt.

Click – thump; click – thump.

The gory metronomic rhythm echoes in the room.

Stumbling around the room, the lizard bumps into the sparse furniture, wobbling on his chopped stump. Then, regaining his balance once more, and with a stubborn determination, he follows me.

I thought that somebody would have barged in by now, especially after our screams and howls.

But either this room is excellently soundproofed or nobody gives a shit to what happens in here, but no one makes an appearance. One thing is for sure, I'm not going to stay here any longer to find out the reason, and he is welcome to explain himself to the humans later.

And with it, I close my eyes, clutching my swords in my hands, pressing my elbow to the torn side, imagining the straight long line of the tall trees outside of my mother's caravan site.

Chapter 13

The cool wind moves my hair and strokes my face. The misty day is filled with the soft hum of the wind and tired groans of the trees.

I open my eyes and scan the late morning around me.

There's no sign of Rafe or my sister, and my wings can't sense any other angelic essence in the opening. I'm here all on my own.

My gorged side moans, seeping with blood. I tuck one sword away and twist at the waist, inspecting the wound.

I exhale with marginal relief at the sight of a small dog bite sized gash. The lizard ripped more out of my sweatshirt than out of me, but the sharp teeth of his tongue left deep and long cuts up and down around the wound.

I shove the other sword behind my belt and with painful breaks, I pull my arms out of the sweatshirt and spin it around my neck, threading my arms through again, pulling it on back to front, at least my bitten side is less cold and exposed now.

I throw my head up to the milky sky, watching the tree tops bend and creak, slaves to the wind, as the wind marauds high between their branches.

I didn't ask Rafe where he's going to take my sister. Stupidly enough, we didn't discuss the meeting plan. We didn't arrange a place to meet and now I'm left to trace back my steps, one step at a time, in the vain hope that Rafe left "bread crumbs" of a clue for me to find and to follow.

It's quiet around me and it's quiet past the line of the trees.

I come closer, peeking around the nearest tree trunk, like a pervert, at the place where my mother lives.

The place is the same retired "ghost town" during the day as it was at night.

Hysterical female TV screams are pouring out of a slightly open window of a nearby caravan, interrupted by a mumbled, stern chastisement of a host and the loud thunder of applause from an audience, daytime TV at its best.

The memories of the night, when I was here last time, come flooding back.

My mother's accusing hateful glare and her psychotic, chanting recitals, the body of my stepfather on the ground with his blood, pooling darkly underneath him, and my sister's small hand, holding the knife and her scared, heart-wrenching whimpers behind my back later.

It all engulfs me, and I can't make my feet move forward, through my past, through and past the line of the trees.

Every time I think that I've made my peace with my mother's hateful rejection, I'm surprised and unprepared at the pain it causes me to see her again, or to even hear her voice.

Through all my "big girl" talk, deep down I know that I have never accepted her rejection and probably never will. Little Ariel is always here, lost and scared, waiting for her mother to find her, to hug her and make it all better, to dissolve the black desolation within with a warm hug.

But mother will never come.

Maybe even death wouldn't break the bond between us? Maybe my quest to find my way back to my mother will die only with me?

Maybe I will be searching for her love forever and will be left forever empty, broken and sore for not finding it.

I swallow past my dry mouth, and out of habit, I drop my gaze down to my feet, as I always used to do when I would speak to her, so careful not to anger her.

Hopefully I'll find Rafe there... Or some clue on where to look for him and Jess... Or a message of some sort...

I mumble in my head, talking myself into walking into that clearing, where about thirty caravans are parked and one of them with my mum.

"He said you might be here", a wheezy old man's voice croaks behind my back, startling me.

I snap my head up and whirl towards the voice, surprised to find myself surrounded by a tight circle of twenty, maybe thirty people and involuntarily, I take a step back, pressing myself closer to the trees.

The group is predominantly male, with only four middle-aged women peppering the crowd.

The people in this group are young and old, large and small, dressed in different clothes of diverse wealth, styles and epochs, like a travelling mob from last century, and at first glance I can't spot a single thing connecting them.

The youngest in the group is a boy, younger than Jess, standing to the right of a very old, frail man, who just spoke. Their ages are a stark contrast.

The boy is dressed in a casual grey hoodie, dark jeans and dazzling white trainers. The boy's arrogant stance oozes disobedience and cheek. A smirk dusts his lips and his neck is tilted to the side as he watches me with interest.

Although this crowd seems to be a weird mishmash, a casserole of accidental people at a bus stop, the power and purpose resonates off these seemingly random ages and appearances.

The group feels strong and organised, unified and regimental, as if brought here by the same business like a mob of villagers on their hunt for a monster, and an uneasy chill touches my spine.

"Who said?" I stammer.

The frail old man next to the boy gazes at me from under his grey bushy eyebrows.

His back is bent low to the ground, must have been frozen in this position for years now, and his head is turned to the side when he looks at me. He leans heavily on his plain wooden walking stick with both of his hands folded on top of it.

The old man wears moth-eaten brown tartan trousers and a navy, home knitted and buttoned up waistcoat, with a faded from the constant washing, dark green shirt underneath.

The old man takes a few shuffling steps forward, barely covering any ground.

"Remember what you've been told?" he rasps at me, but as I say nothing he helpfully adds, jogging my memory, "no more running, chasing or it will be worse?"

He takes long breaks between the words, opening his mouth like a fish gulping for air.

"Tut-tut-tut", he clicks his tongue at me in a soft displeasure, folding his face into something, that he probably calls a smile.

The unease grips the pit of my stomach, bringing fear in its wake.

No more running or it will be worse...

That was the promise then, and now the debt collection on the promise is in full swing.

I take a step back.

This whole interaction is menacing in its soft discordant silence, a cosy weak old man with threatening, authoritative words, the silent people around him with calm, relaxed faces in this accidental mob and the little child with a smug taunting smile at the forefront.

"Why didn't you listen?" The man continues, taking another shuffling step forward. His thick cane hits the damp ground in time with his steps. "Well, sweetheart, this is your 'worse'."

Following the advances of the old man's words and his steps, the rest of the group has moved forward, gradually, one small step at a time, snaking around and behind me, closing the circle tighter. But it's only now that I notice that they've tightened the circle even further.

I spin on the spot inside that enclosed space before returning to look at the old man again.

My hands reach behind my back to my swords.

The swords leave their hiding places, tearing jeans' belt loops on the way out.

Keeping his neck twisted up and to the side, and his gaze firmly on me, the old man reaches under his blue waistcoat.

Following his silent signal, all mobsters as one, keeping their gazes on me, reach to their pockets or behind themselves. And I swallow, take a step back and almost trip, when all of them produce black coiled whips or two feet long black poles with a half-moon or a two tine fork atop.

It is mind scrambling to see a sleek stock broker in a business suit uncoiling a black whip, or a weary looking woman in a stretched, bobbling jumper and in a frumpy skirt hold tight in her grip a black metal pole, which looks remarkably like a cattle prod.

Bearded bikers in black leather trousers and jackets, and groomed, over tanned young men in skinny jeans and tight shirts are flexing their whips and poles at me. A pampered elegant woman in a chic black designer jumper and tight pencil skirt, with practiced moves twirls a black pole with a two toothed fork at the end. She throws her sleek ponytail to the side of her neck, and with a relaxed flick of her wrist, the black pole in her hand extends another foot longer. Her gaze meets mine and she gives me a gorgeous, dazzling smile.

"The perfect equipment for herding an animal", the old man announces, uncoiling his whip onto the ground.

The shock floods in like a tsunami.

"The Scouser", my mind helpfully whispers, before it swoons and passes out, leaving me blank and empty.

Panic squeezes my heart and dread arrives last, with pragmatism calculating that they outnumber me by a mile and I'll have no chance in hell against all of them.

I swallow, scanning this mob, which now looks like a coordinated military battalion of trained and blood-thirsty soldiers, dressed up in civilians' clothing just for shits and giggles.

That's the way to play a mental warfare!

Even the arrogant boy is holding a weapon. The calculated look in his steely eyes has washed away the child.

I stumble back, glance over my shoulder, but they are behind me as well, and tighter now. I am surrounded and locked in.

I whirl around, taking a step back, away from them, but I have nowhere to go. I'm sealed in this lethal tomb by the mob.

I spin on the spot, spreading my arms with the swords wide like a dancer, warding off any of the monsters from coming closer to me, but they don't need to come closer to hurt me.

A bright click of a whip sounds behind me and before I have a chance to face it, pain rips at the tip of my bottom wing, tearing through my wing and my body, as I finish my useless turn.

I stumble and sway, scanning the crowd.

The little boy in the grey hoodie grins at me.

The whip in his hand rests on the dirty ground, its tip painted dark red.

Another sharp slap of a whip rings to the side, followed closely by the next.

The pain erupts at the side of my top wing and at my gorged side.

"Aaah!" I cry out into the cold silence.

Another crack of a whip, rushed by the next, and then another.

I twirl towards the sounds as fast as the pain allows me, throwing my arms with swords out. But I miss it all.

A new wave of pain cuts at my body and another rogue tail of a whip catches me on a cheek. Blood pools and begins to trickle down my chin.

My heart hammers in my chest. I need to do better if I want to survive.

I listen to the air around me, and the next time I hear a foot moving over loose stones on the ground, somewhere behind me to the left, I throw my hand with my sword out, low and to the side, then rapidly cutting with it upwards. Two black whips' long tails fall to the ground next to my foot with a soft "whoosh" of a deflated balloon.

The memory of my customary nightmare comes to me.

What is it with this essence and the gang of executioners?

A clap of a whip kisses the ground and almost instantly comes another whip clap, and each of them is harvesting a deft agony in me, ripping at my torso, at my legs and wings.

The burning tears fall, leaving me in a murky fog.

I try to listen to their movements but the stupid pain dulls my senses, weakening me. I try to fight it but I know that I'm failing.

I no longer cry out at each strike. The strikes are now joined together, like beads on a necklace, and I can't feel a break between them.

The strikes are fused together now into one ceaseless assault. I only weakly whimper, stumbling blindly, trapped, covering my face with one hand and swinging my sword blindly around me with the other, hoping to make contact with their weapons.

Rage is standing on her knees, murmuring rushed supportive words, begging me not to fall, painting dark pictures if I do.

She is a wise girl, my Rage. She knows that falling will be the beginning of the end. And I'm standing, blinking through the pain, afraid to fall down, to stop spinning and give them a chance to pounce on me.

I stagger weakly inside the circle, still gripping my little swords, when a bright zap of energy connects with my lower back, twisting and pulling my muscles all over, bringing me to my knees as my eyes roll back in my skull.

"And even the largest of bulls would fall", the old wheezing voice croaks, "a slave to a throe."

The circle has become tighter.

I can feel them like a swarm of wasps around me and I have no energy to get up.

I was trying to imagine another place in my head earlier and to take myself out of here, to transport myself on my wings, but maybe because of that first cut to the wing, or maybe because of my poor imagination, or maybe something else, but I couldn't do a thing. I can't take myself away, stuck in this gruesome nightmare.

And now on my knees, with pain blanketing my body, I have a sickening sense of déjà vu, like I'm living my usual nightmare, only living it with an amended cast and in real life. And at this moment I wonder if the Scouser lizard is really behind this battalion of death or maybe angels are in play after all.

And just like in my nightmare, the one that is in charge comes forward, away from the circle of bodies.

This one is the old man and not an angel, and his moves are accompanied by the dull beats of his walking stick and his shuffling steps.

I study the rippling, white luminous surfaces of my swords in my hands on the ground.

I'm not going with them. No matter what.

I promise this to myself and to my Rage.

I rummage in my mind, trying to come up with some solution, some sort of plan to find a way out, but I don't have any more cards left to play and I know that time is running out and I'm counting the last minutes of it.

But there is still one body I can reach. It's mine.

"I'd rather be dead than go with them".

A sudden gust of wind blows through the trees and over the ground, moving dry brown leaves along the ground and under my fingers.

"Ariel? Ariel, where are you?"

A soft frightened whisper brushes over me, brought over by the wind.

"Ariel? Ariel?"

My sister's small voice cries around and like smoke, it dissolves into thin air, rising up and floating through the trees.

"I'm scared, Ariel."

Jess?

Jess?!

She can't be here! She shouldn't be here!

Blind panic pushes at me and I raise my head, swinging on all fours, sweeping my gaze over the surrounding mob.

I try to see through them, past them. I'm looking between them, scanning their tight crowd. I need to make sure that they don't have her.

"*Ariel?!*" She cries again and with it I push myself further up, now kneeling in the dirt and swaying.

My head spins with the pain of my body and the agony of my soul.

I know she is my weakness. I know she always will be used against me.

She will be used to play me, but that no longer matters. In reality, it never has. I will do absolutely anything for her. She is all that I have left, all that I ever had.

"Throes will follow us in life and will follow some in their deaths", the old man rasps above me with a grandfatherly wisdom and sadness about an unruly grandchild.

He shares his secret with me. The veiled and obscure wisdom of his words makes me wonder if he was a priest, or a "man of God" of some sorts in his "previous" life, and I hate him for it even more.

In all my life I haven't seen one good thing from religion.

"Some were chosen to suffer in life, but some are cursed to suffer through eternity", he wheezes.

He is close now and I can smell the fetor of decomposing flesh behind the stale odour of mothballs.

Lizards!

Well, that answers that question.

Tips of my damp hair are smothered in mud, and I reach with my arm to my forehead and wipe at my face, pushing the hair away.

I've always felt it easier to handle a situation when I have more information, when I know everything.

Like when you're a child and you see a scary monster shadow on a wall, only to discover later, after flicking a switch, that it's just a pile of school uniform on the back of a chair. And then climbing out of a warm bed and throwing the clothes on the floor, with another flick of a switch, destroying the monster completely.

But I see monsters again, like many years ago, and this time I know what they are.

The wind dies and I can no longer hear Jess, but wherever she is, I know one thing for sure, she'll never make it without me.

I try to push the sword at the ground to steady myself, but the stupid angelic sword just glides easily and without any resistance into the ground and I yank the sword back out.

The "old man" lizard hovers above me.

I'm nauseated, sensing him with my abused, bleeding wings and with my skin, but I push through it as I raise my head to him, meeting his gaze.

The rest of the crowd of everyday monsters stays behind, obeying the hierarchy of command.

"Only the fate can tell how much suffering will be bestowed upon one. But sometimes even a measure of time is not long enough to measure the suffering...", he starts a new wave of his ramblings, reaching down to me as if he is about to pet me, and the revulsion causes my fingers to tighten the grip over the swords' hilts.

No time will be long enough to measure what they have prepared for me.

I drop my gaze to his hands. One of his hands rests on his walking stick, while the other holds a pole with a half-moon at the end.

A white buzzing light like an electricity spark, dances between the moon's twin picks.

That's probably the thing they zapped me with.

I pull my abused muscles at the ready. But I still don't know what for, when he utters next to my ear: "... for us and our kinsfolk."

My arm and my body react faster than my brain.

With my head still bent down, my body turns and twists.

My arm dives low and then shoots up, and a few seconds into the flight, it slows down its upward travel when it makes a connection with the body.

But I push it further and higher. I grind my teeth, forcing my arm to finish its lethal leap.

I slam my eyes shut when I'm showered with a cold thick mucus from above, but I don't stop, pushing my arm higher, reaching up with my body, until my arm comes through, released at the other end and three heartbeats later, the two bodies crash to the ground with a second's delay, their fall vibrating through my knees.

Chapter 14

The sounds of the world burst in, the agonising squeal of the dying animal on the ground, which quietens with every new heartbeat, the hisses and roars around me, the claps of dozens of whips on the ground and the electric energy of hate, anger and fear, that crackle off the crowd.

Now their emotions are reflecting mine, and I am pleased.

I'm still on my knees on the ground in an exhausted stupor, when I'm assaulted with a new shower of whips' bites, which are gorging at my body from every side and angle, and I can't hold it in anymore and I scream.

But my scream turns into a roar as this pain births something new inside me, and this new thing demands blood.

The familiar buzz descends over me, stealing the sight, world's sounds and smells and the ground begins to rumble under my knees like an empty stomach of a giant.

If I'm going to die – you're going to die with me.

My hate and anger are mounting and with it, the white buzzing noise in my head and the vibration to the ground.

The wind picks up speed and begins to roar around me, and the ground begins to shake like it did in the cave and the showers of assaults over my body stops.

I wipe at my face and open my eyes.

I'm in the centre of it all.

I'm surrounded by a tight circle of the mob and the mob is surrounded by a violent, roaring wall of wind, which spins dirt, trees and debris, spinning it all in a tight vortex of a tornado around us. Under my gaze the tornado grows stronger, faster and darker. It rises taller, as the furious wind picks up pace. It reaches to the grey sky and begins to rotate dark clouds above. Its wall grows thicker and denser. Its roar grows cacophonous and deafening.

But it's calm and quiet at the centre of the vortex where I'm kneeling and the gentle wind tenderly moves my hair.

The earth quakes and vibrates underneath me. It rolls and rumbles.

The ground moves and sways, and suddenly, with a loud bang of an exploding pressure cooker, the ground ruptures, as the cracks snake away from me in every direction like rays on a drawing of a sun.

With the screeching noise of grinding stone, the sides of the cracks begin to rub and then with another violent roar, the ground splits open around me. The chunks of the ground cave in, disappearing into the depths of open ground, taking the unexpected mobsters down with them.

The mobsters' screams and cries are disappearing inside, swallowed by the bottomless ground, which carries the echo of their eternal fall.

The last standing mobsters shuffle unsure on their small islands of the remaining ground.

Who is the animal now?

A bloodthirsty grin lifts my lips and I want more of that mayhem as the power surges through me.

Some human lizards try to push through the wall of tornado, but the wall is too violent and too strong for them to get through.

Some of them have abandoned their weapons, yearning only to preserve their lives.

I rise unsteadily to my feet. My body and wings are oozing blood but now I want *their* blood to have my fill, to appease me.

The white buzz spreads inside my head, clouding my vision in a frosted haze, waking something new in me.

Even my Rage is scared of this new, bloodthirsty creature now. For the first time, she stands back, sheepishly offering to hold my purse.

I have called on the wind. I have opened the ground. Now I want to finish them off.

The buzzing in my head increases and the pressure builds inside my skull, and I'm sure that if my head was made of glass, it would have exploded into a million of tiny shards by now.

My vision tunnels, fuzzing out, and a weird feeling of disjoint between my body and self descends on me, as if I was pushed back, away from the front of my consciousness.

As if a gate, holding back something important, finally swung wide open, and the flood of memories pushes in, mounting my anger and outrage.

Now I know what they are.

I know where they came from, and most importantly, I know *what* I can do to them.

"How dare you?!"

My voice roars above the rattle of tornado and it has the steely commanding tones I've never heard before.

The last surviving mob members stop their shuffling and spinning on the spot in search of an escape, and look at me with big surprised eyes. I think that this commanding tone is a surprise to them as well.

"How dare you rise against me?! How dare you conspire against me?!" I bellow above the wind.

"Have you forgotten to whom you owe your servitude? Have you forgotten who created you and who is your keeper? Forgotten what I can *do* to you?"

The veins bulge on my neck. My voice bawls with the righteous indignation, but my locked out mind is struggling to process what I'm saying.

"Have you thought of me weakened? Thought of this shell as easy prey?"

My authoritative voice rings with anger, while at the back of my mind, I weakly wonder if I'm about to pop something.

"Baza might be commanding you now, but I'll forever own you. You are my thralls for eternity, always were and always will be! Never forget that!"

The wind picks up pace, growing violent with my anger, and now lashing my hair around my face.

"Remove your stolen skins. They aren't yours to keep! *Nabalkutu bar!*" I roar, commanding in the language I don't know and don't understand, but these words are familiar somehow.

But more to the point, the lizards know exactly what I demand from them, as the surviving monsters reach for their necks, just as the Scouser did earlier, unclipping their gold buttons at their throats. In unison, they sink their fingers into their throats, under their skins, removing their human faces.

The empty human skins like Halloween masks are cast aside.

Lizard heads sit atop of male and female human bodies and the body of the arrogant boy, who is still stands on one of the remaining islands, sports a large scaly green lizard head on top of his childish frame. His lizard head is large, alien and disproportionate to his body.

I want to slam my eyes shut against these monsters, to close my ears to the wind and run away from this horror show, but this gate has freed something new. Something ancient, something fearsome and bloodthirsty was allowed through.

Under my terrified gaze, the lizards as one begin to strip, removing their human clothes, and soon, the pack of naked human bodies, topped with the lizards' heads, surrounds me.

Please, please, let me pass out!

But I am not allowed to pass out and it's not the end of their morbid strip show.

Continuing their synchronised baring, the lizards grab hold of the edges of their human skins, just around their necks, and rip at it, with all the force, as one might at a shirt with buttons flying and fabric tearing.

Only here, it is human skins are breaking with sharp rips, snaps and crackling.

The tiny beads of blood float in the air around us, caught by the wind.

"Khaaleen!" I command and the lizards yank their dinosaur claws out of the skins of humans arms, leaving those inside out like sleeves on a too tight jumper. The lizards then roll the human skins to their waists, down their legs, exposing more of their scaly, greenish or yellow skin.

One by one, the wasteland lizards are emerging in their full gory glory, leaving the abandoned skins on the ground.

My mind sways weakly, begging to be allowed to pass out now, but my body is too strong.

The greenish yellow lizards stand upright on their small islands of remaining land, swaying blindly. Their tongues whip out, scan the air and go back into their teeth holes.

The lizards are under my control.

I know that these green creatures are scared, but regimented and trained, they know not to burst into a panicked scurry. From what I've seen in Uras during the Baza's proud army demonstration, these are more intelligent.

I scan the naked lizards in front of me.

"Damiq", I call to them.

The lizards wait at the ready for my next command. I am in charge, no one is disputing it now, none of them are thinking about their weapons or even considering their earlier plan.

"That was the first and the last time your kind will rise against me. Woe betide any of you or your kin to insurrect ever against me, as An be my witness in this oath", I throw my arms to the sky. "If you ever do so, I, Uriel, The Harbinger of Chaos, The Keeper of the Gates, The Begetter of Life, The Dam of The Ends and *your* creator, vow to dissolve your entire species into the ash of oblivion."

I sweep my gaze over the still lizards.

"So heed this warning, and may my deeds be the sign to the rest of you and the reminder to your master!"

I feel my face stretch into a wide bloodthirsty smile as I roar, *"Adi la basi Alaku!"*

The ground vibrates and shakes, low and deep at first. The deep rumbling rises from the depths, pushes to the surface, increases in the intensity and volume, and once it is here, right under my feet, the remaining islands collapse, caving into oblivion, taking all of the screeching lizards with them.

Their cries quieten and disappear, falling into the pit of the earth.

Now it's only me left standing on my small island, surrounded by the dark doughnut of oblivion and the faint stench of sulphur from the fiery place whiffs from the open ground.

The wild tornado begins to slow its mad spinning. The broken trees and debris begin falling to the ground, released from the vortex.

A bent bike drops from the sky with a metal thud. It lands on the edge of the cleft, balances there for a moment as if thinking what it should do next, and then, as if finally persuaded, it tipples over into the opening with a jolly ring of its bell.

I take a careful step forward, to the edge of my island and look into the depth of the caved ground.

The sheer drop of the ground is phenomenal.

It goes down forever. The ground of the opening is black, swallowing all light. It's only when I look for a tad longer, I can see a thin orange thread of a river of fire, running along the bottom of that canyon.

The dust begins to settle and the wind dies down, and I can see the devastation around me.

The line of trees, behind which I was hiding only a few minutes ago, spying on my mother's house, is gone. Ripped out, snapped and broken in pieces trees litter the ground.

The caravan park is no longer hidden behind the trees and I can see the damage the tornado has caused. I'm relieved to see that all the homes remain in their original places, and the messed up lawns, broken benches and missing chunks of the roofs are the only signs of damage.

In the quietness of the aftermath, the caravan park is coming alive.

Just like scared children, that poke their heads from under a duvet, the residents emerge from their mobile homes, unsure, descending down their short stairs. Some petrified faces peek from around the homes, gauging if it is safe to come out now.

After a quick scan of the area, it doesn't take them long to spot me, standing on my little island, past the messy line of ripped out trees, surrounded by the ten feet-wide trench of the caved ground.

Unsure residents don't dare to come closer to the trench, freezing where they stand, staring at me.

They look at me and I look at them.

"Ariel."

I turn my head to the voice.

Jess and Rafe stand across from the sunken ground.

He holds her hand in his, and seeing her small lanky form again, safe and sound, next to Rafe, brings tears to my eyes.

It's the relief that she is okay and with me. It's the hope that maybe we will be alright after all. But it has a sting of jealousy that Rafe is the one, who is holding her hand.

Rafe's livid accusing glare is raking me and the devastation around.

I am well aware that it's too late to care about the exposure.

I've dumped the tonnes of heavy ground and took the lizards down with it. I've created so much chaos that I doubt any more of my stunts will make difference at this point. So I open my bleeding wings and I soar across the ravine, to my sister. I can't wait to hug her again, to remind myself why I am doing all of this.

Her wide eyes sparkle and shine like diamonds, when she sees me flying, and the look of wonder on her face is washed with pure joy, when I place my feet on the ground just a few inches away from her.

"Jess", I mumble, unable to summarise the happiness, relief and hope that I feel, looking into my sister's small face with dark circles under her eyes.

"I see you had a good time", Rafe's acidic sarcasm wakes me and I pull my gaze away from my little sister to look at him.

"How come everything is my fault?" I snap.

"I didn't do any of that", I sweep my hand at the chaos, annoyed at him. "I think it was your girlfriend who stepped in and told them what for. Besides", I add, changing the subject, "did you know that I can command these lizards and apparently I own their arses?"

"No, I didn't know that. But whoever has created them, holds ownership over them and I wasn't sure if it was you, An or Mik'hael, or Baza. But can we please go and discuss it somewhere else?" he cuts.

"Sure", I rebuff, "but what am I supposed to do with this?"

I nudge my head towards the small and silent crowd of the residents observing us.

"I'll handle it", he bites, rolling his eyes.

"As usual", he mumbles under his breath, but I can still hear him.

I want to answer him back to his usual dismissive shit, but I decide to leave it today.

"Let's go", he commands.

"Hold on tight, Jessie-boo", I murmur into my sister's hair.

I bend down and lift my sister, wrapping my arms around her, pressing her tighter to me, feeling the tingly warmth of happiness spreading inside me.

I have my family back and I know that my little puppy will be safe with me and maybe, hopefully, one day she will be happy, forgetting this life like a bad dream.

I open my arms and Rafe steps into my embrace as well, now we hold Jess tight between us. I nod to Rafe and all our wings open wide around us, ready to take us to the sky.

And before we soar, I turn my head towards the stunned crowd and I see my mother, now standing at the forefront, silent, with a gawking open mouth, as she watches her daughters floating away from her, disappearing into a foggy sky and I can't stop watching her, hoping, no, wishing for her to call me back.

But like everyone else's faces, her face dissolves, eaten away by the distance between us and when we are high enough, a thunderous explosion of a white luminescent light covers the ground where the residents stand, and Jess hides her face in my chest and starts to sob.

Chapter 15

*W*e fly above fields, over my town and past the forest with tall, hundreds of years old trees.

I take it slow carrying my precious cargo and Rafe.

His wings move in sync with mine, and they are trying to help carry us, but I fly as if I'm the only one who can keep all three of us up.

I guess the habit of relying only on myself will die with me.

Jess quietened a few miles back. Her legs are wrapped tightly around my waist like when she used to do when she was little, when I would carry her upstairs to bed.

I bend my head and smell the top of her head.

Her hair still carries that child's scent, which is currently hidden under the sour smell of an unwashed body and... abandonment. I never knew that abandonment could have a scent, but I can smell it on her right now.

"There", Rafe calls to me and my gaze follows his hand, which points to the edge of the familiar forest.

I drop my eyes at the sight of the forest where I nearly killed us both, wondering if I should read anything into Rafe's choice of our new hiding spot.

But I say nothing and a few seconds later, Rafe tugs at my waist, calling for me to descend with him at a small field on the edge of that forest.

"I thought this would be the best place for us to hide, and I was hoping that you would check here for us", he explains once our feet touch the ground. I can't hear any undercurrent in his voice, but I've been a shit judge of characters all of my life.

He releases Jess, strokes the top of her head, stepping away from us, and walks towards trees and deeper into the forest.

Jess is still wrapped around me like a vine.

She tucked her head against my chest and wrapped her limbs around me the second we took to the air, and she hasn't open her eyes or emerged since, like a hurt tortoise, she's hidden inside her shell.

But she is not heavy, so I follow after Rafe with Jess still wrapped around me.

Weaving past trees and not that far in, I come to a small opening with a brown carpet of late autumn grass, hidden underneath a carpet of brown leaves and yellow pine needles.

A large dark green tent is erected in the middle of that opening, which is surrounded by large pine trees, hiding the tent under their dense canopy. The top of the tent is covered with a generous layer of dry brown autumnal leaves, twigs and snapped pine branches.

I'd imagine it would be impossible to spot the tent from above and would be just as difficult to see it through the line of trees.

Rafe stands by the flap.

"Jess", I call, "Jessie-boo, you need to let go, sweetie."

Without lifting her head off my chest, she shakes "no", rolling her forehead over my clavicle and chest bones, hugging me tighter with her twig limbs.

Without another word, Rafe lifts the flap and disappears inside the tent.

I want to follow him, I need to ask him a few questions about this girlfriend of his. So I come closer to the tent, trying to fold over, to see if I would fit into the tent with Jess around me, but Jess's body is too odd and unbalancing on my stomach, pulling me down.

I kneel in the dirt.

"Jessie-boo, why don't you let go of me and stand up, huh? We can go inside the tent and see Rafe?"

I stroke the top of her head, cooing above her. But she doesn't let go.

"Did Rafe put the tent up? Did you help him? Why don't you show me inside it, sweetie? Jessie-boo?"

Her grip on me tightens.

"Jess, you have to let go, baby. I promise, I'm not going anywhere and you are going to stay with me from now on, but you need to let go."

But she refuses to move, as her legs strangle my waist. Her arms are like a rope around my neck. I try to push her body away from me, but like a boa constrictor, she only tightens her hold on me in response.

"Jessica Davies", I suddenly say in our mother's stern voice, even surprising myself, "that's enough!"

Jess jolts in my arms. She lifts her face to me with panic swimming in her eyes, and her hold weakens.

Her shocked and scared eyes are wide open, as she pushes at my shoulders and my chest with her hands, and the longer I hold onto her, the madder and more urgent her pushes become and I let go.

Unfolding her legs, she slides off me. When her bum hits the ground, she kicks her feet at the ground, trying to rise, desperate to get away from me. She scatters as her panicked gaze is locked onto mine.

"Jess, I..."

I bend down, trying to hug her, but she is too lithe and my arms close over empty air. She is up on her feet and without another look, she sprints deeper into the forest.

Shit!

I fumble with my legs and finally I am up, running after her, but she is just too fast.

She moves like water around the trees, darting from side to side. She is running for her life.

"Jess! Stop!"

"Jess! Please stop!"

"Jessie-boo! I'm Ariel, remember? Jessie-boo!" I call after her.

And then she slows a bit and turns her head, glancing at me. Her big eyes are hopeful and unsure, but her legs are still carrying her forward.

"Jess, please stop!" I scream, but it's too late, Jess rams into a tree at full speed.

And like in a slap stick cartoon, she wraps her arm around the trunk on the impact, then after one second delay, she opens her arms and falls square on her butt, and then two seconds later, she flops back onto the ground.

"Jessie!" I scream.

I cover the last few yards as fast as I can, dropping to my knees in the mud next to her.

Jess's eyes are closed.

"Jessie, Jessie-boo", I murmur above her, calling to her, moving damp hair off her forehead, stroking her ashen face.

"Jess?" Panic changes my voice, turning it into a shrill as I begin to tap her on her cheeks.

I slap her cheeks harder and a moment later, her eyebrows jump up, her eyelashes flutter and slowly she opens her eyes.

I exhale loudly as sweet relief floods me.

I sink to the ground next to her. I'm afraid to touch her, afraid to scare her again, so all that I can brave is to lift my hand and gently stroke her face.

"Are you okay, baby? Can you hear me? Where does it hurt?" I coo, shuffling on my knees closer to her.

She stares into the canopy above her and I wonder if she even hears me.

"Jessie-boo, are you okay?"

I take her face in my hands, carefully turning it towards me.

Her gaze moves with her head and when it falls to my face, for a scary second I think that she can't see or recognise me. But then, her gaze narrows on me, her face wrinkles, her eyes close.

"Ariel", she whimpers and begins to cry.

Thank god!

All worries about her injuries are forgotten, I scoop her little body in my arms, pressing it against mine.

"I'm sorry, sweetie-pie, I'm so, so sorry", I mumble into her hair, rocking her with me, "I'm so sorry."

Jess's cries get noisier and like a little baby, she opens her mouth and bawls, clutching me closer to her.

I rock her in my arms and murmur sweet nonsense to her, as her little body warms in my embrace, and in turn, it warms me inside. I stroke her back and this time I'm not telling her to let go of me.

We sit like this for hours.

"Under the sky
My sister and I.
Trees above us and bottomless sky

Here we'll live – my sister and I", I sing to her, while rocking her in the dark autumnal forest.

The sky light moves above the tree and begins to fade.

My wings are wrapped around us, keeping us warm. Jess fell asleep a while ago, with her legs flopped and spread on the ground and her body in my arms.

I lost the feeling in my legs a while back, but apart from gently shuffling under Jess, I'm too afraid to disturb her.

Rafe came through the trees only once.

He stood there, a few yards away from us, silent and brooding, watching us, and then without a word, he turned around and walked away, ignoring my smile.

It is obvious that Rafe is not a happy bunny right now, and something tells me that it was probably my fault as well, but I am too tired to concern myself with it right this second.

As I sit here, in the cold and silent woods, listening to the wind playing with the tree tops and the occasional caw of a lonely crow, while hugging my sister's little sleeping form, I ponder on what to do next. I wonder what am I supposed to do now, what will be my next move and where will be I running now? Or if I have anywhere else left to run?

As Baza so eloquently put and the lizards openly dictated, I will not be allowed to run forever.

Everyone is coming at me to collect their dues. Only Mik'hael is missing from this debt collecting party, but I'm pretty sure that he won't be much longer either.

My plan to hide on Earth is now in the gutter, discarded and useless, floating down the drain.

It's like running in a lethal maze, doors slam shut behind me, cutting off my way of escape, forcing me to move forward into the unknown.

I look down at Jess's sleeping face.

I wanted her with me, to have her near, so I could keep her safe, but keeping her now seems trickier than I first thought.

It's bad enough to be on the run, chased by those who are controlling the Earth, *thank you, Scouser, for this little titbit!* and be responsible for myself, but to be responsible for a loved one, who looks up to you for guidance, which you can't provide? That's tougher by tenfold.

I wonder if there's anywhere left for me to go or if I should simply dig in and hide in the tent in these woods forever?

Again I stand at the end of another road.

Another bridge was burned behind my back, another return route was cut off.

I throw my head back, staring at the dull tendrils of evening light in the sky. It's already dark down here.

∞ ∞ ∞

"Ariel. Ariel?"

I snap up from my sleep. My eyes are wide open but dazed, as I spin my head, looking for the source of the call.

"Ariel?" A small hand touches my neck.

Jess. Of course.

I exhale and relax, looking down at her. My heart is still beating fast against my ribs.

Her face is ghostly pale in the light of my glow.

Her eyes are bulging as she reaches to my skin and pokes her finger at my jaw.

Oh, shit; glowing. I clean forgot.

I try to dim my glow, but maybe because I'm still rubbish at controlling my powers or maybe because I was startled awake, or for whatever other reason, but I can't turn the glowing off, shimmering in the dark like a bloody firefly.

"You're glowing", she whispers, sharing this big secret with me.

Bless. I wonder if I sounded just as shell shocked and scared when I saw Rafe glowing for the first time.

"I know, Jess", I stroke her head and yawn. "It's just one part of the things."

"What things?"

"Do you remember how we got here?"

She looks up at me and I see her thoughts go back, one step at a time.

"I ran."

"Yes" I yawn, "and before? How did we get to these woods?" I push.

I need her to remember. I need to tell her.

She is coming with me, no matter where I go now, so she needs to be ready for anything that this screwed up angelic world would throw at us.

Her facial expressions are called by the memories, the further back she goes and more she remembers.

Jess starts with a calm and relaxed expression, progressing onto a 'drawn eyebrows' stage, which promptly followed by the bulging eyes, when the final response of self-preservation sinks in and she tries to scatter away from me.

But I'm not planning to let go out of my hold, one head injury is enough for today.

"Do you remember?"

She doesn't answer, just continues pushing her legs at the ground and her arms at me.

She remembers.

"Jessie-boo", I rush in, "do you know how sometimes, even when you can't see some things, these invisible things still might be there? Like you know, bacteria? Or a black hole? Remember, how sometimes you need to have special equipment to see something? Something that might be really small or really big? Or really far away?"

She doesn't answer, still pushing at me.

"But it doesn't mean that these things don't exist, right? It just means that we need special equipment to see it all? Maybe a special gift..." I'm going with Rafe's style of explanation here.

I keep her body tight to mine. She needs to hear me out. I keep my voice as even and calm as I can, and begin to stroke her back, and thankfully, the longer I speak, the more she listens.

Her arms relax and bend at the elbows, as she lifts her face and nods at me.

"Well", I take a breath in and continue, "sometimes, we might not even have the equipment yet, but it doesn't mean that things are not there, that they don't exist", I rush.

"Agreed?"

She nods again.

Here I go. I will try not to sound completely nuts, but that ship might have already had sailed.

So I just rip off that plaster.

"The angels are real", I bleat.

"What angels?"

"You know, the ones in the Bible", I mumble. I seriously don't want to bring religion into this or to validate my mother's hysterics, but there is nothing else I can think of, to which I can relate that crazy life I'm living.

"But these angels are not holy or anything. They are just a different type of people", I gush.

What the hell? "Different type of people"? What, like aliens? I huff at myself. I seriously should have practiced this speech prior.

"You know? More like people from another country", I inwardly roll my eyes, as I try to downplay and simplify the whole angelic bullshit. I really don't want her to freak out, she will have plenty time for that later.

"They are just like us. The only difference is that they live high up in the skies and they can fly. That's all. They can do a bit more than you and me, but not much and they are just like us, really", I gaze into her big trusting eyes, hoping that my story is not freaking her out and it's making sense.

"And you know what else?" I add nonchalantly.

"What?"

"As it turns out, by completely random coincidence, I am one of them", I smile at my sister, "and this", I wave my hand over my glowing face, "is just another, small part of it. I am one of them, so I can fly, I can glow, I don't know what for yet, I don't really need to eat and I can go up to their homes in the skies. They have whole palaces up there. Right above the Earth", I point to the sky.

"What? Like aliens?"

Sounds about right. That's what you get for the "different people" bit.

But I can work with it.

"Yeah, like aliens. They live on their spaceships above the Earth, and now and again, they would come here for a visit. You know, like going on holidays."

"Are these aliens good or bad?" she starts quizzing me. Her bright eyes are on me as she has forgotten about her need to run away from me, so I carefully let go of her.

"Are people good or bad?" I ask her in return.

She thinks about it for a moment.

"Some people are good and some people *are* bad." The shadow comes over her pretty face.

"Exactly. Just like people, these "angel aliens" have good and bad among them."

"But you are good?" Her question is more of the confirmation, and my stomach drops.

"Of course I am good, Jessie-boo", I stroke her face with my hand.

"Like a superhero?" she beams at me.

I am taken aback by her sincerity and her trust in me, but mainly, by the complete belief that I am the "good one". I swallow.

"Sure", I nod, "like a superhero, a glowing, flying superhero."

"Oh", her mouth forms the perfect "O". "You're a superhero", she whispers in awe.

For better or worse, Jess has just assigned me a side.

"Yes, I am. Guarding humanity from bad aliens", I raise my chin up.

Taking Uriel's essence into account, I suppose I am not that far off. I wish I was standing up at this moment, so I could do the "superhero stance" for my sister.

"And Rafe is one of good ones as well. He's helping me. That's why he was looking after you while I couldn't. He is a good one."

I stroke her hair.

"Can we fly? Now? Can you show me something else you can do?"

Her excitement is so infectious that I feel light laughter coming up.

"Not now. First we need to get back to Rafe, but later, sure, we can go for a flight."

Her attention is back to my glowing face.

She strokes my cheek with her warm finger then she brings her finger to her eyes, probably inspecting it for the residue.

"You know what else the glowing is good for?" I whisper.

"What?" she leans closer, her big eyes open even wider with wonder, secrets, fun. She can't wait to hear what more I will tell her.

"Going to the toilet in the woods at night."

A wide grin takes over her face and little giggles come out. Quiet at first, they grow louder, and she presses her little hand to her mouth, suppressing them, but her eyes still shining bright.

A smile tugs at my lips too.

"When you're camping and you need to do your business in the woods, how are you going to hold a light? Tricky, right?"

She nods. Her grin, her open happy eyes, I love making her laugh. I can make toilet jokes all day long if that is what it takes.

"But like that", I say, pointing to my face, "your hands are free to find the biggest leaf and wipe."

She laughs louder.

"But as King Julian said..." I begin.

"Who wipes?!" We finish in unison.

Jess's crystal laugh rings in the quiet of the woods. I smile, looking down at her. I squeeze her tighter for a second before releasing her again.

"Shall we go back and see Rafe? He's probably worrying about us."

"Okay."

She yawns, stretches and climbs out of the nest of my crossed legs.

My rise is less graceful, but eventually I'm up too.

I yawn, rising on my tippy toes, reaching up with my arms, and suddenly, my wings flash open around me. Jess takes a small step away from me, not in fear, but in awe.

I feel less pain in my wings and at my gorged side, thank you, angelic healing powers, so I turn and stretch, as Jess gawks at my shimmering purple wings.

I walk towards the tree where Rafe stood by earlier looking at us. That must be the way to our tent.

Chapter 16

"Thank you for keeping your promise", I whisper, careful not to wake Jess.

When we came back, the tent was warm and three sleeping bags were rolled out.

Again, I can't believe how thrifty and resourceful Rafe is.

"You are welcome", he says in a way of acknowledgement, "I promised it to you after all."

But the pause of unspoken words sings in the air before he quietly adds, keeping his head down, "but please, don't put me in this position again. I have sacrificed a lot for this essence", he lifts his eyes to me, "for you, and I know that I will sacrifice a lot more, everything, if I have to. But as I told you before: this essence is bigger than you or your family, or any of your Apkallu possessions, no matter how important they might be to you."

He gazes into my eyes and I feel like an errant child.

"I told you", he starts, but then cuts himself off, "I *asked* you to make a decision in the cave. I asked you, if you can be part of this war, if you could put the essence first before your needs. I have explained stakes to you, I have warned you.

"By choosing your sister, you have not only abandoned me, you have abandoned the cause and everyone, who risked their lives and safety for this essence. And above all, you have risked the balance."

He rakes his hair, looking past me.

"Uriel used to raise millions under her flag. Millions! Her powers were so infinite that she could give life and take it away. But above all, she was just. Some creatures feared her, many loathed her, others respected her, but they all knew that she would never put her own needs above the others."

I sit there, speechless, stunned. I can't believe he reprimands me, again.

"I know all of this", I snap. "It's not the first time you're telling me this. What's with the lecture again?"

"It's not a lecture. It's a matter of things."

"What things?" I rebuff. "The daily retellings of Uriel's great accomplishments and Ariel's epic failings?"

I glare at him.

"What do you want from me? To say that I'm sorry? Here you are, sorry!" I practically spit it at him.

"But you listen to me too, mate. In the cave I did what I had to survive and I'll do it again. If you expected me to roll over and die, and to make yours", I jab my finger at his chest, "and everyone else's lives easy then you're out of luck, pal. One thing I have learned how to do well is to survive!"

I pull back, shaking my head in disbelief.

"I can't believe we're having this conversation! Again!" I throw my hands up. "Every time you speak to me, you open your mouth only to lecture me. You keep ranting on and on about the essence and how important it is to you, to the world and the whole bloody universe, blah-blah-blah", I roll my eyes.

"But I'm here, with you, ain't I?" I scowl at him, "not with Baza. I didn't stay with him and I didn't run away to him. Doesn't that mean something?"

Silently, he stares back at me, but I'm on a roll.

"And you're talking to me like this, after everything we've done together! After everything *I* have done!"

"We're having this conversation *exactly* because of everything you've done."

I feel like a rug has been pulled from underneath me and I've been spat on.

And the next second, I'm blind with rage.

My bloodthirsty girlfriend Rage still cowers somewhere in the corner, mindful of my latest performance, but I can hear her egging me on from the shadows.

I crawl in the tight space of the tent, closing the distance between us, leaning into him. His cheerful smell of ocean and fruit hits my head, spiking my anger.

"Listen... you", I hiss, "Don't you dare... Don't even dare go there! You don't know me. You know nothing about me! You're in no position to judge me! No one is!"

A distant thunder rumbles in the sky and wind picks speed, pushing at the tent.

"Sit down and calm yourself, Ariel."

I want to kill him and it takes all of my self-restraint not to hit him right now.

"Let's get one thing straight", I bare my teeth at him, "my sister is all the family that I have left and I'll do absolutely anything to keep her safe. Your essence, your 'balance of power'", I mimic him, "your holy war means nothing to me. Nothing! It's got nothing to do with me. And don't you dare lecture me ever again on how inferior I am to your wonderful Uriel, because next time, it will not end well for either of us!"

The wind roars outside, blowing leaves against the tent, bending and creaking, centuries old pine trees.

"Talking of your sister", he interjects, "did you tell her?"

"Tell her what?"

"About you, about what you are now."

It takes me a second to realise what he is talking about.

"Yes I did."

It's clearly not what he expected to hear, as he visibly deflates, and I'm pleased to have one on him.

"What? Everything?"

"Everything that she needs to know right now, yes."

"What does that mean? How large is that mystical 'everything she needs to know' measure? She needs to know all of it. What if something happens, happens to you? More of the earlier ambush? How are you going to explain it to her?"

"Again here you are with your bloody lectures." It's now my turn to throw my head skywards. "Why not just to say, 'Well done, that's a good start'? But no! You have to start another lecture. Nothing is ever good enough for you, no matter what I do or how hard I try. And of course, I know that she will need to know everything, but even you can't be that cruel and ask me to dump it all on her at once. I will tell her everything, but slowly and one bit a time."

I saw him wince at "you" and "cruel".

I take a breath, calming myself.

"Besides, she doesn't need to know that her sister is a freak, who can start earthquakes and annihilate the entire humanity, if she chooses. I'm still her sister and that", I sweep hand over myself, "hasn't changed it, not even a single bit. I'm still me."

"But what will happen when more lizards come calling? Wouldn't you want to spare her your shock and turmoil of when you were told?"

"I am never enough for you, am I? Never good enough and never will be, no matter what I do. You will always treat me like a child, like I am inferior to you" I scream.

"Ariel, control your emotions please", he barks and jerks his head upwards, to the raging wind outside the tent.

I glare at him.

The truth is that I don't know how I am going to tell her the entire truth. I know that she'll be coming with me now, no matter where I go, and she will see things, but... I am afraid of her seeing me in a different light, seeing me differently. I'm afraid to lose her.

I throw open the flap of the tent and climb out into the raging storm and almost trip over at the unexpected sight.

I take a step back, leaning my suddenly dampened back on the tent.

How?!

What now?

Please, not again...

Baza stands in the small clearing just a foot away from the tent.

His face and hands are aglow with a cream pearly light.

He sports a sharp mauve pinstripe suit with a waistcoat underneath in the same fabric. His silver beard is trimmed just as neatly as I remember, and it looks almost white in the light of the evening dusk and his creamy glow.

Today Baza has a black bowler hat on his head and a white sleek dandy walking stick in his hand.

Behind him in a wedge formation, slipping deeper into shadows of the woods, stands a battalion of his angels, the grey, faceless ones, the same as he was parading in front of me in Uras.

Sealed in their matte, dark grey tactical gear, with grey skin tight masks hiding their faces, with shadows and trees hiding their bodies, these soldiers look nothing more than shadowy ghosts.

I don't know how many of his angels are here. This army is hard to see and impossible to count, as most of them are slipping into the shadows beyond.

Like pawns on the chessboard of Baza's game, these angels are masked and faceless. They are stripped of their identities.

Unified and uniformed, they could look cloned, if not for the differences in their heights, body builds and the colours of their wings, which all shoot rigid up to the sky.

"Dear Ariel. I'm so happy that you're alright", Baza calls to me. His face is picture perfect grandfatherly concern, his voice trembles.

He opens his arms wide, ready to welcome me in his embrace.

But I don't rush into these open arms, rooted to the spot where I stand.

Unfazed by my rejection, he drops his arms, still keeping the wide smile.

"When I first heard of what these ibnatums have done, I was beside myself with worry. At first I was appalled. I was furious that these animals have forgotten their place. But then seeing your glorious work..."

His eyes light up.

"Excellently done", he smiles. His hands give me two slow claps.

The shock wears off and I can remember how to speak again.

"Uh, thank you?"

"And I believe you've found your sister after all", he folds his arm over his chest and a soft god thanking smile stretches his lips, "I'm so pleased that I was able to reunite you with your kinfolk. I can only imagine the worry it must have caused you", he shakes his head and sadness casts the shadow over his face.

"Yes, thank you."

I'm like a broken record, but I wish he would just cut to the chase. I know there's a reason why he is here.

"I could've not done it better myself, sweetheart. What a truly masterful way to whip the stupid creatures in line!"

"Pardon the pun", he adds, apologetically shrugging his shoulders, without a doubt referring to all the whipping I had to deal with.

His round belly rumbles with a soft musical laugh the next minute. "They thought they could force their freedom from you. The simple ibnatums expected to catch a human with a bit of an essence for a sparkle, but instead they have found you."

He stretches his arms to me again.

What the hell is it with the arms? He has totally had some stage training by the looks of it.

"Will you just cut the crap, Baza", Rafe calls behind my back and I jump up. "What do you want now?"

I didn't hear Rafe coming over.

"Rafael, I think we both can agree that Ariel can speak for herself", Baza cuts Rafe off and turns his attention back to me.

"Every time I see your work, sweetheart, I'm more convinced that not only the Uriel's essence is in you, but that *all* of the essence is in you, and that the essence is as strong as it was before."

"You know", he drops his voice a little, "sometimes there could be issues during the essence transference, powers lost or weakened, new ones arisen to replace the old, some as pathetic as turning water into wine... And yet here you are, just as powerful and glorious as Uriel herself! And the latest demonstration of your powers on the ibnatums? Truly breathtaking!"

He takes a step closer. His white walking stick sinks into the wet ground.

"So I came here not only to extend, but amend my offer as a way of recognition of your great power. I no longer offer you a seat at my Council, oh no. Now, I ask you to *lead* my Council with me. I offer you to stand beside me. I offer the great power to you, a worthy one to match your power. And to solidify our partnership and as a gesture of good will, I will release all of your ibnatums from my service and all of them will be yours again to command.

"I know I still have twenty million human years left on that lease, but I'm happy to waive it off in our partnership, and they all can be yours again. I no longer offer you my army. I'm giving you your own army! I offer you the full alliance, vote and the decision making with it. You will have your autonomous say, and finally, you will have the army to reflect your great powers. We could conquer anything together! The two of us can do anything! We will make history!"

Shock wears off and with it, I'm finding my voice and my strength again.

"Baza, we've been here before, remember? Why do you think I've run away before? Because I don't want to join you! I don't want anything to do with you. I thought you would have cracked that code by now."

"Rushed and hot-headed like all youngsters", he shakes his head at me.

"Sweet child", he starts again, "you can run all you like, but the time for alliance is coming, and your choices are sparse. It's either Mik'hael or me. And trust me, I am more flexible and far easier to work with than him. Mik'hael is old school, too rigid in his principles. I doubt he'll let you keep your pet sister. You are a young child, a baby in our terms, so you don't understand the gravity of the decision before you. I am doing you a favour here. I am honest and upfront with you right now, and I am telling you that you will not withstand the wrath of Mik'hael on your own. Ever. That much I can promise you", he chuckles.

"You don't have an army. Your ibnatums are mine now", he begins to list, "your followers question you, otherwise you wouldn't be here all by yourself", he adds, pointing his walking stick to the tent behind my back. "You no longer have worshipers for energy replenishment. You are still very shaky with your powers and I wonder how much of your powers you even know about. Do I need to continue?"

Rafe comes closer and I can feel his breath over my shoulder.

"I would've expected Rafael to do a better job in preparing you for our world. If he cared enough for your survival, he would have told you the same thing I'm saying now. You will not survive on your own."

"I'm not on my own."

"You mean him?" Baza points his white stick to Rafe behind me. "I am not including your mangled companion in your possible alliance's choices, because that would be futile and just outright cruel for both of you, cruel to raise hopes up, when there are none to have. The weak and damaged archangel is no good for anything or anyone, irrelevant of how powerful he was once.

"I need the 'Pledge of Propinquity' from you tonight", he cuts.

"And what if I don't give you that pledge?"

He raises his eyebrow at me, "Then someone is going to die tonight."

The softness disappeared from his eyes like a morning fog under the first rays of sunshine.

"Trust me, dear child, it's not a threat. It's just a sound business decision on my part and that's why they are here", he nods behind himself, "to oversee the outcome of our... conversation, shall we say."

He folds his hands over his chest again, gazing deep at me. He takes another step closer.

"You see, Ariel, if I can't persuade you to join me, then at the very least, this way I will make sure that I preserve the current balance of powers, until I am ready to take on Mik'hael or until Uriel's essence is reborn in a more agreeable host.

"This 'hide-and-seek' game went for far too long. You're making a fool of me, and the ibnatums' clumsy rising earlier are the first warning bells. And I am determined to keep it as the first and the last disobedience of my subjects. Sorry, sweetheart, but I need to hear your answer now, but think hard on what I have promised before you make your decision."

"I'd rather die than go to that place of yours, and see all these lizards again, hear all these dying humans screaming, dealing with you and your smarmy type. Butcher, you, lizards. And you know what?" I take a step closer to him, closing the space between us.

"I know that I would pay for that 'Pledge' later", I whisper to him, "Sooner or later I will pay for it, because nothing is ever black and white with you, nothing is ever simple. I may be human and stupid, as you say, but I am learning."

He studies me for a moment.

"That you are", he admits. He raises his eyebrow at me, appraising me. His eyes are slits, his back is straight, and he looks taller somehow. He no longer looks cute and homely.

"Fair enough", he closes his eyes briefly, acknowledging my decision.

"Goodbye, Ariel. It was nice to meet you, however brief that was. I wish there was a different outcome to our conversation, but as you humans say, such is life."

He opens his four gigantic black wings and takes to the sky, leaving me and Rafe in front of his angelic battalion.

Chapter 17

The battalion of angelic death is silent and menacing. It is faceless, regimented and strong.

We are screwed for sure.

"Seems like your wish will finally come true", I whisper to Rafe over my shoulder, keeping my gaze on the grey angelic ghosts.

"What wish will that be?"

"Me dead, that one. And then everything will be alright in your world again."

"*Zu ku Izi*, why do you think your death is what I desire?! I just wish for you to make the right choices."

"*Your* choices."

"Nothing wrong with that."

"Argh, what's the point even trying talking to you?"

It's hard to argue with someone without seeing their face.

"Indeed, right now it's not the time for it. Give me one of your swords."

"What? No! They're mine."

"I need a sword, so I can help you fight. Or would you prefer to fight them by yourself while I do needlework?"

"Fine", resigned I pull out one of the swords and hand it behind my back.

Rafe's hand brushes over mine and the sword leaves my grip.

"Jess, child, come and stand behind us", Rafe calls towards the tent.

I turn and see Jess standing in the tent, holding the opened flap in her hands. I don't know how long she's been there or how much she heard.

I turn my gaze to the forbidding wall of the grey angels.

"What are we going to do?" I ask Rafe.

"The same thing you've been doing all of your life, we're going to fight."

I glance back at him. He is not kidding. Two against however many.

"Shit, shit, shit", I swear under my breath. "We are not going to win this one, are we? What are they going to do to my sister?"

"I really doubt they're going to kill her. Although..."

"Although, what? Can you bloody finish your sentence?"

"I wouldn't discount them taking her to Arllu."

"What? What for?"

Panic kicks at my ribs. I'm already regretting my decision.

I want to call Baza back.

I thought my sister would be okay, I thought that her soul would be safe as she was not selling it, but now Rafe is telling me this?!

Oh no.

I spin to face Rafe.

"Maybe I should make this deal with Baza? Maybe I should take it?" I plead with Rafe.

My head is ringing. I am swinging on my feet and I can't breathe.

What have I done? What have I brought my sister into?

"Remember that little girl, who saw you?" Rafe whispers, gazing deep at me.

"Huh?"

"In the hotel you mentioned that a girl saw you and your wings?"

"And?"

"Are you telling me that you will be willing to swap your sister for that little girl and for millions of other little children like her?"

His quiet voice is not a match for his livid stare.

Of course not, but... What have I done? I think I might be sick.

I close my eyes for a moment, looking for the strength that I simply don't possess.

"Okay, then we better win here."

Silence.

"We're going to win, right?"

He says nothing, staring back at me.

"We'll do our best", he whispers. "Here we go."

He comes to stand next to me, but I can't draw my gaze away from my sister's face. Her big frightened eyes are on me, looking for reassurance and help and by sheer miracle, I manage to squeeze a smile out of myself.

I hold her gaze for a second longer before I turn back to the grey battalion.

Rafe widens his stance next to me.

I glance at him, pull my sword out and copy his move.

He arches his back, rotates and stretches his shoulders. I copy him.

He clicks his neck while twirling the little sword in his hand. I move my neck, leaving the sword twirling bit out.

"You see", he says without looking at me; his gaze is glued to the grey lethal mass in front of us, "This is precisely why I wanted you to tell your sister everything about us."

I turn back, glancing at my bug eyed sister, standing immobile behind our backs.

Now she stares past our bodies at the grey faceless army.

"Jess", I call to her, but she can't hear me.

"Jessie-boo", I call louder, "look at me."

When she manages the pry her petrified gaze off the angels and look at me, I can see only panic swimming in her eyes.

"It's going to be fine. I promise", I smile, "just stay behind me and Rafe, okay?"

Her slow nod answers me.

I only can imagine how she feels and I doubt she is okay, but as much as I want to scoop her in my arms and give her a tight hug, I know that right now is not the time for that. I'll deal with her mental scarring later.

If there will be any "later"...

Following the silent instruction only heard by them, the wedge of faceless angels shuffles forward.

Only now do I notice that they are a lot closer than they were before.

The front row spreads wider, then breaks in half and angels slide silently to the sides, encircling us. The row behind them takes their place and then slides to the sides just like the ones in front of them. More coming forward, more of them are emerging from the shadows of the woods.

They are silent and barely visible. They are precise and regimented.

Rafe's twirling of the sword looks less impressive now.

Shit. We're done here.

"Shall I start an earthquake? Or make a tsunami? Shit, there is no water..." I ramble on in a hot urgent whisper like I'm possessed. "How about a tornado?"

I don't know any other natural phenomena I can command, and even those I commanded on cue were always a spontaneous response. I don't know if I'll be able to do it now, but I'm willing to try.

"No", Rafe answers, keeping his gaze on the grey ghosts spilling around us. "What's the point? They'll just fly up."

"Maybe rain? Or hail? Lightening? I've never done those, but if it will help..."

"It will affect us as much as them."

"We need to do something", I plead to him. "How are we going to fight all of them?"

Rafe turns his head to me and the penny finally drops.

There's no way we'll outfight all of them.

"I'm going to pull as many as I can towards me. You keep Jess near. When I give you the signal, you grab Jess and go to Uras. There you will seek Domiel and Dumah. I've been in touch with them and they're waiting for you. Stay away from Chamuel, and for An sake, take care in there!"

"Come with us! We can all go to Uras right now", I whisper to him, "I can take both of you."

He darts his gaze to me before returning to his stealth mode.

"Ariel, be serious for a minute. If we all go there, Baza will be right behind us. We wouldn't have the time or space to manoeuvre, but the two of you might have a chance. I will buy you some time."

The grey masked mass has finished shuffling forward, but as I spin to look around, I note that they haven't closed the circle around us. I guess there's no need to encircle such a weak and easy prey.

As if following another silent command, all of the angels as one draw their identical dark swords, raising them above their shoulders at the ready.

A chill touches my spine at the sight of the silent lethality of this battalion.

The identical angels in their identical gear with their identical weapons continue their encircling of us. Even their movements are identical, so robotic and mirrored that for a split second I wonder if these are "real" angels, or maybe just a product of magic, cloning or bionic science. Or maybe they're a result of my crazy imagination and I need to wake up right now.

And suddenly, the next moment, the silent pandemonium erupts, as five angels separate from the front and rush towards us.

They don't cry their battle cries, don't yell instructions to each other. They simply run at us in a complete silence, only twigs snap under their feet and the wind picks up the pace, howling louder.

"Back!"

Rafe shoves me behind him, then takes a long stride forward and throws his sword up to meet an angelic sword of the closest grey angel.

Hypnotised, I stare at the dark blade of the angelic sword.

Its black blade ripples and moves like a black fire and like a fire, it has a blue outline on the blade, and the shades of blue and red playing and interchanging at the tip of the sword.

The two swords collide with a loud hollow sound of a large gong. Two small explosions are born of this collision at the point of impact, one of a pure-white light and one small ball of red fire.

Rafe pushes at his sword, twists his wrist, then his arm, guiding the angelic sword down with his and once it's there, he thrusts his sword into the angel's side.

Without stopping or slowing, Rafe spins and both of his left wings open wide as they brush over a second angel.

The pained and dying cries in two different voices sound with a second delay.

The first angel drops to the ground and a wide, gashing wound opens at the side of the second angel, as blood pours out, washing his grey gear in red, as he stumbles back.

Wow. I didn't know his wings could do that.

But without easing or slowing to admire his handy work, Rafe finishes his spin, tossing his sword into his open left palm while stepping towards the third angel, and the moment his hand closes over the hilt, the sword draws a line in the air from left to right, next to the angel's neck.

When I think that the sword hasn't reached its target, the angel opens his hand, releasing his long black sword, and throws both of his hands to this throat.

The gurgling sound leaves his throat together with his blood through his fingers. His hands are on his neck, trying to stem the flow of his blood, or as if trying to stuff the source of life back in.

I spin to Jess.

Her shocked eyes follow the fall of another body.

The thuds of falling bodies, the whistling of the wind in the trees and Rafe's heavy breathing are the only sounds in the clearing and this dark, unsettling silence tastes like iron.

"Jess, look at me. Look at me!"

She lifts her big wet eyes at me.

"Close your eyes and keep them closed. Do you hear me?"

She gives me a slow small nod and shuts her eyes.

"Keep them closed."

When I turn around, two more angels are strewn on the ground and Rafe holds an extra sword in his other hand, the long black fiery sword from one of the angels, and blood seeps from the shallow cut on his right cheek.

Another group of "greys" break away from the main formation, slithering toward us.

This group is larger than the first and, like silent grey water streaming around a rock, this group separates into two as it comes closer to us. One half zeroes its attention on Rafe while the other half is coming my way.

Shit, shit, shit!

I'll give them one thing: they don't discriminate against girls!

And as they come closer, each group breaks further into two and then a few "grey ones" open their wings and take to the sky, floating just above us and the ground, sealing us inside the dome.

I throw my arm out with my sword, swinging it from side to side and up above me towards the "greys", swatting my sword around me as if I'm swatting flies.

I reach behind me, nudging Jess's body closer to Rafe's, stepping after her, when one of the "greys" takes a fast step towards me. He is like a blur, his moves are faster than the processing power of my mind.

The flick of his wrist is barely visible and suddenly pain erupts at my hip. Stunned, I drop my gaze just in time to see the tip of his sword leaving my body.

Another step forward from another grey soldier and another dive of the black sword towards me, but this time, woken by the pain and led on instinct, I swing my hand and my short sword collides with his.

With my peripheral vision I register another shaded grey body sliding closer to me on my right, and the next second, the reds and blues of the tip of a black sword enter my vision.

My sluggish brain demands a movement from my body, but my body is too slow to react.

That's it.

My brain yells to brace for pain, when suddenly I'm shoved back as someone's elbow jabs at my ribs and losing balance, I fall to my knees.

I lift my head and watch two swords cross and clash above my head. I twist my neck enough to see Rafe's arm above me wielding one of the swords.

But Rafe is too busy to deal with all of them and we are outnumbered. We are surrounded from every side and every corner, we are sealed in by them. But still determined, Rafe twists from side to side, jumps, ducks and dives, blocking assaults from every direction.

Legs sealed in grey armour enter my vision.

They shuffle, stepping closer, advancing on Rafe and without debating any further, I swipe my short sword in front of myself in a wide arch. This trick worked once and I pray for it to work again.

And with a heavy thud and an agonising roar, the body falls to the ground.

He is next to me. His body is inches from mine and I can see the grainy texture of matte diamonds of his protective armour over his legs and torso.

My gaze travels towards his head, away from the growing pool of blood where his legs once were, and breath leaves me and my head swims, when I see a pair of pale blue eyes, framed by blonde lashes, looking at me through the narrow slit in the mask.

He is alive, and he is a human. He is human enough to me for having these eyes and I can't bring myself to do anything else, I just stare at him. I can't move away, wanting to come closer and help, whispering all apologies I can muster and I can't move forward to finish what I so bravely started.

His pale, powdery blue wings spread underneath his body. The tip of his left wing is almost touching the tip of my bottom wing, and I can feel a sweet zap and a tingle of an angelic essence radiating off it.

He is not a lizard, he is an angel, and I wonder why he is fighting for Baza. Or knowing Baza well enough now, I ponder what Baza might have on him.

We look at each other and neither of us saying a word.

Our gazes are locked. Mine is scared and unsure and his is deep and studious.

I can feel a thought behind these intelligent eyes. I can see a surprised flicker of a careful recognition and then a soft of whisper, like fog, slithering into my mind in a soft male voice.

"*So you are truly Uriel*", it breathes out in wonder inside my head.

"*I never thought I would see you again. Do you remember –*"

His words are cut mid-sentence and his eyes fly open in pain before they glaze over in death.

My heart flies into my throat, calling for my usual nauseated response.

I scramble back, watching Rafe pull out a long black sword out of the "grey" angel's heck.

"Grab his sword", Rafe commands and I crawl towards the fallen angel, scooping his sword in my hand.

What does he mean "do you remember"?

Do I know him? Does he know me?

Correction: did.

I sober, but I don't have time to dwell on it or to think, as more of the "grey ones" are filling in for their fallen comrades.

I've never learnt how to wield a sword, and now I'm left to defend and protect myself and my sister in this heavenly world, which belongs to the world of ancient myths and legends, which my clumsy body and scared mind are not equipped to deal with.

Still on my knees, I hold the two swords in my hands, both are so different to one another.

The Mia's short sword shines with a white, almost translucent light and the sword of the "grey soldier" is a light absorbing black blade of rippling fire, with blue and red outline, and a cold black metal hilt.

I'm expected to stand up and fight. I'm expected to stay alive, and right now that means to fight and... win.

Just like these two swords, this life was shoved into my hands. The life, which is born from the different universes, lived in the different times, lived and survived by the different rules. These alien to me "terms and conditions" were flung, shoved at me, just like these magical swords.

This new life doesn't forgive, doesn't give second chances. The second chance in this world is a chance to live another day and then *that day* might be the last.

This new universe is cruel and unforgiving, and this lifestyle is most certainly not for the fainthearted.

This is a primordial universe of elemental, ruthless beings, who resolve any problem with blood. This universe and the human world have absolutely nothing in common.

Now I am in it, gullible, unprepared, untrained, weak. Finally, with all the clarity of bright sunshine, I can clearly see that I will never outrun this life. I see that running will achieve nothing in cutting my ties with this universe. I will never be allowed. I'm chained to this life, chained to my fate.

Somewhere high in the skies – or maybe by a sheer fate – this life was chosen for me, just like the colour of my eyes.

I'll die in this life and in this universe. I will die with it as I'll die with the colours of my eyes, and right now only one thing matters: will I die fighting and die today or will I live to fight another day?

I twist my neck and look up at Rafe, who is a few feet away from me, fighting for both of us. Rafe, who was wiser to accept the inevitable, wiser to accept these chains that linked us.

I bet running from this life would've been easier for him.

Yet he is still here, proving his loyalty to me and to the ancient part of the universe I don't know.

Jess is next to him. Her eyes are still shut while Rafe is jumping, spinning and dancing around her, warding off the attacks of a dozen of black swords.

But he is getting slower.

His breathing rasps heavier and his movements are losing fluidity and speed. The sweat trickles down his temples and fresh bleeding wounds mar his body.

A twig snaps near me and I turn my head in time to see a long black sword descending towards me. I twist sideways, throwing my long sword upwards. And like trains meet at a station running on the parallel tracks, our swords part ways, but mine makes a connection and find its target, sinking into flesh.

Forever chained to my fate, which I can't outrun...

Without a glance at the "grey", I yank my sword out, turning, twisting, rising to my feet.

Another blue fiery tip jabs at me, slicing a few feathers' tips off my wing. Another sword drives forward, and just in time I manage to slide to the side, throwing my sword forwards for protection.

I spin on the spot, erratically throwing my arms and rotating my swords. It's not Rafe's calculated lethal dance, but more of an adrenaline pumped survival jig.

But still, my swords make occasional connections, and now and again the hollow gongs of the clashing swords echo around me. But I'm not managing to ward off every attack, as the shallow slashes and a few stab wounds begin to mark my body and my wings. And I cry out every time as pain blossoms around my body, and tears roll down my face with every wound, but I'm afraid to fall to my knees again. I am afraid that next time if I fall, I will not get up.

The grey circle is tighter around us. A few "greys" take to the sky and hover above us, blocking out the night. Moving the air, their wings produce a whooshing, hissing, strumming sound above us, and now it feels as if we are enclosed by a dome of a swarm of insects.

The dome above us is solid, yet breathing, and alive with the bodies.

Now and again, Rafe throws his arm with the sword above him and then with a cry, a body would crash to the ground, whimper for a bit and die. But his efforts are not enough, we are surrounded and outnumbered.

The wind has quietened down, led by my mood and the slow realisation. Funny how some realisations come too late.

I cry out again when another searing fire cuts at my side, and almost instantly, another fire tears through my wing.

Rafe's agonising roar echoes mine.

I doubt it will be much longer now... Poor Jess. I hope she'll be okay, I hope they let her go.

My bitter experience slaps my naïve mind.

Will they?

And another sickening realisation punches me, stealing my breath.

They are not going to let her go. Baza will see to it.

The memories of the bright light of the Hell lighthouse, of the naked hoarded humans, their agonising screams and of the monsters herding them, flood my mind and I spin around looking for my sister, who still stands behind Rafe with her eyes shut tight, her trust in me is complete.

She trusted me then and she trusts me now. She trusts that I will look after her, that I will protect her, that I will make sure that she's okay. She trusts I will keep her safe.

And suddenly I can't swallow past this glaring realisation and a new, sickening, choking resolution. My mind can barely process it, and it takes a few long seconds, before buzzing words form only one prayer in my head, delivering only one thought: "*I hope her soul will go to heaven...*"

I hope she will be allowed in, even after killing my stepdad. I hope there is a Heaven. And if it is there, I hope Baza will never reach her there. I hope nobody will. I hope she will just be left be. It was always my job to look out for her and I am determined to do it until the end, until *our* end, even when I can't protect her any longer.

I slash and stab around me, spinning in a mad frenzy, trying to save my broken cursed soul from what I've decided to do should we both die. But I'm losing this battle just like so many battles I've lost before.

Suddenly, with a sharp cry, a grey body drops from above, landing somewhere into the depths of the "grey" crowd.

Then another body falls, heavily hitting the ground only a few steps away from me, then the next and the next after. But I can't stop to watch them or even to question this sudden "bird flu" outbreak, I am too busy fighting the greys around me.

But the dome above our heads is thinner now and with a quick glance, I can see a dark milky sky and a solitary star above.

With the last slash at the grey near me, I dart to Jess's side.

"Keep your eyes closed, baby. I'm here." I guide her hand to my waist, "just hold on to me", and I shove the bottom of my sweatshirt into her palm.

A few more bodies drop to the ground like stones with sharp, unexpected cries and I twist my neck, stealing glances upwards. I tuck Mia's short sword at the waist of my jeans, keeping only the long one in my hand, while hugging Jess to me with the other hand.

The angels above us are no longer zoomed in on me and Rafe. They turned their backs to us as chaos entered their ranks.

For the first time since the assault began, they are shouting something to one another, barking in their angelic language, and now and again, a single voice would be cut and then another body would drop.

The pile of bodies littering the ground is growing.

The metallic smell of blood wafts through the air. The blood coats the yellow grass in the clearing, seeping into the ground.

The unexpected attack on the home front has brought discord into the angelic battalion, their advance on me and Rafe is now half-hearted. They swing their weapons at us while stealing glances to the air above, jumping out of the way of another falling body.

A few angels open their wings and take to the sky, eager to find out the reason for the "bird flu" and maybe, plug in the holes.

Rafe sneaks glances upwards as well, while pushing at the ones left on the ground, pressing his advantage, as the wall of bodies around begins to thin out.

"Aaa!" Another grey body crashes to the ground.

Pushing Jess along with me, I shuffle closer to Rafe.

The breastplate and pauldrons of his black tactical gear glisten in the darkness, awash with the earlier rain, and now with blood. Like a glorious lethal dancer, he spins and turns, throwing wide arches with his swords around him.

I push Jess closer to him and cower with her behind his back.

The "greys" are still dropping from the sky and finally, through their weeded out ranks, I can see an unexpected reason for this plague in the form of another "grey" soldier slaughtering his own.

Sealed in a grey matte gear, with his face hidden under a grey mask, he floats above the ground on his four pure white wings, whilst stabbing, slashing, butchering. His two black fiery swords dance through the air and not a single "grey" can outfight or outrun him.

Another cry and another fall of another body to the ground, the crunch of the bones against the ground next to us and more blood.

Jess spins and hides her face against my chest.

"Keep your eyes closed, sweetie", I coo.

Only a handful of "greys" are still standing: two of them are battling Rafe, while three others are floating in the air, trying to bring down the traitor. Now only a few occasional hollow gongs of clashing swords echo around the clearing.

And before long the clearing quietens. The air grows still, as the monotonous November rain settles and the wind dies.

The last body falls from the sky with a sharp cry.

The last "grey" on the ground is battling Rafe, but hearing the fall of the last of his comrades, he freezes for a moment, sweeping his gaze over Rafe, Jess and me. He raises his gaze to the renegade on the white wings above him, then spins on the spot and takes off running into the already black woods.

Rafe yanks me closer to him and steps forward. Both of his swords are raised upwards towards the grey traitor.

The rebel has settled, floating above us on his four wings.

He doesn't rush or dive at us, but waits, probably playing his sick "cat and mouse" game.

He is quiet, studying us through the slits in his mask for a moment longer, before under our cautious gazes, the traitor unexpectedly begins removing his skin tight grey mask.

Chapter 18

"Ta-dah!"

Sam's pretty face is looking down at me.

His arms are open wide and the beautiful arrogant smile blossoms on his lips, resurrecting that gorgeous little dimple of his, as he descends gracefully to the ground.

Sam's blonde hair is dishevelled and a glossy sheen of sweat coats his perfect skin.

"Pagru di mursu sadhu!" Rafe growls next to me, not even trying to hide his hostility.

"Wow!" Sam throws his hands in front of himself, taking an exaggerated theatrical step back. "No need for that."

"The overall performance felt a bit forced, especially the big reveal", the poison drips off Rafe's tongue.

Sam narrows his eyes at Rafe in response.

"If I had hoped to hear anything from you, it would have been 'Thank you for saving our lives and saving the essence of eminent Uriel from being captured and extinguished again!' and not that hostile tirade."

Oh no, here they go again.

"What are you doing here?" I snap at Sam, interrupting this feud before it got out of hand.

"Are you not happy to see me either, Mermaid? Damn! I was hoping for a warmer reception, I must admit."

"Is that your sister?" He changes the subject and takes a step closer, "she does look like you. Only skinnier." He tilts his head to his shoulder, mulling it over for a moment then adds, "like a stray dog."

"Why are her eyes closed? Is there something wrong with her?"

"Nothing is wrong with her", I snap at him. "Jessie-boo, you can open your eyes now, sweetie."

She moves slightly and opens her eyes. She cautiously turns around, glancing over from Rafe to Sam, before taking a small step back, pressing herself closer to me. Her gaze is still locked to Sam's.

"Hello, Jessie-boo. I am Sam. I'm your sister's friend", he says, bending down, resting his hands on his knees and bringing his face to Jess's level.

"Not a friend", I interrupt.

"I think I am a friend", he raises his eyebrow at me. He straightens up and sweeps his arm over the ground, littered with bodies.

Following his arm with her eyes, Jess surveys the clearing for a few long, quiet seconds and suddenly a high-pitched, hysterical shrill rips through the silence.

"Come on, Jessie-boo, come on." I drop to the ground, cooing to her. I turn her around, pressing her face into my chest. "It's okay, it's okay", I gush, "I am here and everything is fine. We are fine. We will be fine. Come on, Jessie-boo, come on."

Sam stands, watching me and Jess with interest, as I rock her, murmuring sweet nonsense to her.

Rafe stands there, watching us for a bit, before without another word, he turns around and walks off, away from us, further into the clearing. He steps over the bodies, bending down over a few of them to pick up an occasional sword or take a mask off a body.

"Remember how you ran away from me after seeing my wings for the first time, Mermaid?" Sam asks, reminiscing.

And when I meet his gaze, the pull of his blue eyes catches me. It sinks its familiar soft claws into me and into my heart. It is strong like a vortex in deep waters and it's pulling me deeper, and I don't want to let go. I don't want to swim up from that depth.

But with a slow blink he releases me, letting me go.

The heat colours my cheeks and I drop my gaze.

Then after a pause he asks, "Can she see my wings? Or yours?"

"No, she can't", I answer, careful not to look at him again.

"But you've told her about *who* you are now?"

That is more of a confirmation rather than a question, and against my earlier resolution, I snap my glaring gaze back to him.

"What is it with everyone and this insistence on telling her about me? What's the rush?"

"Ah, I get it. So I'm not the only one who thinks this isn't a good idea?" he sniggers at me and I'm annoyed even more by the melodic sound of his laugh.

"Mermaid, if I may. You came here to find her", he nods his head at my sister, "and you have achieved it. I'd imagine you had a plan of some sort for what you will do next, and if I know you well enough, I would suggest it was a misguided idea of living on the run with her here, in Apkallu. Only this plan has sprung a leak, a huge leak, if you ask me. Living on the run doesn't work well if everyone is able to find you pretty easily. So, would I be right to assume that you are out of moves and ideas by now?"

I glare at him, saying nothing.

"Am I right?"

He doesn't give up.

I look at Sam, then scan the dark woods, taking in the bodies around us, whimpering Jess and Rafe's back, bent over one of the greys.

I am put on the spot and I feel cornered. It is as if they have been talking behind my back. Like they were discussing my "misguided ideas" and this right now feels like an intervention.

Anger spikes, bringing a wary Rage in tow, who is still skirting around the walls, unsure of the new me.

Of course he is right! They are both right.

Rage nods her head at me, agreeing with me entirely.

Sometimes it feels like they might be reading my mind, but that does not give him, or him, the right to pull me up on it, in nicer words calling me an idiot.

Rage bobs her head at me like a dashboard puppy, the girl is still cautious around me. Fair enough, it's not like I can blame her.

"I didn't plan on it, did I? It just happened. They all just found me somehow. It's not like *I* invited them", I start, but his eyebrows shoot up in a silent, arrogant question and I slam my mouth shut.

"Oh, shut up!" I snap at him, but he just laughs.

A moment later he sobers.

"Ariel, can I please speak to you in private? I know it's very ill-mannered of me to have secrets with company present", he darts his eyes to Rafe and his arrogant smile grows, "so I ask only for a few minutes of your time. Is that okay with you, Jess?"

Exasperated, I sigh, briefly closing my eyes, and nod at him.

"Jess, can you please see Rafe and stay with him for a bit?"

I watch Jess run to Rafe and once she is at his side, Sam takes a few steps away from the tent, away from the pile of the bodies and I follow him.

Suddenly he stops and turns to me, opening his arms wide and before I know, I am swallowed by his warm embrace. His arms and his gorgeous scent envelop me. His hands stroke my back, while his breath caresses the top of my head and I begin to melt, against all my decisions and will. His usual scent of pine and moss, intensified by the wet November woods makes me lightheaded.

I breathe in, relaxing in his arms, soothed by the security and the warmth of his hold.

"I was so worried about you, baby", he murmurs in a hot whisper, stroking my back, "I only heard of the ibnatums' rising once it was done. I'm so sorry that I wasn't there. I didn't know. I wish I could have stayed with you. I was so worried." He strokes my hair and I can feel his head bending, his lips on my forehead.

"I rushed here as fast as I could. Thanks to An's guiding light, I came just in time." His tone changes, when he adds with some steel, "I've asked Rafe to look after you, to keep you safe. He gave me his word! He was told to heal himself, to provide better..."

He takes in a breath, calming a bit and then continues, "But I guess everything has just got out of hand lately and even the archangel can't keep you safe anymore. I don't know what else to do, how else to keep you safe, how else to protect you", he breathes out.

I raise my head, looking up at him. The pull of his eyes and his scent, the warmth of his arms and his embrace... I am falling again.

"I've missed you", he whispers, "I wish that all the craziness would stop for just a minute and give us some time..."

His soft warm lips cover mine.

He tastes of sweet and slightly bitter forest fruits. I taste the wild blackberries on my tongue, just like the ones I used to pick up in the woods behind my house in summer.

My head is swimming and I am drowning in his scent, his warmth, his tenderness, and I want nothing else but to stand like this and think about nothing, care for no one. Just to be myself for a moment, without the ugly past and a messy future.

The crisp scent of pines is exploding in my head like fireworks.

I like him so much...

But the metallic tang of blood slithers onto my tongue and into my head. It covers my yearning for him, bursting that stupid happy bubble, bringing with it the memories of lizards, pulling their human skins off, my sister and the dead body of my stepfather at her feet.

I push at him.

"No. No", I wipe my lips with my thumb, "No, Sam. I am not dealing with this right now."

He looks at me.

"It's all just too much", I shake my head, "too early, too messy, too soon I guess. You're right, it's all getting out of hand here, everything!" I ramble on unsure how to explain, "I can't deal with this as well. The whole angelic thing was thrown on me and I am still finding my way in it all, trying to swim up but every minute I am dragged down by another undercurrent. I'm learning about this whole new world. New creatures, new places and none of it seems too friendly, everyone wants to kill someone else. It's a viper's nest and most of them are after me. Even creatures I've seen only once, from a distance, apparently hold a grudge against me and want to hurt me. I have my sister with me now. I have to look after her, it's not just me anymore."

I take a small step away from him, away from the hold of his scent.

"I don't know who is a friend and who is an enemy. Everyone lies to me." I say that, looking into his eyes. He needs to hear me. Maybe I am stupid, but I am growing smarter now.

"Ariel, I would never –"

Jess's shrill cuts the silence and Sam's sentence.

I spin around in time to watch Rafe's body crash down, face forward, while still hugging Jess's small body and bringing her down with him.

Jess continues to scream, crushed on the ground under Rafe's weight.

We sprint towards them and the first thing I notice is a long slit at the back of his black protective vest and his white pearly skin shining through. But the skin is dimming as blood fills in.

The cut is clean and sharp, curved between his shoulder blades.

Rafe mumbles something, while trying to raise himself up on his arms and get off Jess, but his arms give way and every new attempt looks even weaker than the one before.

Without discussing it, Sam bends down to Rafe as I reach for Jess. Sam grabs Rafe under his arms, lifting him up, as I reach under, pulling my sister from under Rafe and off the ground.

"It's okay, it's okay."

How many times have I said that to her since finding her in the caravan park, holding that bloodied knife? And how many more times will I?

Rafe weakly whimpers as Sam places him on the ground, turning him face up.

I take a few steps closer, pulling Jess along with me.

Rafe wheezes like an old man and his suddenly pale face stands out against the black glossy breastplate of his vest.

"What's happened?" I ask everyone, sweeping my gaze from Jess's face to Sam's, to Rafe's. I let go of Jess and I sink to my knees next to Rafe.

Rafe's white lips move without making a sound.

Incredulous, I look up at Sam, but he says nothing. He just stands there looking at me with pity.

"Jess", Sam says, tugging her to him, "come with me, darling. Your sister needs a minute."

I don't need a minute. Why would I need a minute? What for?

He wraps his arm over Jess's shoulders, leading her away from me and Rafe.

Rafe takes another ragged breath, which expels a sloshing sound from his slashed chest and his lips move once more, this time producing some noise. His voice is weak and barely audible, and I need to lean in to his lips to make out the words.

"Sorry, Ariel. I didn't see him... and when I saw, it was too late. I figured you'd rather have your sister than me."

He takes in another sloshing breath.

"You see, I kept my promise. Even when I told you otherwise, I would have always kept it, Ariel."

My head spins. The heavy dread pulls somewhere at the pit of my stomach. I hear his words, but I refuse to believe what he is saying.

"I know what it means to lose the only one you love, and I would never wish it upon you. No matter how annoying you can be sometimes", he tries to laugh, but only the gurgling wet sound escapes his chest and his throat. "I just didn't want you to think that you have carte blanche on your actions."

He stops for a second and in the silence of the woods, his laborious breathing mirrors mine.

"A profound loss like this tends to kill the soul and I didn't want that for you", he raises his head. He barely manages it, but he keeps it up, needing to tell me something, something that he thinks is important.

I lean closer to him and a fat rain drop falls from above and lands on his cheek.

"Then Baza would have won", he wheezes, "but now he hasn't. I saved your soul. I saved them and us."

These words ring of a goodbye and I can't bring myself to speak.

I can't move my tongue. I don't know what to say. I can't believe it.

Another drop falls next to the first one and only now I understand that it's my tears falling down.

His words, his breathing, his pale lips... It feels surreal like a bad joke, and I want to shake him to tell him to stop mucking about, to stop winding me up.

I'm afraid of what he is saying, or more precise, of what he is implying here, but I'm too afraid to admit it, afraid to assign this moment its ancient name.

"Sam", my voice is a whisper, when I lift my gaze to Sam.

His answering gaze is full of sadness and sorrow and I want to hit him.

Rage is back, swinging her arms, demanding for Sam to keep his dirty lies to himself.

"No", I shake my head, warning him from saying it, warning him off.

"No. Don't even say it. Don't even think it! He can't. He just can't!"

That's not happening to me. Not again.

I'm afraid to be left alone, again.

I am afraid of this abandonment grief that I felt when my dad left, when he just went, without as much as a glance back, leaving his children behind like unwanted toys. I can't feel this again.

I can't be abandoned again. I don't want to be alone again. I don't think I will manage it again and survive in one piece.

Shock, fear and grief are spinning in my head, punching at my chest and I wonder if that's how heart attacks start.

But the sweet denial floods in, saving my sanity. It whispers its reasoning and stories, reassuring and bright, and I have never been so happy to see it and believe any little lie it is willing to give me.

"Aren't you angels, immortal?" I babble to Sam, raising my wet face to him. "You should be immortal. He definitely should be. He was Uriel's soul mate. That must mean something, must count for something, right?"

My words are hot, rushed and hopeful.

I don't want to hear the silence. There's something heavy and solid in it, something final and true and I'm scared of it.

"He can't be killed! He burned his wings in this lava place but he lived. So he must be strong, stronger than others! He said that this place is bad for angels but he lived!"

I plead with Sam, praying for him to agree with me but he just stares at me.

"Stop looking at me! Just stop! Do something!" I yell.

"Ariel, there's nothing I, or anyone, could do now", he whispers.

He glances at Rafe's body on the ground and says: "His essence is gone."

"What?" I look at Rafe's pale face, but I am afraid to touch him.

"I'm sorry, Ariel."

"No! No, no", I lean to Rafe.

Rafe's face is white and looks oddly frozen, and I can no longer hear his raspy breathing or the gurgling in his chest.

"No!" I grab hold of his shoulder and shake him, "come on! Get back! Get back into your stupid body. Come back!"

His body is heavy and rigid in my hands, and his head lolls and flops unnaturally with my violent shakes. But he is not awake, he is not telling me to get off him, he is not swatting me away. He is not telling me how useless I am and how disappointed he is in me.

The "cotton wool" vacuum wraps around my head, dulling my senses, the noises of the woods and Sam's voice.

Only now do I realise that I trusted Rafe more than I knew. He was the only one who was honest and upfront with me. He was the only one who put his cards on the table; only he left me to be me.

The silent vacuum encroaches towards that invisible edge, hangs there, then slowly tips over and begins to ring.

The throbbing grows inside my head, pushing at my ears and it feels as if they are about to burst. This ringing vacuum spreads into my chest and I'm afraid that my chest is about to cave in.

I fall to the ground next to Rafe's body.

I feel in pain and adrift. I am alone, lost in the darkness of what I am now and without him I don't know where I need or should go.

I look at Rafe and the dark grey bodies, littering the clearing past him. If not for Rafe, mine and Jess's bodies would have been among these.

Sam stands beside the battlefield, hugging whimpering Jess to his side. I sweep my gaze over my sister's small body. Still in her outgrown and worn-out blue plaid dress, Jess hugs Sam tight, gawking at Rafe's lifeless body.

"Sorry, Ariel. There's nothing we can do now", Sam says, but I don't listen to him.

I have Jess with me now. I have to be smart for both of us. The luxury of solitude is long gone. The freedom to be an idiot has evaporated. I need to get up and keep on going. I need be strong for her, but I don't know how.

I lift my head up, scanning the dark night sky, covered by thick winter clouds. Maybe my plans before were bad, but right now I don't even have a plan.

Through the clouds, a lonely star plays a "peek-a-boo" with me.

"There must be something", I say to the star. I am not asking Sam. I can hear the craziness bubbling in my voice but I don't care.

Sam stops stroking Jess's hair. He lets go of her and comes over. He squats next to me and takes my face into his hands, turning my face to him.

"There are not many ways for angels to be killed, but once it happens and the essence leaves the body, not much can be done. And his essence has left."

"But my essence was brought back."

I want to argue with him. There must be a way. I am living proof that there is a way. I can't just let go.

"In your instance, Ariel, Ophanims were called upon, who in return decided to bring the essence back", he moves his hand off my face and strokes my hair.

"Can't we call them again? Ask them to bring his essence back?"

I gaze into Sam's eyes, pleading with him. I sound weak and desperate even for my ears.

"No", he shakes his head and his voice is gentle and soft. "The extinguishing of his essence doesn't bring the imbalance to the forces", his pity is loud and clear. "His essence is not that significant. Although he is one of the archangels, his essence is not going to tip the scales. Besides, his essence was already weakened when his wings were seared off in Hannom. He didn't replenish his essence since and it was just a matter of time before they made their move to take him out."

I can't listen to this right now. All my fault, again.

The guilt punches at me, stealing my breath.

My fault. Always my fault.

But there must be something, something, anything.

"There must be something" I plead with Sam.

Again I have no one and it's my fault that I lost one that I had.

241

My chest hurts so much.

"Ariel, nothing can be done now. An essence doesn't just come back. It's not much different from a human life, once the life source is taken, that's it", he says, stroking my hair.

"An essence has been returned, or given, only twice since the beginning of time. Once when An gave a part of her essence to Mik'hael, when he saved her children of Humanity, and the second time when Ophanims brought your essence back. That's it. It's never been done, apart from those two instances."

He strokes my hair, soothing me, but I don't need his pity any more. The hope begins to flutter in my head as his words begin to sink. Maybe that's the way to fix it all.

"Can't I ask An to help again? Maybe she'll help him?" I sit back on my heels.

His eyes look at me with a deep sadness as if I've finally lost my mind, as he softly shakes his head.

"An doesn't get involved anymore, with anything or anyone. She is not going to help you."

I refuse to give up. There must be something that could be done.

"But how did she give her essence to Mik'hael?"

He sighs, shaking his head, but answers, "It worked because they were connected, and they were connected deeply. He was her child. Only a few bonds can be strong enough to share and give an essence. The bond between a parent and a child, and the bond of the soul mates. These strong bonds are the ones that are called "The Twin Flame" or "Great Arcanum", and only these bonds *potentially* can withstand the essence transference or share."

"My essence and his were soul mates", I suggest. At this point I'm open to any idea, no matter how crazy or far-fetched it might be.

I am up on my knees in front of Sam. On the knees, we are almost the same height and his face is just inches away from mine.

"Can't I just give him some of mine?"

I need to do something. I must. I can't let Rafe die because of me. He lost his life, protecting my sister, protecting me. His essence was "weakened" because of me.

He can't die today.

Chapter 19

"Just give him some of mine", Sam huffs, repeating my words and mulling it over as if it is a joke he doesn't understand.

A sad smile pulls at his lips, but the longer he looks at me, the faster his smile perishes.

Sam's eyes bulge at me, as if suddenly I spoke in tongues or grew a second head and sprouted a tail for a good measure.

"You're not serious, are you? Surely, you are not! Because that would be just outright crazy", he barks, calling for my sanity when I can't find any.

The longer he stares at me, the more animated his face becomes. The emotions on his face are slowly churning like wheels stuck in mud. The bafflement and incomprehension gives way to a spark of understanding, followed by shock and disbelief.

The final emotion to arrive in his head and to take over his face is fear, a pure, undiluted fear. His face turns pale under my gaze. Now he sees that I wasn't joking.

The show of emotions on his face is truly entertaining to watch. I've never seen such defined and animated emotions on anyone's face change so fast, and I've never seen such a colourful and broad display of so many of them in just two seconds.

Staring at me, he tries to shake his head, but his moves are so slow and jarred as if he broke his neck or forgot how to move. His bulging big eyes look at me as his white lips move slowly to form a '*No*'.

I can't hear the word, he doesn't make a sound, but I can read his lips, although I don't even need to do that. The '*No*' is written all over his face.

"Why not?"

I wipe at my itchy eyes and wipe my nose with my sleeve. I want to see him better through the haze of my tears.

But I need to hold myself together. Finally, we are standing here and discussing a possibility, a plan, a magic miracle solution, no matter how small or far-fetched, which might bring Rafe back. And now finally, I feel a tinge of hope stirring inside.

"What's the big deal?" I snap at him as he still says nothing. "You just said it yourself that it can be done. We have everything we need for it", I begin to list, folding my fingers. "Mine and his essence were soul mates, flames of whatever thingy, that's one. My essence is one of the larger ones, so I don't think I'll miss some of it, that's two. I don't know if it matters, but my essence was the daughter of An, who gave her essence to someone else, so this whole thing should work, that's three. So the only questions left for us are how are we going to do it and how much to give."

But it seems that I'm talking to a frozen statue with a disbelieving face, as Sam sits immobile and doesn't utter a word.

"No", he croaks eventually. The statue has finally found a voice.

He clears his throat and punches at his chest with his fist to dislodge the shock.

"No!" he barks. "No, no, NO!" he roars now.

The weird sense of déjà vu comes over me, as I watch him wailing the 'NO' as I was, just a minute ago.

"You can't do this", Sam screams, grabbing my shoulders and shaking me. My head lolls.

I push his hands away and wrestle out of his hold.

"What you mean 'I can't'? You just told me that it can be done and in fact it was done by the people, sorry, angels! who are related to my essence. I don't know, related, spawned from, people, angels, whatever", I bark. "Is my essence strong enough to bring Rafe back or not? Is it large enough to give him some of mine? I think the answer is "yes" on both counts."

I'm baffled. I don't bloody understand where he is going with it. I don't understand what his problem is, but more to the point, I really hate when someone tells me what to do!

"That's not the point!" he roars.

"For God's sake", I roll my eyes upwards, "Why is that not the point? Can you just follow through and keep on bloody topic? You said and I do quote", I do a 'bunny rabbits' with my fingers in front of him, "not much can be done for him now. Only the essence transference can bring him back."

I'm annoyed now and the louder he yells, the angrier and louder I go.

"I don't understand you. One minute you say that a large essence, *like mine*, can bring him back, that potentially it can be done, and the next second you tell me that I can't do that! What the hell?" I glare at him.

"If there is even a slither of chance, I'll take it!"

Now we are both yelling, glaring at each other like two angry goats.

"What you are talking about, what you are trying to do is not something to play with. It's dangerous, it could end badly. But more to the point, you will lose a part of your essence, maybe half! Yes, your essence is large, but it's not infinite! You will no longer be as strong as Baza, but even that is not the main problem. You no longer will be equal to Mik'hael! You will be weaker than him! That essence transference may as well kill you now, because after it's done you will be as good as dead."

He takes in a sharp breath and closes his eyes. I know when someone is exasperated with me, the routine hasn't changed much.

He exhales, opens his eyes and takes my face in his hands again, leaning in closer. The fierce light dances behind his eyes.

"You don't understand what you are saying. You don't understand what you're offering to do. You don't understand the impact it will have on you and everyone else on every plane of existence!" he whispers.

"Sam, it's you who doesn't understand. I don't often make sound decisions. In fact more often than not my decision-making sucks, but this essence, this..." I gesture to my chest, "what happened to me, it is a mistake. It was always a mistake. I don't have a right to this essence. And I am not the best person to have it. Not the smartest or the wisest, with all my past... I know it was a mistake."

I need him to understand.

"You know, "easy come, easy goes"? It's about this as well. This essence is not mine. I don't have any claim to it. With everything that happened to me, I should have been dead a long time ago. In fact, I am surprised I'm still here.

"Rafe has more rights to this essence than I do. The essence was always a part of him, it was his. It was attached to his essence, and I always felt as if I stole it somehow. But the main reason, the main issue", I pause, waiting for him to hear me, to understand me, "it is Jess. Rafe kept his promise to me twice and I know that if anything ever happens to me, he wouldn't leave her. Now I'm convinced that he wouldn't break his promise to me. I know that he wouldn't abandon her.

"I don't want her to be abandoned and discarded like I was so many times. I don't want her to feel as unwanted, disposable and...

dirty as I felt. I want someone to be there for her, someone, who would care for her, someone strong and reliable, someone who will give her a hug and will make her feel less scared and alone. Someone who will protect her."

I raise my hand and softly touch his cheek. His skin next to mine is velvety and warm, and I want to stay like this forever, looking at his beautiful face while losing myself in his bright blue eyes, watching as a soft wind strokes his blonde hair. I want to feel him next to me.

But instead, I pull my hand away.

"And quite frankly, I wouldn't bet on my long-term survival in here", I smile at him and glance at the battlefield behind him, "essence or not, I need to think about Jess."

I try to lift the mood a bit. "How cool will it be if she had her own, personal, real life guardian angel?"

But he doesn't crack a smile and his dimple is nowhere to be seen.

"Sam, if I disappear, no one will notice, apart from Jess, and no one would care. And if we are being completely honest with ourselves, my chances of surviving this whole angelic mess are pretty slim. I know it and you know it, and it is okay", I rush before he interrupts me, "it could have been much worse. All that we're talking about right now is death, and it's not the worst thing that can happen to someone. I can promise you that."

He released my face a while ago, and now his hands rest on his knees as he watches me.

I shuffle closer to him until our knees touch. I want to be closer to him. I want his scent to fill my lungs again. I want to taste the blackberries of his lips. If he is right about this turning out badly, then right now, it would be my last time so close to him.

But I don't reach for a kiss. I just stay where I am.

I breathe in and out, gathering my strength to tell him my plan in full. I can't unravel now. If he sees me weak, he will try to persuade me against this idea and I know that I will let him. I am scared.

"If I survive the transference, I will need him to help me fight and teach me how to survive. My chances for survival with him are there", I raise my hand above my head, "and without him are here", I sweep my hand an inch above the ground.

"I need to do it for Jess, for myself, and even if I lose the essence, it still might be the best outcome for everyone."

Even for you, and me.

I reach to him and lay my hands over his chest. I keep my hands there for a few seconds, enjoying his warmth under my hands. Finally, he looks at me and he... hears me.

"Sometimes we are given that one big chance in life, the chance to make a difference, a difference for ourselves and for others. But not always can we see it, not everyone can spot this chance. But if the chance was given to you and you have managed to see it in full, it's always up to you to seize it and find the bravery within yourself to take that step."

His eyes are on me. His pull, his scent, his warmth... I wish everything was different. I wish I was different, maybe less broken and screwed up.

"I know how incredible it was for me to receive this essence, even if I didn't want it, but now I need to be smarter about it and realise when it's time to step back."

I pull my hands away and sit back on my heels.

"But you are not giving away the essence", Sam croaks and his voice doesn't sound like his. He shakes his head at me, "you are talking about *splitting* it. If you survive the transference, which is a big "if" by the way, you will be weaker for battles to come. Can you trust him", he nods his head at Rafe's body, "not to betray you in these battles? Would you trust him to have your back? Would you trust him not to betray you by joining Mik'hael? Because that would be the end for you."

"I know. But I have to trust someone. I've trusted you." I say it, letting it hang there for a second.

I force my lips into a smile. I can't go there, not again and not now, but I read a new sadness in his eyes and I know that he knows what I mean.

"Okay", he nods.

I lean into him, stealing a quick kiss. His lips are soft and warm and the scent of pines sings in my head and I can taste blackberries on my lips again.

I want to stay for longer. For a fleeting second I close my eyes and imagine that none of these angelic things even exist. I imagine that I don't have to fear lies and scheming games, I imagine myself prettier, happier and less broken, and him loving me for no reason, just because it's me.

I let my ridiculous wishful thinking ride for a bit longer, as I know that it's either not going to be much longer for me, or at the very least, after this "transference" I will lose the substantial chunk of my essence, and with it, my appeal to him.

And that will be fine too.

"Thank you", I whisper into his lips.

I pull away.

"So how is it done, then?"

He takes a deep breath, gazing at me, "if you're sure."

I nod.

"Okay. Have you had any Uriel apparitions lately?"

"Apa – What?"

"Is Uriel still around? Can you feel her? Can you hear her? Did she manifest herself at all?"

"Yeah, when the lizards came at me, I think she took over and was talking to them, as there was no way I could've known these things or could speak that language. And then she killed them all," I mumble. "She was inside my head, talking for me, moving for me. She just took over."

"So she is still around. Not like I'm surprised, mind you", he shakes his head. "I didn't think she'd leave him behind."

He rises to his feet, takes a few steps away, then turns around and marches back, deep in his thoughts.

"Sam", I call to him.

He snaps his gaze back to me.

"The best way to go about it, and to make sure that everything is done safely and you're not dead by the end of it, is to let Uriel take over and perform the transference. On the plus side, I would imagine she knows how to do it. Also, the good thing is that you are unlikely to lose the entire essence, as Rafe's essence was never as big as Uriel's. But there is one large, glaring negative in it all, you will have to submit yourself to her control."

"So, do you think she can do it?" I rise to my feet.

"I don't know", he snaps at me, "I never met An or Mik'hael and as a result, never had a chance to ask either of them how these things are done. And there is no manual on the essence's transference, so I'm flying blind here."

Woah, horsey! Chill, man.

"Sam, it's me who may be dead by the end of it, not you", I point out.

"I'm sorry, Ariel. It's just... I'm not sure how to do what you've asked me to do. And apart from you relinquishing yourself to Uriel's mercy, I have no idea how to go about it and it frustrates me. You're not listening to the voice of reason. You're dead set on going through with it and I can't convince you to rethink."

He stops, looking hopeful, "are you sure you want to do it? Why not just leave it?"

I shake my head and he exhales.

"Thought so. In this case, if you're dead set on doing it, your best bet is to step back, bring Uriel to the forefront, let her take control and pray to An that she knows what she's doing."

"How do I do that?"

"I don't know. How did she come to the forefront last time? What did you do then?"

"She came when I nearly got captured by the lizards", I answer.

And maybe, it was her sabotaging my wings when I nearly killed myself.

But I don't tell him that.

"And before that, it was in the cave in that fiery place, when she wanted to kiss Rafe", I mumble under my breath, gauging his reaction.

Slowly, his eyes fill with blood and his jaw begins to move, straining the tendons on his neck.

"Damu mursu sadhu", he seethes under his breath, and his voice shakes with such raw anger as he practically spits these words out.

He marches to the nearest tree and punches at the trunk.

The hundred year old pine tree groans, receiving the punch, squeaks, and then, with a piercing splitting noise, the trunk begins to crack and a moment later the tree falls, miles away in the distance, deep in the woods, raising a cloud of screaming birds.

His hands ball into fists at his sides and I'm afraid of him, of him hitting me.

I take an involuntary step back away from him.

But he just glares at me for a few seconds before spinning on the spot and walking away from me.

"Sam?" I call after him.

Where is he going? What's going on?

"As we don't have lizards at our disposal, and you are bloody set on going through with this ridiculous thing, you might need to kiss Rafe in order to entice Uriel to the forefront."

"What? I don't want to kiss Rafe!" I shake my head, stupefied. "And besides... he is dead!"

I glance at the unmoving body next to me.

"I don't want you to kiss Rafe either!" Sam glares at me, closing the distance between us, "finally we are agreeing on something. So are you happy to leave this whole idea alone?" There is hope in his voice.

I turn my head and scan the world around me, the world that is my world now. The world with the bodies of angelic assassins, the angry beautiful angel in front of me, the dead one on the ground and the stupefied Jess, who is quietly rocking herself where she stands as her lips move without making a word.

I take a breath and close my eyes for a second, steadying myself: "No, I need to do it."

I don't look at Sam. I spin away from him and walk over to Jess.

"Jessie-boo", I hug her tightly to me, "I love you, Jessie-boo. I love you", I whisper.

I rock her and begin to sing softly in her ear, so it's only her who would hear the song, which is intended only for her.

"Under the sky
Here I lie,
Under the sky
My sister and I.
Trees above us and the bottomless sky
Here we'll live – my sister and I."

Her little body shakes next to me, but I need to get on with this essence transference crap.

"Sam, can you please hold her?" I snap at him.

I want to be the one holding my sister, and it's not his fault for all the mess I am in, but I'm a bit busy right now, gambling our lives away.

Sam comes over and I turn Jess to face him, pushing her closer into his awkward embrace. Like a puppet master directing a doll, I raise his arms, one at a time, and wrap them around Jess.

Sam's grey breastplate and pauldrons are cold and rigid, and Jess looks uncomfortable as if hugging a fridge, but right now he is all we've got.

"Can you please stay with her?"

Sam just nods.

I kiss the top of Jess's head, turn on the spot and march to Rafe's dead body.

I kneel next to him, looking for the courage to touch his body.

Okay, just get on with it, Ariel.

Yes, life is shit; it is unfair and full of crap we don't want to do! But you know what, Ariel? Suck it up!

Just suck it up and get on with it! Save your whining and complaining for someone else and just get on with it!

I close my eyes, breathe in and out, and again, gathering the nerve to push for the last step.

I don't think Uriel will be far away, she probably felt my despair when Rafe died.

Still on my knees, I shuffle closer to Rafe's body.

I reach out and take his face in my hands. His skin is still warm under my hands.

I imagine him sleeping like he was in the cave. I imagine kissing his warm lips like Uriel wanted me to do then.

I force myself not to pull my hands away. I can't afford to be weak now. I lift my gaze to Jess. She is snuggled in Sam's embrace, with Sam's murderous face above her head glaring at me.

Okay, Uriel, you better get your butt in here and get this sorted pronto!

With another deep breath like that of a diver before a jump, and before I get cold feet and change my mind for good, I close the distance between our faces and my lips touch Rafe's.

Come on, Uriel. Where are you? Get your arse in here! It's your boyfriend I'm trying to resuscitate!

I'm looking for her inside of me, when a weak whimper, followed by a cry, resonates at the back of my skull, echoing somewhere deep in my head and my heart.

Chapter 20

*H*ere she is.

I call her to me, enticing her to come forward, and in answer to my call, her cries rise inside my head with the force of an upcoming tsunami and her sorrow threatens to engulf me.

Wispy white shadows dance behind my closed eyes. The thin tendrils of the living white vapour swerve and bend, wrapping themselves around each other, merging and dissolving the next second. They move in, gliding forward, as if blown towards me by a wind. They slither like snakes and bend like stalks of wheat in a field. Some of them are multiplying, when a few thin white slivers split in the middle lengthwise. Their numbers are growing and their bodies thickening.

And the louder the cries grow, the thicker grows the vapour.

The vapour is solidifying. It's no longer a wispy fog, now it feels material like cotton wool and I think if I reach out, I will be able to touch it.

When the cries turn into heart-wrenching wails, the white fog morphs to form the outline of a female face.

The moment is finally here. That's what I've been calling for but I am scared, regretting it now.

My hands and arms are locked, holding Rafe's head and I can't command my body to move, I can't pull my lips away from his.

I feel powerless and bound to Uriel's mercy.

In my head I think I'm thrashing out of her hold, regaining my independence and self-control, but actually I don't manage to move a muscle. I am disconnected and detached from my body, suddenly watching my body from the sidelines. It is as if I am trapped behind thick glass and I cannot break through it.

I can hear myself hyperventilating in my head, but not a sound escapes my lips, still sealed to Rafe's.

The female face, constructed out of the fog, is now clear and defined.

I can see a slim face with high, slightly flat cheekbones, betraying some Asian descent. Her nose is slim and straight, and the corners of her full lips are drawn down and her eyes are shut as she cries.

Her thick hair is plaited and pinned in a crown atop of her head but I can't tell the colour of her hair, her skin or her lips, as she is made entirely out of the white fog.

Her ethereal face grows and expands, rushing towards me like an approaching freight train and I know that her force will crumble me just like the force of a train would.

Her face charges at me and when her foggy face is only an inch away from mine, her eyes fly open.

If I had any control left over my body, I would scatter and try to disappear as I look into the black and red abyss of a living searing fire, into the oceans of blood and black, light consuming emptiness, but I can't move a muscle.

And the next second I stop breathing, swallowed by the abyss and my life stops.

∞ ∞ ∞

I wake surrounded by a glowing soft milky haze.

I feel warm and snug as if wrapped in a weightless duvet.

The haze is above and around me, and I'm startled at the realisation that this living haze is under me as well and I don't have solid ground under my feet.

I look down.

I don't have feet, I don't have a body and all that I can see is a milky fog.

I am the milky fog!

Panic. The crippling panic takes over.

The pressure rips, rupturing me from within and I open my mouth and wail, but not a sound comes out. My mouth of mist is frozen in a silent scream.

Slowly, as if through a thick barrier or a wall, my sobbing voice comes to me.

I can recognise my voice, but I can't understand why it comes from a distance or why it doesn't scream in time with my panic.

My voice softly whimpers, rumbling incoherent nonsense in an unknown language. My voice says the words I haven't uttered. My voice echoes around me, living a life of its own.

"Rafael, *ki zalag-um*, my love, why would you do this? I asked you to be careful. I asked you to be wise for both of us", my voice whimpers behind the thick glass. "It is a long road to walk, especially on your own, and you couldn't have saved every abandoned dog along the way."

I can feel Rafe's hair against the skin of my palm. I can feel the softness of his skin on mine when my hand slides over his and I can taste the salt of my tears on my lips.

It is the weirdest of feelings. I feel disjointed and distant.

Through this glass wall, I can see myself leaning closer to Rafe's dead body, kissing his lips. My hands are all over his face, stroking his skin, his hair. My hands sneak behind his back and feverishly dance over tip of his wing. I'm touching Rafe as a blind person, who is learning the world by the touch.

But it's not me who is touching him. It's not me, who is crying, mourning lost love.

Powerless, I'm locked inside the glass box, unable to do anything to affect the outside world in any way. I want to throw my fist and punch at that glass wall, but I am an incorporeal fog and I can't do anything.

"I knew they'd come for you, but I prayed to An that it would be much later", my voice whispers. "I spent every moment of my time in Udhad praying you'd keep yourself safe. I always knew that the call of honour is strong in you but..." She falls quiet for a moment.

"Oh An, how much I hoped that self-preservation would be greater."

My hands travel over the plastic of his black breastplate. I see my white fingers with short bitten nails tenderly stroking the surface of his protective gear.

My hair falls around my face as I lean and kiss him again.

But I see my hair much further ahead from myself, as if I've taken a back seat, and this is a very unsettling feeling.

His lips are now even colder than they were before.

I pull away from him, raising my head, zooming in on the one I am looking for.

"Samael", my voice rings with steel above the dead silence of the clearing. "What are you doing in here?" I demand with an authoritative right that no one would be dumb enough to question, and Sam is not that dumb.

He raises his right hand, pressing his four fingers to the middle of his forehead and bows slightly.

"Uriel, it is an honour to see you. I hope that Udhad is not too dull for your liking."

He says polite words, but the arrogance and challenge are dripping off his tongue, and even I know that these words were chosen carefully to provoke something in Uriel.

But she doesn't acknowledge his challenge.

"What are you doing in here? And what do you want with the shell?" she demands. Wait! No, *I* demand. No, Uriel demands in my voice.

I listen to this exchange. But what is the *"shell"* and where is it?

Jess is still glued to the Sam's hip, now gaping at me with her large and frightened eyes.

"Beyelai", Sam answers, bowing down but keeping his mocking gaze on me, or should I say *her*? "Since when did my frolicking become of interest to you?"

"Since the moment the shell inherited my essence, everything concerning her became of interest to me", she snaps. "She is me now and I will not tolerate her allying with your kind."

Wait. Am I "the shell"?

"With all due respect, Uriel, it is much too late for these proclamations. You have relinquished the hold on this shell, and your essence is under her command now", Sam answers with another light bow.

"Although", he continues a moment later, narrowing his eyes at her, "have you relinquished the hold or were simply overpowered by a mortal? I wonder..."

My hands ball into fists by my sides.

But Uriel is not the only one who is angry right now.

I'm livid as well. All these demands on me from day one, all of the expectations, survival and suffering, and yet still to her and to all of them, I am just a "shell"?

I let her come forward. *I* have allowed her to do this. Without me calling on her, welcoming her and allowing her to the forefront, she would still be in that hell hole, where she came from.

I called on her to help to save *her* boyfriend, her soul mate and that is what I am getting as a "thank you"? To be told that I am only the lowly "shell" to her, who should be told what to do and who to ally with? She thinks that she is still in charge. She still thinks that she is the Mighty Uriel, thinks she still calls the shots?

I'll show her "the shell"!

The anger mounts inside of me.

Rage gingerly pokes her head above the line of trenches she has dug for herself. My good mate nods in agreement but since that incident in the clearing near the caravan park, she is wary of me.

The silent scream freezes on my lips but the anger pushes like a slow rising explosion from somewhere within my haze, somewhere at the core of me.

I want my body back.

I will not give my life to anyone ever again, not without a fight, and they had all better wish that I am dead this time.

I bawl and my milky haze starts to vibrate, ringing like a pinched guitar string. But the guitar string is thin and weak and the noise is barely audible but my haze is getting louder, it refuses to stay behind and be silenced. It pushes to the forefront, demanding to claim what is mine.

My vibrating haze fills the glass box. It expands, bringing a deeper sound with it, and with it mounts the pressure within the box, which slowly turns into a pull, a suction.

My haze is expanding by *sucking* something into my glass box with me.

The suction grows stronger with the noise, and suddenly, as if an elastic string was released, something slams into my haze.

Suddenly I feel another presence in my glass box with me.

It feels as if my haze is mixing with someone else's. Mine and the stranger's hazes brush against each other as they whirl and spin. I'd imagine that's how a goldfish might feel, when another fish is dropped into a small glass jar with her.

Only it feels as if I am sharing a jar with a predator, or a piranha.

But that's okay too, it is not the only predator in this jar.

The haze around me is agitated and angry.

It lurches, twirls and spins, bouncing from wall to wall of my glass box, slicing through the air, looking for a way out and every time it rushes past me I can hear a female shriek and see a glimpse of Uriel's distorted face.

Her face is a frozen mask of agony with her eyes wide open in shock and her mouth frozen in a scream.

She pounds at the walls of our glass box, erratically swinging, but the walls of the box are too thick and she bounces off again, this time rushing at me.

"*You*", she shrieks and my ethereal haze flies into a corner.

"Put me back! Release me forward immediately! I need to save him. I will take all of your essence and give it to him if I must, but he will not die today."

"It is all of your doing", she screeches and her mist comes forward, condensed, forming a clearer outline of her face. "His death is on your hands! If you were not so irresponsible and weak, not so pathetically human, he would still be alive."

She yells and thrashes around me and my haze rips as if caught in the blades of a propeller.

"He is all that I have left! He is all that *you* have left! There's no one else who would help you and take your side the way he did!

You already killed him once and now you're killing him again", she shrieks.

She spins around me like an angry wall of a tornado and her haze begins squeezing mine. Her haze moves faster, gathering the speed, and it's now strangling me.

"None of it would have happened were it not for you. None of it would have happened if you were not so weak, so... human!"

She seethes, spitting the last word at me. I bet for her it is an insult.

But I am done taking it.

I fly at her haze, ripping it in two.

"Human? Human?!" I yell.

"Better to be a human than back stabbing, smarmy, scheming angels that you all are. Care for nothing, anything or anyone but yourself. Selfish, greedy! Thinking that you're just so-o-o much better than us. Everything and everyone might as well rot in hell as far as you are all concerned. Humans are just cattle to you, pets, toys, pawns for you to play your perverted games with! All our sufferings are just a joke to you, a funny game you watch to entertain yourself. And if the game is too boring, then why not go down there and stir up some shit? Why not make their lives even worse than they already are?"

I finally say all that I wanted to say for so long, to all of them, but she is a good point to start.

Her black eyes grow wider and angrier the longer I speak.

"Don't you dare even think about lecturing me!" she roars, and the walls of our glass box vibrate.

"Me! Me? Of all angels?! I was the one who always stood by you, who stood behind you, supporting your kind, ignoring the stupid childish games you were playing with each other. I stood beside your kind through all of your small minded wars, through every plague. It was me who led you to many of your discoveries that you enjoy so ravenously now. For centuries I was there for you, protecting you, helping you to grow your knowledge, sometimes even against my better judgements. It was me, *me!* who stood between humanity and every Arllu ruler and I stood up to my family for you!

"I was willing to sacrifice my life for you all! I am the one who stood up for your free will, the will to make choices, and what have you done with it? What have you done with my gift?! You chose to kill, rape, abuse, steal, cheat. You have created Hell on Earth. You, humans, did it! Not angels! *You!*"

The memories of my life before angels rush in, giving me a sobering slap.

She is right. I wasn't hurt by angels. Humans did that to me.

And my anger subsides, giving way to embarrassment and regret.

"But I am still not your shell to command", I bristle, hanging on by a thread to the fight I started so stupidly.

"And I never expected you to be. I never asked for it. I stepped back releasing my essence into your hold. I no longer have any command over you, nor did I have to begin with. I gave my life to protect humanity's free will, why would I stop now?"

"But what you said to Sam..." I mumble, embarrassed at my rushed decision to pull her into the box with me.

"I said that because I know his kind better than you do. He is fallen for a reason. Their morality was compromised. While some of them were exiled, some actively chose to sell their Qal, just like some humans did, and the fact that he is in Baza's service means that he sold his Qal to Baza."

She sighs.

"I am trying to protect you and my essence", she is calmer now, but more irritated. "For someone who suffered as much as you had, you are very naïve, Ariel."

Her urgent haze stirs around me, still held inside the box by the force of my haze.

"Ariel, you need to release me now, I need to save him while I still can. The time is running out and the longer we wait, the harder it will be for the essence to attach itself to the body. Please let me save him", she pleads with me.

She is right, I am naïve. And I am about to trust her implicitly right now.

As if sensing my doubt she adds, "Please release me, Ariel. I swear to An and on the eternal shine of my Qal that I will not take more than I need to save him. I promise you, I swear on my Qal, you're making the right decision saving him, for yourself and for your kin."

Too naïve, too trusting.

I release my hold on her haze. I float back, towards the farthest corner of my glass box, telling her to go.

Chapter 21

$\mathcal{M}$ y body leans into his. My lips hover above his, as my voice, commanded by Uriel, begins to chant.

"Em-nam kud Anshar, wabalu seru ina ditallu Qal Rafaelsu ihtan anu Isnarkabtu Shiimti ak essentu-uri. Cacama", she whispers above him, her breath brushes his lips.

She draws in a sharp breath.

"Em-nam kud Anshar, wabalu seru ina ditallu Qal Rafaelsu ihtan anu Isnarkabtu Shiimti ak essentu-uri. Cacama", she repeats these words again, releasing her breath into his open mouth.

She takes in another breath and repeats these words again, and again, and again, releasing her warm breath into him.

And slowly these words find the pulsating rhythm of a tribal song, and when they do, she begins to mumble faster, hotter and more urgent, until the words turn into a pulsating chant.

These words are fluid like water and soothing like cool silk. Her quiet shamanic voice, my voice, is getting quieter and smoother with every new word. The tone of her voice changes, becoming evanescent and ephemeral. Her voice dissolves the words into the air and I can no longer hear this chant with my ears. Instead I hear and feel it with my... haze.

My haze throbs with these chants. These chants are pulsating inside me. My haze vibrates and hums with her words.

I have never heard these words before in that alien language, but I can understand them. Somehow, I know them now and I know of their power.

Reality begins to shift around me.

I no longer see the usual world past my glass wall. In fact, the glass walls of my box are now gone, dissolved, and unrestricted, my haze floats unstoppable into the world.

But the world is no longer there, or at least, it's not the world I know.

The world around my haze morphs and pulls away, stretching at the sides. It's not the breathing and living world I know. It looks like a photograph, like a picture frozen in time.

And when my drifting haze, released from the box, hits that photograph, my haze like acid begins to dissolve the world and reality begins to bubble and hiss, disappearing under my stunned gaze.

The world around me is eaten away by my essence and I can't stop it. I float around, spreading like a misty fog on a cold morning and consuming the world like a virus.

Everywhere that I've eaten away at the reality, I leave behind a dark grey empty vacuum.

And the more I consume, the wider grows the vacuum and the stronger grows its pull. Under the vacuum's pull, the wisps of my haze rip off me, one sliver at a time, sucked into that grey emptiness.

My acidic mist spreads, creeping, crawling, towards where Sam and Jess stand.

I try to yell at them, trying to warn them, but I don't manage to produce a sound. I push at my haze, but I can't stop it and the image of them disappears under my horrified gaze and I scream again, afraid of what I have done.

I want to stop my haze from eating at the world, but the chanting words vibrate around me, taking over and creating the stronger pull from this growing, empty, grey vacuum.

My gossamer head is filled with the chants and the hissing noise of the dissolving reality.

The grey nothingness encroaches, erasing the last images of the world and I swear I can smell the stench of that fiery place, the stench of rotting eggs and ammonia, and my shocked mind weakly wonders how I've ended up in that fiery place again.

But all that I can see and feel around me is the grey vacuum.

And the growing vacuum tugs harder.

It rips off wisps of my milky haze and pulls them into a vortex of the grey oblivion, and the larger and stronger it gets, the thicker the chunks of haze that are leaving me. And thicker the chunks, the more it hurts. If at the beginning, it felt small and annoying, like a mosquito bite, now the pain resembles a feeling of a few hair strands being pulled out, and it's increasing.

I want it to stop. I want the oblivion to leave me alone and let me be.

I'm afraid to be swallowed by that grey emptiness, afraid to be destroyed like candyfloss, torn bit by bit by a child's hand, and to become nothing more, just a memory.

And I scream. But even my scream turns into another silent and floating tendril of fog, which disappears inside that grey bottomless hole.

The chants vibrate the air, the grey oblivion and my haze with it. My haze hums like a string.

The pain descends over me, ripping me apart and I can't do anything to stop it.

I agreed to it, but now, as my gauzy white essence breaks and it's worse than any physical pain I've ever experienced, I wonder if that was my last bad decision and I am about to die.

The white chunks of my essence are torn off, leaving behind the bleeding and weakened soul and there's less and less of me left with every pull. I cry, I weep, I wail. I am hurting.

That must be it. That is probably what death looks and feels like.

The shredding pain is now gone, giving way to a weak and sombre ache.

I close my eyes, relinquishing myself to the vibrating chants and pain.

∞ ∞ ∞

The chants suddenly stop. The vibrations stop and the grey oblivion ceases its pull.

The silence and emptiness ring around me.

"Get up, Ariel. It's over now."

A tendril of creamy smog floats around encircling my weak haze. It dives around me, waiting for me to wake up.

This tendril is warm and soft, and a golden shimmer comes off it that my haze doesn't have. This tendril is like a ray of warm yellow sunshine, reflected by dozens of crystals and suddenly I can smell ripe fruits and sea salt of the ocean.

"My gratitude forever will be yours", Uriel's voice echoes around me. "Until end of days, for as long as An's light shines in Sarukh or until the last shine of my Qal, whichever one may come first, I will always remember your sacrifice. I pledge my true bond and I swear my eternal loyalty to you until Udhad brings us both to nought. My oath should be witnessed by all."

She stops speaking, but I still feel her presence around me.

"I will never forget what you have done today nor will I ever be able to repay you in full, but I swear my support to you, for as long as I live", Uriel quietens for a moment, "or until Udhad swallows the last of me."

She floats around me, stroking my haze with hers.

"Ariel, my essence is yours now and trust me, I have made my peace with it", she says, "in fact, I would not be able to take it back no matter how hard I might have tried."

"But heed my warning, child. With this essence, you are me now. All of my previous battles and all of my earlier wars are now yours to fight. All my promises and oaths are yours to keep! All that the essence had sworn on is yours to fulfil. All my sworn allies and foes will come to you to collect their debts, and I am sorry for that.

"I am sorry that you are left to play my game and I'm sorry that you are hurt. I would never have wished it upon an unprepared one, but the fate of Ophanims was delivered and the road was mapped. Everything that this essence is, it is you now. The path can't be changed nor can the journey be annulled. From now on you have the power to steer your fate, but you have no power to change what you are. You are the essence now. You are me, the primeval archangel."

I can feel a soft stroke on my cheek.

With her every new word, I want to cry.

Maybe these are tears of relief after the pain, maybe her words are finally sinking in, I don't know which one... But all that I want to do right now is to tell her that all of it is a big mistake, and that there must be a way out.

But deep down I know that if there was a way for her to get her essence back, she would have taken it by now. I know that Rafe would have found a way to bring his soul mate back. If there was a way for Rafe and Uriel not to rely on a weak human for their politicking games and battles, they would've taken it.

I hear the truth in her words and I know that I am here to stay, or at least for as much as the essence is concerned.

The path can't be changed...

The next heartbeat punches at my ribcage with the sobering realisation that I knew it all along, just didn't want to believe it. I was lying to myself, imagining a way out, hoping to outrun it all, pretending, playing games.

"You are what you are, and you need to find a way to accept it. You need to accept the whole of you, because it's all that you will ever have. You are the only being that is forever with you and the only one you will never outrun. You are forever with yourself, until the last breath leaves you, escaping into Udhad, and it will be a miserable existence if you don't accept yourself, *all* of yourself."

She brushes around me, warms me.

"And forgive", she breathes.

My weak haze ripples, breaking in many places at once like fine lace under strain.

"The essence might have commanded *what* you would become, but it's your decision *who* you'll be", Uriel's voice whispers.

"The long path ahead of you is far from over. But you can shape it and you can lead it. I've been listening through Rafael and..."

She pauses for a moment and when she speaks again, I can hear a weak smile in her voice, "I'm pleased that this duty has fallen upon you. With the wisdom and kindness I've seen in your heart, I believe that our battle is far from over. I believe that everyone, on every plane of existence, still has a chance. Surprisingly, your heart is still full of benevolence and that shows the strength that is you. The great sacrifices that I've witnessed are driven by it and it gives me a great hope."

She is silent again, warming me with her glow.

"If I had met you earlier, I would've assigned the guardianship of a few hundred souls into your care", I can hear a cheeky smile behind her words.

She is quiet, probably searching for words to say but I'm afraid of what else might come at me, what else I might hear.

"But fear not", her voice rustles, "you can call upon me and I shall come from Udhad should you need me. I will show you the power that is your essence. I will teach you as much as I can. All that I ask of you in return is to keep Rafe safe. And you would not be able to do so if you were still human.

"So as you can see, my generosity is tied to my agenda. I can recognise when rewards outweigh sacrifices. I would not have lasted this long in Sarukh otherwise", she coughs a dry laugh, and it is a sound of a light silvery bell.

She is quiet and when she speaks again, I can hear sadness in her voice. "But it's not going to be long before I disappear from Udhad forever, but until then... An be my witness as I vow my aid to you.

"And I am sorry for lying to you and telling you that I am able to take the entire essence from you. In truth, I cannot and nobody can now. You letting me in and willing to share your essence with Rafe is the only reason why it worked."

She stopped speaking.

No more chunks of my essence are leaving me. Whatever is left of me is mine now, I guess, to keep if I want to.

My haze is filling in, thickening, shaping, solidifying. I can sense the world around me building itself up, like a monochrome puzzle, one piece at a time before colours begin to seep in too.

The world comes rushing to the forefront and the earlier actions play up in reverse as if an invisible 'rewind' button was pressed.

The noises of the woods come through next. Crows' rasping in branches of groaning and bending trees, the heavy breathing of two people and Jess's soft whimper.

With a sudden punch that makes my head ring, I'm shoved back inside my skin, and I wake up and open my eyes to my lips still sealed to Rafe's.

I pull away, scanning the forest, taking in a deep breath of succulent November air.

The wet November forest never smelt more delectable. The grey colours of a miserable English winter were never deeper and fuller. The crows and magpies have never sung sweeter.

It is as if I see, hear and smell everything for the first time.

Maybe it's the stress, maybe the sweet relief of seeing a miracle of the world around me again, but tears fill my eyes and I begin to cry.

I fold over Rafe's body and I sob.

Another fork at the end of another road forced me to make another decision. But this time I was asked to accept myself, the whole of myself as I am; to accept all of myself, with my ugly past and shame, with my pain and doubt, and to stop hiding, running away from myself.

"Don't, little one", Sam's hushed voice says, "she needs space to accept the changes."

I lift my wet face and look at Sam, then at my little sister, whose little face is as wet as mine, riddled with desperation and fear.

She is lost and afraid, just as I am.

She will have no one if she doesn't have me, and her turbulent life would fall on another twisted and unknown path and no one would ever promise that it would be a better one.

She will be left alone in the darkness with the demons of her past, and I fear that she will drown in that misery. She will be another desperate child on the run from her inner demons only to run into the hands of the real ones, the ones of flesh and blood.

I turn my gaze back to Sam.

He stands immobile, waiting for me speak, waiting for my move.

He knows well that whatever just happened, it would have forced another decision from me and he isn't wrong.

His solid arm is wrapped over Jess's shoulders, grounding her to him. His lips are set in a tight line and his eyes cautiously follow my moves.

I wonder if he is scared of me as well.

And surprisingly, this thought pleases me.

I want him to be scared.

I want everyone to be scared and afraid of me because *I am* afraid of that crazy monster waking up inside me. Now I am something new, unfamiliar, something I have never lived with before.

I narrow my eyes at him.

"I am done running", I tell him. "I see that I will never be allowed to leave nor will I ever be left in peace. I am what I am, and maybe it's time I accept it. And *I am* going to accept and live with it.

"But I will do better than that. I will make this path my own. This path will serve me and I will bend it to my will. I will make it work. And everyone, whoever thought that I am easy prey, had better think again because I am done running and hiding. I am done being scared."

My voice grows stronger with every new word spoken.

"I was told I am the most powerful archangel? Then I had better show to everyone what I can do, but they ain't going to like it and that much I can promise!"

I'm telling him, Jess, and everyone out there who can hear. It is a warning to anyone who'd listen.

I'm done being scared and playing someone else's games. I'm done running, done hiding, done being afraid, done questioning and doubting myself. I'm here now to survive and take back what is mine, to take back my life.

I'm ready to play their games, only I'll be playing them on my terms. I'll be dealing the pack from now on and *I* will be calling the shots, and anyone who disagrees with it had better move over.

I'm not planning to fight Uriel's battles, I'm planning to fight mine. I'm planning to fight for myself, for my life and my future. The oaths that she swore are not going to be mine for long, her promises are not mine to keep.

I'm taking my life back, all of it, every last shred and sliver of it and everyone had better come to terms with it.

"I'm taking my life back. I am not going to run. I am going to stand and fight! For everything that is mine, for everything that I want. I will take back what is mine and I'm starting with Uras. Was it Uriel's? Fantastic, now it's mine and I want it back. And that back stabbing bastard Chamuel has twenty four hours to pack up and move out, and take his mug with him. That is as much as I will allow him. I want him gone and anyone who wants to walk out with him are welcome to do so, but that will be the last of my graces!

"From now on, I expect loyalty from everyone, who chooses to stand beside me", I look at Sam. I hope he hears what I'm saying, "and anyone who can't deliver that loyalty, had better be gone. I might have been placed on this 'chosen' path, but I will walk it my way. I will carve my future and anyone who disagrees with it, had better move over."

I'm glaring at Sam as he is the only one here.

Whoever he plays for, whatever his motives are, however he feels about me, it's all irrelevant now. Now he can go out there and spread the word. If he was ever attracted to that mediocre, scared little girl, he is out of luck now as she is gone. There will be no more "scared girl".

"I'm done being stupid and gullible. Done! And I am done being a victim. I want everything that is mine. I want it all back and then some. And I *will* take it if I have to. I have survived plenty and I will survive this one too!"

It is one of very few promises that I've ever made. But it's the one I'm going to keep.

Rafe's body is slowly warming up under my hands and his mouth opens, drawing in his first breath and I take it as a sign.

Glossary of terms used in "Heavenward" and "Hallow" and translations of some Celestial words and phrases used in both books.

Beyelai – owner, master or a deeply respectful term, addressing someone who holds a higher celestial position.

Kyriotes – a term for "free-will" subordinates.

Malakhims – a term for Baza's warriors, all of which are angels.

Uras – the name of Uriel's castle.

Sarukh – Heaven.

An – The "creator" – or God as we know it – the female.

Ophanims – The keepers of universal laws, who sit above all factions.

Hinnom – The endless lakes of fire

Ibnatum – a term for a slave, but used in derogatory terms to describe a paid soldier for Baza. This term would include, but not limited to: lizards, worms, angels etc.

Arllu – Hell.

Apkallu – Earth.

Udhad – the void-like place, which sits autonomously from other planes and realms, where beings without a soul or an essence, are dissolved by the consuming void.

Qal – the "light of the essence".

Great Arcanum – "Twin Flame" – the soul mates concept in old religions.

Adi la basi alaku – the instruction issued by a Celestial master, owner of your essence, which dissolves an essence into nothingness, after which an essence will disappear forever.

Ki zalag-um – "My heavenly celestial star". The term used to address one, who is a part of the family.

BOOKS IN THE "CELESTIAL CREATURES" SERIES:

THE BOOKS ARE AVAILABLE VIA ALL MAJOR PLATFORMS & BEST RETAILERS!

"HEAVENWARD", BOOK 1: https://books2read.com/u/bWzWlx

"HALLOW", BOOK 2: https://books2read.com/u/m2vkw6

"HARBINGER", BOOK 3: https://books2read.com/u/bx8n1l

"HALO", BOOK 4 (AND FINAL): https://books2read.com/u/3nvW56

Acknowledgement.

As usual, all my gratitude goes to my family: to my husband and my two daughters. Without their support and encouragement this book simply wouldn't have been written.

I want to thank all of the "Heavenward" readers, who took a chance on the story, read it and enjoyed it.

My immense gratitude goes to all of the fantastic book bloggers who participated in the "Hallow" blog tour and who made the "Hallow" release so much fun. I've met these wonderful people along my writing and publishing journey, and I am happy to call them my friends. Guys, you rock!

Ancient civilizations always have fascinated me, so it's really not a surprise that my books have a heavy dose of it. A lot of theological and ancient civilizations' research went into both books. The research was carried out into Jewish and Christian eschatology, Jewish beliefs, Christian doctrines and old Sumerian beliefs and language, and of course, the Bible's Book of Revelation. So I would like to thank all researchers out there, who dedicated their lives to these topics and fields. Without all of your books, mainstream and academic articles, and life-long researches my world of the angels would have been much poorer.

I need to say a huge "thank you" to my supportive and enthusiastic friends: Gina Ginnaw and Cheryl Butler. Thank you for your interest in my story, thank you for beta-reading it for me and thank you for your wonderful friendship. I am honoured to call you my friends.

I need to say a huge thank you to Melanie Fraser – blog tour organiser-extraordinaire, for organising fantastic blog tours, for her help with finalising this manuscript and for being such a wonderful friend. I am lucky to have met you.

And finally, the massive gratitude goes to the fantastic linguist Fred Hamori for his tireless work on understanding and translating "dead" languages. His articles on the Old Sumerian language were used and adapted to create my angels' language. I have used the listings of some Sumerian words and their English translations made by Mr. Fred Hamori.

If you would like to purchase a signed copy of "Heavenward" or "Hallow", please visit author website at www.OlgaGibbs.com. There you'd find more information on the upcoming books as well.

ABOUT AUTHOR

Olga Gibbs lives in a leafy-green town, nestled amongst the green fields of West Sussex, England. She lives with her husband Richard and their two daughters.

When she is not dreaming up new adventures for her imaginary characters, she does outreach work with teenagers. She loves adventure and travel, as it's during our time away from ordinary, something extraordinary will happen.

If you would like to purchase a signed copy of her books, please visit author website at www.OlgaGibbs.com. There you'll find more information on the upcoming books as well.